BATTLE BORN

A Novel by

JOE VAN RHYN

Published by El Cid Publishing, Las Vegas, Nevada 12/25/17

ISBN: 978-0-9986798-3-9

The author may be contacted at: joevanrhyn@cox.net

Additional information about the author can be found on his website: www.joevanrhyn.com or on Facebook @ Joe Van Rhyn, Author.

EL CID PUBLISHING
2722 Horseshoe Drive
Las Vegas, Nevada 89120

I dedicate this book to
my wife, Elaine, and to my children,
LuAnn, JoAnn, and Rick.

I thank you for
the love, respect, and support
you have given me
throughout my life.

The War is Over

Being in civilian clothes felt good, but Nora frowned at the gaunt, tired face she saw in the mirror. She straightened the collar on her cotton blouse, shifted her gray gabardine slacks, and downed the last swallow of gin. She rinsed the glass and set it on the sink ledge. Finding a comb in her ditty bag, she made a half dozen passes through her cropped hair and added a fresh layer of bright red lipstick. A circle of rouge on each cheek added color to an otherwise winter white face.

She sashayed across the room in step with the calypso beat of the Andrews Sisters singing on the radio, part dance and part alcohol-induced stumble.

"Drinking rum and Coca-Cola," her voice blended in perfect harmony as she sang along with the girls. She mumbled through the second line and finished big with, "working for the Yankee dollar." In one motion, she grabbed the handle to her tattered suitcase and tossed it onto the bed. Her fingers defied her as she struggled to unbuckle the straps. Success came with a burst of anger. "Dammit to hell." She threw back the straps and flipped open the top.

Sliding the brown jacket off the hanger, she draped the garment across the bed and folded it so the medals and combat ribbons laid flat. She folded the skirt and placed it in the grip. Laying the jacket on top, she smoothed the wrinkles and straightened the lieutenant bars on the epaulets. Her finger circled the rim of one of the brass buttons and she recalled the first time she wore her dress uniform. It was September 12, 1942, the day she graduated from basic training. She recalled how proud she felt standing on the parade grounds with hundreds of other nurses undergoing their first full dress inspection. Although a mere three years ago, it felt like a lifetime.

She picked up her cap and placed it on her head, tilting it to the proper angle. Her expression turned serious. Her back stiffened. Full of pride, she brought her hand to her forehead in a crisp military salute.

She relaxed her hand and slid the cap off the back of her head. Folding it, making sure not to bend the Corp emblem, she placed it in her bag.

Nora's hand trembled as she retrieved the glass from the bathroom sink. It shook worse when she took the pint of gin from on top of the dresser. Unscrewing the cap, she emptied the last of the fiery liquid, a full three fingers, into the goblet.

Looking at the bottle, she studied the costumed figure that adorned the label. "I bid you adieu, Monsieur Beefeater. You've been a faithful friend, helped me through some pretty tough times." She raised the glass in a farewell salute. "But alas dear fellow...it's time to go our separate ways." Holding the neck of the bottle between her thumb and forefinger, she watched as it slowly slipped from her grasp, hitting the bottom of the wastebasket with a thud. She leaned for one last look at the empty soldier lying in the basket. Was this truly the end of their relationship? Would she be able to function without his helping hand?

She swirled the mind-numbing contents around in the glass before casting the whole of it into her mouth. The distilled heat barely fazed her. It wasn't always that way. When she first turned to her bottled friend to help deal with the carnage of war, even small sips would send a burning sensation through her entire body. After endless days of seeing men, some younger than she, die painful deaths or having to console the lucky ones only missing an arm or leg, she needed a touch of his magical elixir to get from morning to afternoon.

She rinsed the glass again and set it on the dresser. Taking one last look around the room, she closed her suitcase and buckled the straps.

***

As she walked out through the main gate of Fort Campbell Army Base and Hospital, the sun hung just above the nearby hills, casting a yellow glow and long shadows. After a final salute to the sentry on duty, she hurried to the curb as the Greyhound bus lumbered to a stop, sending a cloud of Kentucky dust swirling in the air.

Nora coughed as the door opened. "Is this the bus to Chicago?"

The driver leaned forward. "Yep, but y'all gotta change buses in Indianapolis. Need help with your bag?"

Without responding, Nora reached down and hoisted the tattered brown case. She climbed the steps, pushing the bag in front of her. She didn't need help; it was like an old friend. It had been her companion as she traveled halfway across America and was at her side on her journey through Europe.

Three uniformed servicemen came running from the base and jumped onboard. The first GI ran into the back of her, almost knocking her over.

"Excuse you!" She stabbed her elbow into his gut.

"Sorry, ma'am," the soldier said, sliding into the first seat.

"Colored to the rear," barked the driver to the Negro soldier who was the last to board. While his two Caucasian buddies grabbed front seats, their black friend walked to the back. Nora was startled when the Negro soldier reached over her and pushed her bag the rest of the way onto the overhead rack. He smiled and continued his trek to the rear of the bus.

Nora sat and took the newspaper from the side pocket of her purse, and placed it across her lap. The headlines literally jumped from the paper. GERMANY SURRENDERS. Her fingers touched the date printed in the header: May 9, 1945. She shuddered as memories of the horrors she had experienced flashed through her mind like a movie house newsreel. The odor of diesel fuel stung her nostrils, but it couldn't wipe away the memory of how putrid blood and burnt flesh smelled. She thought of the young men who lost limbs to the surgeon's saw, and those who exhaled their last breaths as she held their hands. She had cried so much these past three years, she had no tears left.

The bus jerked as the driver accelerated up the road. Nora watched as the last bit of daylight eerily illuminated the rural landscape. The leaves on the trees flowed to and fro as if waltzing in the wind. Fields of early corn and wheat sprouts gave promise of life and a bountiful harvest. She folded the paper and held it to her chest. It's madness. Bullets couldn't stop the stupid war, yet now, with the stroke of a pen, it's over.

She fumbled in her purse and brought out a sheaf of papers. An empty miniature liquor bottle slid from the fold. She couldn't recall how it got in there or how long she'd been carrying it around. She surreptitiously dropped it back into her purse. Skimming across the heading and official seal of the cover page, she paused when she came to her name: NORA JENSEN. Other words caught her attention as she glanced at each sheet: 2nd Lieutenant, Nurse, and Honorably Discharged. *I only had to sign once to enlist, six times to get out. I guess that's the end of it. Why am I not happy? It's all I dreamed about for the past six months, but what am I going to do now?*

She put the papers back in her purse and tried to assemble the events of the past week in her mind. Seven days ago, she was a triage nurse at a field hospital outside of Rome. Six days ago, she accompanied a number of seriously wounded on a medevac flight back to the States. Then two days ago, with a recommendation from her CO and because her hitch would be up in a few months, she was given the option to muster out. Everything had happened so quickly she still hadn't fully digested all the changes. She felt guilty about abandoning the doctors and nurses she worked with back in Italy, yet very happy to be free of the army, a lifestyle of rules and regulations she found herself running contrary to on many occasions.

Darkness enveloped the rolling behemoth; heads bobbed in unison as the bus bounced along the highway. Nora was about to nod off when the bus slowed.

"Rest stop," the driver announced. "Ten minutes. Get out and stretch your legs; restrooms for whites inside, behind the building for colored."

The Negro soldier walked past, exited the bus, and walked to the rear of the combination restaurant-gas station. As Nora stepped off the bus, she caught a glimpse of him opening the door to a wooden outhouse. Her insides churned. There wasn't any of this blatant discrimination when the wounded were brought in. Everyone bled red. She stopped momentarily at the front door and read the sign posted in the restaurant window: "Colored fed at rear door."

The driver sat at the counter, smoke curling from the lit cigarette in his fingers. He was about to sip his coffee when Nora tapped him on the shoulder.

"How long to our next stop?" she asked.

"We'll be in Indianapolis in about four hours," he replied with a slight turn of his head.

Nora caught the waitress' attention and ordered two cups of coffee to go. The Negro soldier was already on the bus when Nora returned. She handed him a cup and smiled. "Where you headed?"

"Lafayette, Indiana. How 'bout you?"

"Don't know. Maybe home – Ely, Nevada. But first, I'm going to see a friend in Chicago."

"Thank you for the coffee, ma'am." He looked back at the outhouse. "I'd forgotten how bad things are here in the South. I hoped it would be different after the war."

Nora studied the battle ribbons on his chest. "You've got quite a collection there: Sergeant...Purple Heart...Bronze Star. That's going way above and beyond the call."

"The sergeant stripes came as a battlefield promotion, mostly because we needed a non-com for what was left of the platoon."

"What about the Purple Heart?"

"I took a bullet in the leg at Troina, Sicily. I was lucky. It missed the bone, just tore up the meaty part of my thigh."

"I was at a field hospital in Catania, on the coast. We got a lot of wounded from Troina. The guys said the fighting was fierce." Nora sat in the seat next to him.

"I didn't get to a hospital; the medics patched me up in the field. The fighting was bad. A lot of guys bought the ranch. I guess by the grace of God I made it through."

"You were lucky." Nora turned away. *How does God do that? How does he pick who lives and who dies? How could this so-called loving God sit by and let all these young men be slaughtered?*

"Yeah, lucky, I guess, but I lost a lot of good friends and it's hard to reconcile in your mind why so many around you get killed and you're spared." The soldier winced.

Nora put her hand on his. "I'm sorry, I didn't mean...but...I've wondered, too, how God decides who..."

"It's okay. I take it you're a nurse?"

"Nora Jensen, 2nd Lieutenant, Army Medical Corps, Serial number 675987342 at your service." Nora huffed. "I guess I don't have to give the whole spiel anymore, I mustered out today. Call me Nora."

The driver stepped onto the bus and came to the rear. "Ma'am, it's not proper for you to be a sittin' back here. Would y'all like to take a seat up front?"

Nora jumped to her feet. "This man is a decorated veteran. He took a bullet for his country and has served valiantly protecting your sorry butt. I think it's horrible how he's being treated. He's the one who should be sitting in the front."

The driver backed away. "Sorry, ma'am, I'm just followin' company policy."

7

The serviceman raised his hand. "It's okay, I'm fine back here." He smiled at Nora. "Thanks' again for the coffee."

Nora returned to her former seat and stared out the window. *There I go again, shooting off my mouth. Why do I keep trying to change the world? I'm tired of fighting, tired of the army, tired of seeing young men maimed, and I'm sure as hell tired of people being treated like shit.*

The rhythmic bouncing of the bus soon lulled her off to sleep. It had been months since restful slumber came that easy. She was used to catching sleep whenever she could. The medical corps wasn't a nine-to-five, punch-the-time-clock type of work. The wounded came in day and night, generally in large numbers. Most of the time, it was long hours of nothing but blood and guts. Was it any wonder she needed an alcohol sedative to reach REM peacefulness.

Indianapolis 2 AM

When the bus jerked to a stop, Nora woke. She rubbed her eyes, blinked, and peered through the slits between her eyelids. "Another rest stop?" She checked her watch. *What the hell...it's two o'clock in the morning. The army must run this bus line, too?* She stretched and read the sign on the building. "Oh crap, this is Indianapolis." Wiping the rest of the sleep from her eyes and pushing a few errant strands of hair into place, she gathered her sweater and purse.

The colored soldier walked by. "We have to change buses."

"I know, but it's a damned poor time to be doing it. I was sleeping so good."

Nora took down her trusted case and staggered off the bus.

The driver stood by the door. "The bus to Chicago is late. Y'all can wait inside. It should be along right soon."

A lot of people milled around in the terminal.

"Nothing's open," said the colored soldier. "I can't even buy you a cup of coffee."

"That's okay; is everyone here waiting for the Chicago bus?"

"Not everyone, some are continuing on to Fort Wayne or Detroit." He put a cigarette in his mouth and offered her one.

9

"No thanks, I only smoke after sex." She felt her face flush and forced a chuckle, trying to hide her embarrassment for saying that to a stranger. "I'm kidding...I don't know why I said...I never picked up the habit."

The soldier smiled, flipped open his Zippo, and lit up.

"Now, if you had something in the form of alcoholic spirits, I would gladly accept your offer."

The soldier shook his head and blew out a large stream of smoke. "We have opposing vices; I don't drink."

"I don't think either one is good for a person." Her dry mouth reminded her it was not going to be easy to be without Mister Beefeater's shoulder to lean on.

A bus with Chicago in large white letters displayed above the windshield rumbled up to the terminal.

"Nice talking to you," Nora said abruptly, picking up her suitcase and hurrying off. Her years in the army taught her to move fast if it involved getting in line. Among the first to board, she stowed her bag, took the aisle seat, and hoped no one would climb past to sit beside her. Outside, people lined up to board, including the three servicemen from Fort Campbell. A woman and a young girl stood off to one side, clutching one another, and showing no sign of letting go. The woman looked frail, her face ashen. Her dark recessed eyes gave further indication she wasn't well. The girl had a youthful figure. Her chestnut hair hung in loose curls off her shoulders. Her cheeks were tear streaked.

The servicemen boarded. His buddies again grabbed front seats while the colored soldier continued to the back of the bus.

The driver climbed aboard and motioned to the girl. "Are you coming or staying?" he snarled.

"Coming," she said, jumping on the first step. "Bye, Mom," the girl yelled. She waved wildly as the driver closed the door in front of her and put the bus in motion. The girl continued to wave until the bus turned and blocked the view of her mother.

The soldiers ogled the young lass as she staggered up the aisle. Doing her best to maintain her balance, she made eye contact with Nora and then eyed the vacant seat. Nora smiled, grabbed her purse, and rose.

"Thanks, I was hoping you'd let me sit with you," the girl said, taking the window seat.

"No problem; traveling alone?"

"Yes, I'm going to Chicago to live with my Aunt Betty." The youngster wiped a tear that gathered in the corner of her eye. "Pa was killed in the war and Mom's got some kind of cancer. She can't take care of me anymore."

There you have it, the girl's whole life in a nutshell. Another casualty of this godforsaken war. Nora took the girl's hand. "How old are you?"

"Sixteen," she said, "on my next birthday."

What a kick in the head. Fifteen years old and being sent to live with relatives. "What's your name?"

"Sarah, Sarah Jean Connolly."

Without warning, the girl buried her face on Nora's shoulder. "I'm afraid," she cried.

Nora put her arm around the girl, much like she had with the young soldiers who came out of the anesthesia missing an arm or a leg. "It's okay, everything will be alright." Nora took a hanky from her purse. "Here, dry your eyes."

"I don't know what's going to happen to me," the girl said between sobs.

11

"For one thing, we'll make sure you get to your Aunt Betty's." *Damn the war, damn everything about it. What kind of loving God would allow a child to be dealt a hand like this?* This was not the first time Nora questioned the existence of a benevolent God.

The girl wiped her eyes. "I'm sorry; Mama told me I had to be strong."

"And you will be." Nora folded her sweater. "Here, rest your head against the window. Try to get some sleep; it's six hours to Chicago."

The girl sobbed quietly and slowly gave into sleep. Nora looked to the rear of the bus. The soldier flashed a toothy smile. She slipped out of her seat, careful not to disturb her sleeping friend, and walked to the back.

"Can you stand some company?" she said. "Sorry to run off on you back at the station. The army ruined me. I hate standing in line."

"Roger that." The man moved to make room. "I don't want to cause a problem."

"If anyone wants to make something of it, they'll get an earful. I'm a little ticked off at the world right now. I'm sorry, I didn't get your name?"

"Neil Jefferson, and you're Norma?"

"Nora, my mother left out the 'm.' Is Lafayette your home?"

"Yeah, first time back in two years."

"Got a girlfriend?"

"Did." The man looked to his lap. "She got herself pregnant and married another guy. I got her 'Dear John' letter the same day I took the bullet. I don't remember which hurt worse."

12

"There's a lot of fish in the sea. I'm sure there will be plenty of girls falling all over themselves when you hit town. The uniform gets them every time."

"Maybe, but I thought she was the one. The war got in the way."

"I know what you mean. I lost a love...sort of."

"A soldier?"

"An Italian winemaker."

The man's eyebrows raised.

Nora chuckled. "Funny, huh? It's a long story."

"We have an hour to Lafayette."

Nora sat back and wondered where to start. "I did a lot of bike riding in Sicily. It helped to take my mind off what was going on at the hospital. I bought a used bicycle from a man in the village and would go riding near the base camp. The allied forces had pretty much secured that part of the island, but you still had to be careful because there were pockets where remnants of the Italian army continued to resist.

"We'd had a grueling week, I had two days off and decided to venture out into the countryside. I was riding through this huge vineyard, somewhere south of Catania, when the chain jumped off the sprocket. Before I could even assess the problem, this handsome Adonis with jet black hair and square jaw appeared out of nowhere. He fixed the chain, then motioned for me to follow him to his cottage with one of the few Italian words I knew — vino. His English vocabulary was limited and I knew even less Italian. Sometimes, eyes and hands can convey a person's feelings better than words.

"His cottage was built of field stone and hewed timbers. It was one room with a sleeping loft. The stone

13

fireplace provided both heat and the means for cooking. The furnishings were Spartan and hand-made. It had a thatched roof and was tucked in a wooded area on land his family had grown grapes for five generations."

Nora paused. "The setting would have made a great oil painting."

The soldier's smile prompted her to continue.

"His name was Antonio Giuseppe Garibaldi. He had this dilapidated motorcycle and he took me for a ride on all these back roads. That part of Sicily is so beautiful. We stopped at one farmhouse and it was like a family reunion. People seemed to appear out of nowhere; they hugged and kissed us both. Within minutes they were opening bottles of wine. One man began playing a squeezebox and another, the violin. Soon we were all dancing and singing. They spread a table of sausage, cheese, and fresh-baked bread. The cheese was absolutely delicious; they made it right there on the farm." Nora paused, wiped her eyes, and stared out the window.

"It was already dark when we got back to his cottage, and I was in no shape to try and find my way back to the base. To tell you the truth, I really didn't want to leave. He lit a fire in the fireplace, opened a bottle of wine, and we laid on the floor in front of the hearth.

"Maybe it was the war, or maybe the wine…" Her words trailed off. She blinked to hold back the tears, then forced a smile. "Do you know how you say, 'I love you' in Italian?"

The soldier shook his head.

"Te amo." Nora looked out into the darkness. "It was a beautiful night."

Nora searched the soldier's face for a sign of disapproval. *Good heavens, girl, first I make the smoking-after-sex joke and now I'm telling a stranger about*

14

shacking up with a guy I just met. This Neil must think I'm some kind of sex maniac. "I know I'm boring you with this, right?"

"No, it sounds like a nice love story."

"I choose to think it was love, but it could have been lust." Nora smiled sheepishly. "But...I'll never know. I returned the following weekend and learned he was AWOL from the Italian army. His family had tried to hide him in the cottage, but a Mussolini sympathizer turned him in."

"Jeez, what happened to him?"

"I was never able to find out. Italy surrendered less than a month later."

The soldier straightened up in his seat. "Desertion in a time of war is a serious offense, He could be..."

"Shot? I know, that's what everyone was afraid of. Anyway, we moved the hospital closer to Rome two days later."

"So, you never...?"

"Nope, I guess the war got in the way for both of us. I do think about him, but as I said, I don't know if it was love or we were both simply trying to escape the reality of the lives we faced."

The soldier looked out the window. "We're coming into Lafayette."

Nora stood. "Good luck, Neil. It's been nice talking to you."

"For me, too. I want to thank you," the soldier said.

"For what?"

"For being kind and making me believe not everyone in America is a bigot or a racist."

Nora smiled and returned to her seat.

The bus rolled to a stop; Neil smiled as he passed by. Nora watched as the soldier was engulfed in a crowd of family, friends, and well-wishers the moment he stepped off the bus. A large banner read: 'Welcome Home Neil Jefferson.' She smiled. How appropriate, she thought, he goes from being regulated to ride in the back of the bus to a hero's welcome. Here it was three o'clock in the morning and all these people had come out to greet him.

As the bus belched out a blue cloud of diesel exhaust and rolled away from the curb, the soldier waved to Nora.

Nora waved back. For her, at this moment, it seemed everything was right in the world. She sat back and studied the young girl sleeping next to her. She ran her finger through one of the ringlets of red hair that hung from the girl's shoulder and wondered, what life had in store for her. As the bus rumbled in pursuit of its Illinois destination, Nora closed her eyes and drifted off to sleep.

Welcome to Chicago

As the first sun rays broke over the horizon, they sent shards of light cascading through the bus windows. Nora stirred and Sara pulled her head off Nora's shoulder.

"I'm so sorry," the girl said, sitting up straight. "I didn't mean..."

"It's okay," Nora said. "We'll be stopping soon. Are you hungry?"

"A little, but after Mama paid for the ticket all she could give me was twenty-five cents. I've got to save that in case I have to call Aunt Betty when I get to Chicago."

"Doesn't this Betty know you are coming?"

"I think so. Mom sent a letter last week. She called yesterday, but Betty said she couldn't talk. I'm not sure what that was about."

What kind of a cockamamie situation is that? Nora didn't want to add to the girl's confusion by asking more questions. "Well, I'm sure I can scare up enough to buy us both a proper breakfast." Money was not an immediate problem for Nora. She was sitting on three months' pay. *Not much has changed. I'm still taking care of the casualties of war, only the wounds are different.*

Nora drank her coffee and watched the girl finish her plate of eggs and bacon. "Well, Sarah Jean, finish your milk

17

and bring the toast with you. We have to get back on the bus. We should be in Chicago by nine."

Sarah grabbed the two pieces of bread and rushed off. Nora opened her purse, took out some cash, and laid it on the bill. Then pulling out a small bottle, she shook two white pills into her hand. Popping them into her mouth, she took a quick swallow of water and made her exit.

"You didn't tell me your name," the girl said as the bus pulled out of the parking lot.

"Nora Jensen, ex-army nurse."

"When I helped take care of Mama, I thought about being a nurse."

Nora had to bite her tongue to keep from expounding on all the reasons this young lady should seek another line of work. "It has its good days and bad."

The girl continued talking, but Nora's mind drifted back to the day she waited with her mom and dad, about to embark on her own life-changing journey. Coming from Ely, a small farming and mining town in western Nevada, no one was more shocked than Nora when she received the acceptance letter to become a student nurse at Chicago General. Like the young girl beside her, Nora remembered how she, too, hugged her mother up to the very last moment before getting on the bus and waving out the window until her mom was no longer in sight.

It seemed like a lifetime ago, maybe two or three lifetimes. She had no way of knowing back then all the human destruction and the less-than-honorable army culture she would encounter over the next three years. She thought about Neil. He was lucky; the wounded from Troina were mostly from gunfire. The invasion at Anzio, a few months later, was supposed to be the one that drove the Germans back to Berlin, but Hitler had other ideas. To keep the allied forces from moving inland, he bombarded them with every piece of artillery he could send.

Those large shells exploding overhead kept the GIs pinned on the beach for months. Bullets generally leave a clean wound. Shrapnel cuts and tears flesh so brutally it's hard to find much left to sew together. As a triage nurse, Nora stood in God's shoes and decided who received care and who was beyond human help. Even some who made it to the operating table didn't pulled through. Each death took its toll, a heavy burden for anyone to carry, but especially hard on this twenty-four-year-old Nevadan.

Nora picked up the last of the girl's conversation. "...and the doctors said it could be a matter of weeks, perhaps even days."

"That's too bad. I'm sure your mom wanted you to be with family. The best way to honor your mother is to study hard and make something of yourself."

"I used to get A's but I missed a lot of school taking care of Mama. Hopefully, I will be able to study more at Aunt Betty's."

"There it is," Nora said, pointing ahead. "The windy city. If you'd like I can stay with you until your Aunt Betty comes to pick you up."

"Could you? I guess I'm somewhat afraid. She's Mama's sister, but I haven't seen her since I was about nine. I don't know much about her or my Uncle Bob."

"I've got time; no one is waiting for me. Do you have any other family, any brothers or sisters?"

"Nope, Aunt Betty is my only relative. Ma's parents are dead, and Pa came from Ireland. His family is all over there."

That explains the Maureen O'Hara tresses.

19

The girl's eyes were glued to the window. "I've never seen so many tall buildings. In Danville, the tallest building is the courthouse. It's only two stories high."

"I thought you were from Indianapolis?"

"Danville, about half an hour away. The neighbor lady gave us a ride to the bus station." Sarah Jean continued to comment on every building as the bus weaved through the morning rush hour.

Making a large swooping turn, the bus pulled into the downtown station and stopped abruptly. A heavy cloud of thick blue smoke rolled out from underneath and filled the cabin with its noxious fumes. The diesel engine wound down, ending the ever-present vibration, and for a moment there was complete silence. Then as if someone blew a whistle, there was mass chaos as everyone on the bus got out of their seats and began gathering their things.

"Stay close to me," Nora said, grabbing Sarah's hand.

The two entered the busy terminal, looking for anyone to show a sign of recognition. Both took a step forward when a woman, waving and running toward them, rushed past and embraced the man behind them. In minutes the crowded room emptied as people made their way out the exits. Nora used her foot to slide her suitcase in the direction of a row of chairs. "Let's sit here for a bit and think this out."

Sarah sat and pulled her case between her legs. "What if Aunt Betty doesn't come?"

Nora's throat was dry. Not just a little dry, but Nevada desert dry. Her tongue searched for moisture in the far corners of her mouth. Her fingers tapped her thigh and her heel joined in by bouncing off the floor. "Have you got your aunt's phone number?"

"It's pinned inside my sweater."

Nora half dragged Sarah over to a row of phone booths. "Do you want to call, or should I?"

"Would you?" Sarah handed her the paper.

Nora dropped a nickel in the slot and dialed the number. After the fourth ring, "I'm not getting an answer," she said. "Do you have the address?"

Sarah pointed to the paper. "It's on the back."

"Bob and Betty Cooper; is that their name?"

Sarah nodded.

"Liberty Street. If I remember correctly, that's not far from here. We can grab a cab and take you over there."

They walked out to the street. "Taxi!" Nora yelled.

The cab driver pulled in front of a narrow two-story house; the siding was weathered and the yard overgrown. The surrounding houses all needed attention, a few appeared abandoned, with wood covering the windows.

"Wait for me," Nora told the driver. Sarah grabbed her suitcase; the two climbed the porch steps. The drapes in the front window were closed but moved slightly. Nora rang the bell. The door opened to the extent of the safety chain.

"Is this the Cooper residence?" Nora asked.

The woman's one eye looked first at Nora and then at Sarah.

Are you Betty Cooper?"

The woman unchained the door, stepped out on the porch, and put her finger to her lips. "You must be Sarah Jean," she whispered. "You look just like your mother when she was a girl. I'm so sorry, she can't stay here."

"Are you Betty?

She nodded. Her face was puffy, her lip was split, and she had a greenish black contusion around one eye. Her

21

dress was torn near the collar and she tried to hold it in place with her hand. "Please, she can't stay here."

"Are you alright? What's going on?" Nora asked.

The door swung open. A burly, unshaven man in suspenders and a dingy strap undershirt stood in the doorway. His arms were covered with an overabundance of hair. Gobs of hair also curled out the arm and neck holes of his shirt. The bottle of beer he carried disappeared behind his back. "Come in, we were expecting you." Betty cowered to the side.

Nora held Sarah behind her and glanced around the room. Papers were scattered on the floor. The throw rugs lay curled and piled in a heap. The chair and sofa appeared to have been pushed out of position.

The man tried to look around Nora. "Are you Sarah? We got the letter from your mama," he said, wiping the beer drip from his chin.

Sarah moved into the small of Nora's back.

"I think she's going to like it here," he said. "We're going to take real good care of her." He looked at Nora. "I guess we need to thank you for bringing her to us."

Nora saw the fear in Betty's face. She leaned into the man and whispered, "Listen you bastard, you touch one hair on that kid's head, and I will come back here and cut off your balls."

The man raised his hand. "You bitch, you can't talk to me that way."

Nora blocked his swing and delivered a quick shot to his ribs, doubling him over. "You're right, we're done talking. I see what's going on here. You're using this woman as a punching bag and God only knows what you have in mind for this poor girl." Nora picked up Sarah's bag. "Come, we're getting out of here." They hurried down the steps.

The man, holding his side, stood in the doorway. "You bring her back; you have no right to take her."

"What am I going to do now?" Sarah said as the cab drove them away.

"Don't worry, we'll think of something." *She's right; what do we do now?*

Help from a Friend

Nora leaned forward, instructed the cabbie to take them to Chicago General and settled back in her seat. "I've got a nurse friend there; she should be able to help us."

Sarah held her suitcase on her lap and stared straight ahead. Nora couldn't be bothered trying to guess what was going through the girl's mind, she was too busy second guessing herself. *Maybe I acted too quickly. I'm barely able to keep myself together; what am I going to do with a fifteen-year-old? That bastard surely would have molested her. You could tell by the way he looked at her. I couldn't let her stay with that creep. I just couldn't.*

Nora and Sarah didn't bother stopping at the front desk, they walked straight to the elevators. To anyone watching, the two women carrying suitcases were typical patient check-ins. They stepped in and both watched the arrow above the elevator door as it moved from first to second floor. When the door opened, Nora walked directly to the nurses' station. "Is Gladys Iverson on duty?"

The girl, dressed in a candy-striped student's uniform, gave the women an inquisitive look. "She's in a meeting; is there something I can help you with?"

"Tell her Nora is here."

The nurse rose and pulled her lips tight.

Nora took note of the girl's attitude and straightened her collar. "I know we look like we came off skid row, but we've been on a bus...for fourteen hours...okay...Please, just tell Gladys, Nora Jensen is here.

The girl disappeared through the doorway behind her. Nora motioned Sarah to the chairs along the far wall. They barely got settled in their seats when a big woman came barging out the door. "Nora!" The woman practically lifted Nora from the chair. They hugged for the longest time. Slowly the woman let go and took a step back. "Girl, look at you, you're practically skin and bones. What happened to you?"

"It's called World War II. Up until a week ago, I was in a field hospital south of Rome, dressing bullet holes in what otherwise were perfectly healthy American boys. It's been a stressful three years." Pushing Sarah forward, "She and I spent the better part of fourteen hours on a Greyhound bus. We got into town less than two hours ago. This is Sarah Jean Connolly. Sarah, meet Gladys Iverson, head nurse and the Terror of Chicago General."

Gladys eyed up the girl. Her expression showed how stunned she was. "She's a nurse?"

"No, we met on the bus. I came from Kentucky. She got on at Indianapolis."

"So, what's the deal?" Gladys was never one to mince words. "You're not AWOL, are you?"

Nora chuckled. "No, honorably discharged."

"Well, you still look like shit. So, what's the story on the girl; she an orphan or something?"

"Sort of," Nora felt dizzy. "She's..."

***

Nora rolled on her side, and slowly opened her eyes. The room was unfamiliar. She tried to sit up, but felt a hand holding her in place.

"Don't try to get up. Just lie there for a while."

Nora recognized Gladys' stern voice. "Wow, what happened? Where am I?"

"My office. You passed out, fell right into my arms. You've got some explaining to do, young lady."

Nora panicked. "Where's Sarah Jean?"

"She's out in the waiting room paging through the latest *Look* magazine," Gladys said. "She told me about her mom and the situation at Aunt Betty's. But before we get to her problem, I found these in your purse." Gladys showed Nora a bottle of pills and an empty miniature gin bottle. "You don't want to be mixing barbiturates and booze. That can be deadly."

Nora shook and broke into tears. "You can't imagine what it was like. The wounded kept coming, day after day. I tossed men's amputated arms and legs away like I was taking out the garbage. I picked shrapnel out of just about every inch of the human anatomy, inside and out. We'd go ten and twelve hours at a time. I would be so exhausted, I could hardly stand, and then I would lie down and couldn't sleep. The pills helped."

"Okay, I understand the pills; what about the gin?"

Nora turned away. "I needed that to numb the pain. I've witnessed more death than a normal person would face in a hundred lifetimes. It never got easier."

Gladys helped Nora sit up. "You're right, I can't imagine what it was like over there, and I'm not here to judge you, but booze and pills are not the answer. You need regular nourishment and time to let your mind and body heal."

"I know," Nora said. "I'm thinking of going home to Ely. Spend some time with Mom and Dad."

"Good idea, some of your mom's home cooking is just what you need."

Nora stood and braced herself on the side of the couch. "Speaking of moms and home cooking, how are your parents?"

"They're good. Dad sold the cows and rented the land. He said he's getting too old to farm anymore. I was planning on going up there this weekend."

"It's Pine Lake, right?"

"I took you there right before you had to report to the army. That fellow Duke asks about you every time I'm up there."

Nora took a deep breath. "I remember your folks' big house overlooking the lake and your mom's apple pie. If I close my eyes I can almost smell the pines."

"It hasn't changed much," Gladys said. "What about that guy, Duke? Did you ever hear from him? I thought you two really hit it off."

"We wrote a couple of times during boot camp. I broke it off when I shipped out. Who knew what was going to happen."

"Well, I don't think he's gotten over you."

Sarah jumped up as Nora and Gladys came through the door. "Are you okay? I was so worried."

"I'm fine," Nora said. "It's you we have to worry about."

"I know, what's going to happen to me?"

"First of all, we are not going to let anybody hurt you," Gladys said. "We don't think it's a good idea that you go to your Aunt Betty's. What do you think?"

"I didn't like the way Uncle Bob looked at me, but where else can I go?"

Gladys put her arm around the girl. "I know some people down at social services; they may have some ideas for us."

Nora squirmed. *Was she talking about an orphanage? No way! That's almost as bad as Aunt Betty's.* "Gladys, maybe we can talk more about this later."

"Maybe I could stay with one of you," Sarah said. "I won't eat much, and I promise not to cause any trouble."

There was an uncomfortable silence.

Nora put her hands on Sarah's shoulders. "How would you like to take another bus trip?"

Gladys choked. "You're not thinking about...You could get into a lot of trouble..."

"You want to tell me she would be better off in an orphanage, a foster home, or God forbid, with that lecherous bastard of an uncle? Let's just say I don't have the highest regard for government run organizations. Besides, no one knows me, and who would ever think to look for her in Ely, Nevada." Nora motioned Sarah to pick up her bag.

"What about your mom and dad; shouldn't you ask them first?" Gladys said. "You could be putting them in a lot of trouble, too."

"Mom will love Sarah and Dad will do whatever Mom says." Nora hugged Gladys. "I was hoping to spend some time with you, but I think we need to git while the gittin' is good.

Gladys grabbed Nora's arm. "Now, listen to me. Get off those pills and stay away from the booze. Promise me you'll do that."

"I will, I promise, and maybe it's best if you forget we were ever here. I'll write in a month or two." Nora picked up her bag and ushered Sarah back to the elevator.

The Bus to Ely

The afternoon bus going west was scheduled to leave in twenty minutes. The girls hustled into the ladies' room.

Nora pushed Sarah into one of the stalls. "Have you got a different top you can put on?"

"What? Why are we doing this?"

"In case someone is looking for us, let's not make it too easy."

Nora changed her top, too. "Come here," she said, covering the girl's chestnut curls with a handkerchief and tying it under her chin. Looking in the mirror, Nora messed her own hair. There wasn't a lot she could do with her cropped hair style. She tried combing it in different directions before finally just bringing it all forward. She heard Sarah giggle and saw the reflected image of the young girl in the mirror.

Sarah tried to keep from laughing. "You look silly," she said, putting her hand over her mouth.

Nora took a second look in the mirror. They both doubled over laughing.

When the door to the ladies' room started to open, the girls immediately sobered, picked up their suitcases, and brushed past the large woman coming in. They looked away so the woman couldn't get a good look at their faces.

The two walked through the terminal, trying to act nonchalant. Slipping into the gift shop, Nora bought them each a pair of sunglasses.

When their bus departure was announced over the public address system, Nora instructed Sarah to move ahead and board. "Let's get on separately, take any seat, I'll be a few people behind you. Once we are on our way we can sit together." She kept a lookout to see if anyone was paying attention to them. *I may be overdoing this, but it's better to be cautious.*

The bus rolled out on time. Nora got up and moved to the seat next to Sarah. "So far so good," she said.

Sarah watch out the window as the bus made its way out of the city. She looked at her ticket. "Where is Ely, Nevada? Is that where we're going?"

Nora pointed to the front of the bus. "It's straight west. It's where I grew up. My mom and dad are there. Hopefully, it can be the start of a new life for you and a chance for me to get back on my feet."

"My mom doesn't know where we're going; I hope it's okay with her."

Nora slumped in her seat. *Oh my god, I didn't think about her mom. If she talks to her sister, she might panic and call the police. I can't believe I didn't think about her mother.* "Does your mom have someone staying with her?"

"The neighbor lady brings her food and checks on her."

Nora looked at her watch and checked the schedule. "We get into Lincoln, Nebraska about eleven; that'll be too late to call. We'll have to wait until we get to Cheyenne in the morning." Nora fussed with her hair and rubbed the back of her neck. *I sure could use a drink right now.*

Damn, why didn't I think about her mom? This could get ugly really quick.

"Do you want to go back?" Nora asked. "We can go back if you want to."

"I can't go back. Mom will die soon, and I don't want to go to Aunt Betty's."

"We'll call in the morning to let your mom know you're safe. And hopefully convince her that you are with people who will take good care of you."

Nora rubbed her temples and although she knew she was being hypocritical, she whispered a small prayer, "I know I've questioned you on a lot of things, but please, don't let her mom call the police."

The bus rolled into Lincoln a little ahead of schedule. Sarah was curled up in her seat sound asleep. Nora got off the bus. She tried to decide whether to call Sarah's mother even at this late hour. Instead, she walked into the gift shop and purchased two miniature bottles of gin. Going to the restroom, she hurried into a stall and feverishly opened one, chugging the full two ounces all at once. She bowed her head. She hated herself for being so weak. She'd promised Gladys and hadn't made it eight hours. She threw the bottle in the trash, washed her face, and put a stick of gum in her mouth.

Sarah woke when Nora returned to her seat. "Where are we?"

"Lincoln, we'll be in Cheyenne about six in the morning. We can get some breakfast and call your mom."

"Okay." Sarah rolled back toward the window as the bus departed the station and was soon back asleep.

Nora put her seat back. Although she felt the effects of the gin, she knew sleep was not going to come easy. *How do I get myself in these messes? I was going to Chicago to visit Gladys and now I'm probably a fugitive from the law. Why me? Why can't I just close my eyes and let all the misery of life pass me by. Why do I think I have to fix everyone's problems?*

Nora woke when the bus came to a stop, and the driver shut down the engine. She looked quickly to her left.

Sarah was sitting up looking out the window. "You're a sleepyhead," she said. "I've been awake for an hour."

Nora smiled. *If she only knew how unusual it was for me to sleep that way.* She brought her seat upright. "Let's get some breakfast and call your mom."

"Mom doesn't have a phone; we have to call the neighbor, Mrs. Halstead."

"You mean we won't be able to speak directly to your mother?" *This could complicate things a bit. I'll have to be careful what I say to this Mrs. Halstead, in case someone has already called the police.* "Let's eat first. We'll call after that." *It will give me a chance to figure what to say.*

"That's good. I'm hungry," the girl said.

The waitress brought their food and Sarah quickly attacked her plate. Nora buttered a piece of toast. "Is this Mrs. Halstead a nice person? Will she give your mom a message?

"Sometimes she's a bit crabby, but she always brought the phone messages from the doctor."

"You do know her number, don't you?"

"I have it in my pocket. I was supposed to have Aunt Betty call when I got to their house."

Nora took the paper and shook her head in disbelief. *Good Grief! It goes from bad to worse.* She pushed her empty plate to the center of the table. "No sense waiting any longer. Let's get this over with." The two walked to a nearby phone booth. Nora rang the long distant operator. Depositing the correct number of coins, she listened to each ring. Finally, a person answered.

"Hello, Mrs. Halstead. I was wondering if you could deliver a message to Mrs. Connolly."

The voice was friendly. "Yes, she has been waiting for your call. We expected you to call yesterday."

"I beg your pardon?" Nora put her hand over the receiver. *She must think I'm Betty.*

"Did Sarah Jean get there okay?" the woman asked.

Nora searched the reaches of her mind. *What do I say? She thinks I'm Betty.* "Yes, Yes. Sarah Jean is safe here with me."

The woman sighed. "Sarah's mama had a real setback. She collapsed when we got back from the bus station. The doctor didn't expect her to make it through the night. I know she was just hanging on waiting to hear if her baby made it safely. She can now go peacefully, knowing her daughter is in good hands. I'm going to tell her right now. God Bless you."

Nora slowly hung up the receiver. Tears gathered. Real tears ran down her cheeks.

"Did Mama die?" Sarah closed her eyes.

"Soon," Nora whispered. "But she will go knowing you are safe."

Sarah put her head on Nora's shoulder. Nora wrapped her arms around the sobbing child. *Maybe this was God's plan all along. Maybe Sarah Jean Connolly will have a normal chance at life instead of being a casualty of it.*

34

Welcome to the Wild West

How long before we get to Ely?" Sarah asked.

"It's about seven hours to Salt Lake City and another seven hours to Ely." Nora looked at her watch. "That should put us there around eight tonight."

Sarah continued looking out the window. "The mountains are so beautiful. This is a lot different than Indiana. It's so wide open, not many houses."

"This is the start of the wild west. They're part of the Rocky Mountains. Wait until we get to Nevada. Wheeler Peak is just south of Ely. It's all pretty wide open in this part of the country."

"The trees all look so different."

"A lot of Pinion Pine. No oaks or maples like you have in Indiana. We also have cactus, sagebrush and mesquite trees."

Sarah appeared deep in thought. "Do you think your mom and dad will be upset that I'm coming with you?"

"Mom is going to love you," Nora said, and gave the girl a big hug. *Dad could be a different story. I'm sure Mom would have done the same thing I did and if Sarah's mother knew the whole story, she would approve, too.*

Sarah continued looking out of the window; Nora settled back in her seat. The tires made a blipping sound as they rolled over the cracks in the road. The rhythmic sound had a hypnotizing effect on her. Nora closed her eyes. "Oh yes, I remember going to Pine Lake," she cooed softly.

The years rolled back to July 4, 1942. Gladys was going to visit her folks for the weekend and invited Nora, who hadn't said a word about enlisting in the army. She was leery whether Gladys would approve. The six-hour drive to Pine Lake would give her plenty of time to break the news.

America had joined the war in Europe in April and the medical corps was in desperate need of nurses. Recruiters combed the hospitals and used every ploy to get nurses to put their names on enlistment papers. Like so many others, Nora was moved by an appeal to her patriotism.

Pine Lake was a small resort town located in the north central part of the state. The lake was large, crystal clear, and deep. It appealed to both fishermen and those who enjoyed the other water activities, such as swimming and sailing.

Gladys had assured Nora a good time, saying the weekend would be full of festivities. "There's fireworks, an outdoor dance on the courthouse lawn, and a moonlight hay ride."

Nora thought it all sounded fun.

At first Gladys was angry when Nora broke the news about enlisting. She sputtered about it until she realized her idealistic friend would have naturally felt compelled to do her part for the war effort.

It was after dark when the girls drove down Main Street. The celebrating had already begun. Music from the courthouse lawn filled the air and the pop and flash of firecrackers exploding came from all directions.

"Let's drop our things at the house first and let Mom know we're here." Gladys said.

Gladys' mom and dad were wonderful people. Their farm sat on a hill overlooking the lake. The house was huge, built by a civil war general who came to Pine Lake after the war. It had eight bedrooms and a porch that wrapped around three sides of the house. Her dad bought the farm during the depression. Like a lot of properties, it was sold for back taxes in a sheriff's auction on the courthouse steps.

Gladys' mom hugged Nora. "We've heard so much about you. Gladys says you're her best student." Her dad smiled and nodded in agreement.

Gladys gave her dad a hug and kiss on the cheek. "Nora and I are going to join the fun on the courthouse lawn. Would you like to join us?"

"Oh, heaven's no," sighed her mom. "That's no place for us; you gals go and kick up your heels. Dad and I will enjoy a peaceful evening on the porch; we can see the fireworks from there."

The downtown was alive with excitement. Locals and tourists alike danced wherever they stood. Some enterprising kids sold lemonade while the American Legion Post handed out mugs of beer, drawn from a half barrel floating in a washtub of ice. The first of the fireworks display exploded as Gladys and Nora made their way through the crowd.

Nora felt a hand grab hers. On the other end of the muscular arm was a six-foot guy with bushy hair, green eyes, jeans, t-shirt, and cowboy boots. Before she could break free, he dragged her closer to the music, pulled her *forward and twirled her under his arm. He twirled her again, holding her hand above her head. The guy did the Jitterbug quite well considering his cowboy boots didn't move as quickly as his body. When the music slowed, he did a lot better with the fox trot.*

"My name's Duke; what's yours?" he shouted over the din.

"Nora."

"Norma?"

"No 'M.' Nora!" she yelled in his ear.

Nora opened her eyes as Sarah rested her head on Nora's shoulder. "Time for a nap?"

Sarah yawned. "I guess so."

Nora rolled her head to the side, closed her eyes, and was surprised how quickly and vividly her memory of that evening came back to her.

When the band took a break, her new-found dance partner bought her a lemonade. "Want to take a walk? It's really nice down by the lake."

Nora saw Gladys talking to a group of ladies and gave her a wave. She pointed to the boy and then to the lake. Gladys returned an acknowledging wave.

A cool breeze came up from the lake. Nora pulled her blouse away from her skin and flipped up her sweaty curls. "I haven't danced that much since high school."

"Where are you from?" he asked.

"Chicago."

"Are you going to be in town long?"

"Just the weekend. I came with Gladys Iverson."

Reaching the water's edge, Nora climbed up and sat on a nearby picnic table. "Is Duke your real name or a nickname?"

"Real. I think my mom was hoping I'd grow up to be royalty."

"Are you English?"

"Irish. My last name is Brady." He picked up a stone and skipped it across the water.

"Are you local?"

"Been here for a couple of years."

"Doing what?"

"Refinishing boats. I work over there at the Boat Works." He pointed to a large building on the other side of the park. "What about you?"

"Just finished nurse's training. This is sort of a graduation sendoff."

"A sendoff to where?"

"Wherever the army sends me."

The playful expression drained from his face. "Were you drafted?"

"I enlisted," Nora said. "I report in two weeks."

The waves splashed against the large stones that lined the lakefront. The cloudless sky was filled with millions of twinkling stars and the light from a full moon danced across the black ripples on the lake.

"Some of the guys from town have signed up," he said. "I'm not sure what I'm going to do."

"I'd wait to be drafted. No sense volunteering to be shot at."

"What about you; it could be just as dangerous for you."

"*Don't be silly. Nurses don't get shot at; we're just there to clean up the mess.*"

Nora opened her eyes and glanced at the girl sleeping next to her. It had been a long time since she thought about Pine Lake and the brash young man, but the memories were crystal clear. She closed her eyes again and returned to that long-ago evening.

Standing at the water's edge, a thunderous salute signaled the end of fireworks. Catching Nora by surprise, she jumped and fell into Duke's arms. She quickly righted herself. "Sorry, I guess I'll need to get used to explosions like that."

Without hesitating, he drew her close and kissed her.

Her first reaction was to push away, but she slowly gave into his embrace. She hadn't kissed that many boys. David Morrison gave her a short peck on the cheek when he brought her home from the prom. This kiss was nothing like that. She felt the warmth of his body as he tightened his embrace. His tongue lightly circled her lips before pressing forward. She momentarily clenched her teeth to block its penetration, but his persistence paid off. She relaxed and felt his tongue probe the depths of her mouth. Her hands moved slowly up his chest and around his neck. Her fingers laced through his hair and held his head to hers. It felt like a hot poker was touching her in so many places and the heat spread through her whole body. Without warning, he pressed a hand on her breast. Grabbing his hand, she said, "C'mon, let go back to the dance."

"I'm sorry, I didn't mean to offend you."

She pulled him in the direction of the music. She knew all about the physical part of whoopee making. Nurses study how life is procreated, but until now she had never felt the desires that coursed through her body in the arms of a man.

He pulled her to a stop as the hay wagon passed by. Two large horses stepped lively as the bells on their harnesses jingled. "Want to ride? C'mon, let's jump on."

Nora squealed as Duke grabbed her under her arms and threw her up on the wagon. He ran alongside and hopped on. They found an open spot among the many couples nestled in the hay. Nora lay on her back and looked at the sky. Duke lay on his side and propped his head in his hand.

"I'm sorry about back there, I..."

He never got to finish his sentence; she pulled him until their lips met. She tasted and savored his tongue as it gently circled her lips. His breath was full and intoxicating and he pressed his tongue deep into her mouth. It was a magical moment. It was as though her heart had taken wings and she was floating on air. A warm tingle reached down to her toes. She found his hand and placed it on her breast. His fingers rubbed gently over the nipple before closing and gently squeezing. Her heart was about to leap from her chest. She unbuttoned her blouse and guided his hand inside her brassiere. His hand was that of a working man, coarse and rough, and she felt each finger as they gently encircled her breast. He pressed himself to her. The rapid beat of his heart matched hers. She gasped for air as her body was about to explode in a burst of passion and desire.

***

"Are you all right? Are you okay?"

Nora felt a hand on her arm. She opened her eyes and saw Sarah's concerned look.

"Are you okay? You were sort of jumping around and breathing funny."

Nora straightened in her seat. "I'm fine, just a bad dream." *No, actually it was a good dream. Do I remember going to Pine Lake? Every wonderful minute of it.*

Nora looked out the window. "This is Salt Lake City, Utah."

"I know, I've been reading the signs."

"We'll grab the Pony Express here. It'll take us to Ely."

Sarah's eye grew big. "Do we have to ride horses?

Nora laughed. "Maybe seventy-five to eighty years ago we would have; now it's just the name of the bus line that goes from Salt Lake to California, with a stop in the great city of Ely, Nevada."

"Is Ely as big as Salt Lake City?"

Nora laughed again. "Oh, lord no. Ely is small, a lot like Danville, but we have the largest copper mine in America. You'll like it there and you're really going to like my mom and dad."

"But will they like me?" she asked, her voice cracking.

"They're going to absolutely love you," Nora said, as the bus came to the stop. "Make sure you have all your things. We have a bit of a walk. The Pony Express terminal is a few blocks from here."

"Are we going to stay in Ely for a while?"

"That's the plan." *Subject to approval from Mom and Dad.*

42

Home Again in the Battle Born State

I never rode on a horse before," Sarah said. "But I'd like to try it someday."

"My daddy is a deputy sheriff for White Pine County. They sometimes use horses if they are searching for lost hunters or have to get off the main roads. Maybe he can take you riding someday."

That brought out a big smile. Sarah settled in her seat and watched the rugged terrain pass by. "This looks like what you see in the cowboy movies."

"You're right. We still have cowboys in Ely. This is the Wild West. Nevada is the Battle Born State, admitted to the Union during the Civil War. There are a lot of big ranches around there and the cowboys still round up cattle on horseback."

"Are there Indians?"

Nora laughed. "Shoshone, but you don't have to be afraid, they're not on the warpath any more. There's no war paint, no feathers in their hair, or leather loincloths. They dress like regular people and they're no longer out looking for scalps."

Sarah rested her head on Nora's shoulder. "When I first found out Mama was going to die, I wondered what would happen to me. Mama said everything would be alright, and I wanted to be strong for her, but I was scared. I was afraid getting on the bus and when we got to Aunt Betty's, I was

43

more afraid than ever. I want you to know I'm not afraid anymore and I want to thank you for all you've done for me."

Nora swallowed hard. "That's wonderful. I will try to make sure you never face that fear again."

It was just past eight-thirty at night when the bus pulled up to Economy Drug Store on Aultman Street. The sun was sliding behind Murray Summit, producing an awesome red-orange lightshow in the sky. A few people milled around, but no one paid any attention to the two women getting off the bus. Nora pushed her suitcase toward the store. "I don't know about you, but I need to use the restroom." They walked into the drug store and headed to the rear. "Mind if I go first?" Not waiting for an answer, Nora opened the door to the toilet and locked the door. She did have to go but was more interested in what was in the bottom of her purse. She brought out the miniature bottle. The first swallow went down quickly. She let herself taste the second, whispered an apology to Gladys, and swigged the rest. She wrapped the bottle in tissue and threw it in the wastebasket.

While Sarah used the restroom, Nora bought some Chiclets and popped a couple in her mouth. "This store is new. It wasn't here when I left in '41," she said to the bubbly gal behind the counter.

"We've been open for six months. You're the Jensen girl, Norma."

"Nora."

"I'm Cheryl Goodman; I was a few years ahead of you in school."

Nora smiled and tried to give the impression she remembered the girl. "It's been a while, hasn't it? Is there

44

still a phone booth down on the corner across from the hotel?"

The gal nodded.

Sarah studied each building as they stood outside of the drug store. "What is that big building?" she asked, pointing up the street.

"That's the high school. That's where I went and probably where you'll go, too." Nora turned and mumbled, "Unless all hell breaks loose at Mom and Dad's."

"I didn't hear you, what did you say?" Sarah said, trying to catch up.

Nora pointed back to the big domed building across the street from the school. "I said that was the White Pine County Courthouse. C'mon, there's a phone booth on the corner, we can call my folks to pick us up."

Nora dropped a nickel in the phone slot. She hesitated before dialing. She had written letters, she knew the address, but wondered if she remembered her parents' phone number. "It was only four digits, but was it 4858 or the other way around?" She felt a warm surge go to her head as she dialed the last number. By the third ring her mouth had dried and her tongue was stuck to the roof of her mouth. "Hello, Mom," she coughed out, "it's me, Nora. Yes, I'm at the phone booth...down from the drugstore...I know...can Dad come and pick us up? I have someone with me. I'll tell you about it when I get there. Yes, tell him we'll wait here for him."

"My dad is coming to pick us up," Nora told Sarah, trying to conceal her nervousness.

"This is a small town, I can see the end of it down the street." Sarah continued to look at the storefronts. "What do the people do?"

"The town is surrounded by ranches and I told you about the large mining operation west of here. A lot of people work for the railroad to haul the ore to the smelters in McGill. I'll give you a tour of the town. It will all look better in daylight."

"I think it's neat. It must have been fun growing up here."

Fun? "Oh yes, it's a great place to grow up." Wholesome is probably a better word.

A familiar pickup truck kicked up a cloud of dust as it came to a stop. The driver jumped out and hugged Nora, practically raising her off the ground.

"Hello, Daddy," Nora said.

The man released her and took a step back. "Why didn't you let us know you were coming? This is such a surprise."

With more to come. "It's been a whirlwind trip...came about rather suddenly."

"Is this your friend?"

"This is Sarah, Sarah Jean Connolly."

Her dad reached down and picked up the suitcases. He put them in the bed of the pickup and held the door open for the girls. "I got to get you guys to the house. Your mom is so excited. I know she can't wait to get you in her arms."

Nora waited for Sarah to jump into the middle seat before climbing in. She patted the dashboard. "I see you're still driving this old '37 Ford."

"Watch what you say. It's got to keep running until we start getting some new vehicles out of Detroit. All production went to the war. The sheriff did get notice we're going to get two new vehicles for the department, but there hasn't been any cars or trucks available for ordinary citizens yet."

Nora's mom was standing outside on the driveway when they drove up. She practically pulled Nora from the truck in her desire to embrace her daughter. "I can't believe you're here. You don't know how I prayed that you would come back to us." She used her apron to wipe the tears that flowed down her cheeks. "My goodness, you're so thin. How long can you stay? Where is your friend?"

Sarah followed Nora's dad out of the truck and came around the front. The headlights spotlighted her youthfulness and soft features. Nora's mom wiped her eyes again. "She's just a child." She looked inquisitively at Nora.

"Her name is Sarah Jean. We're traveling together." She took Sarah's hand and brought her forward. "Sarah, these are my parents, Harriet and John Jensen.

Not waiting for a formal introduction, Nora's mom put her arms around the girl and hugged her tight. "C'mon, let's go in the house. Are you hungry? Thirsty? I've got some lemonade in the refrigerator. How did you get here?"

"Came on the bus from Chicago." Nora pulled out chairs for both her and Sarah.

John took the seat across from them. "Are you a nurse, too?"

"Don't be silly, John, she's too young. Can't be more than fifteen." Harriet set a glass of lemonade in front of each of them. "Your last letter was so depressing about all the wounded. You didn't quit the army, did you?

John laughed. "You don't quit the army."

"Actually, I mustered out four days ago," Nora said. "Honorably discharged, I might add. With the war over, they let me out a couple months early. I'm sorry about the depressing letters. There was a lot going on. I was in a bad frame of mind."

"Because of that Italian fellow?" her mom asked.

"Yeah, him and all the other men who died in the stupid war."

"So, tell us about Sarah," her mother asked. "It's such a pretty name. Whose daughter is she?"

"Right now, no one's," Nora said. "Her dad was killed in the war and her mom recently died of cancer."

Harriet put her hand on Sarah's head and stroked her hair gently. "You poor child. Are you going to live with family?"

"That didn't work out, either." Nora proceeded to tell the whole story of how they met and the experience of meeting Aunt Betty and Uncle Bob.

"You just took her and brought her here without asking anyone?" her dad asked. "That could be considered kidnapping. My God, I'm a deputy sheriff; I've sworn to uphold the law."

"Stick your badge in your back pocket, John. What was Nora to do, leave the child in the hands of that pervert?"

"Of course not," he said. "But she should have gone to the authorities. Worked through legal channels."

"And where would that put her?" Harriet said. "Orphanage? Foster home? That's no place for a young lady."

Nora smiled. *I knew Mom would feel that way.*

"I understand, but it puts me in a bad position," John said.

"Don't worry, if anyone ask, we'll tell them you didn't know a thing about it." Harriet helped Sarah out of her chair. "C'mon, let's get you out of those clothes and into the shower. We need to get that diesel smell out of your hair."

Sarah looked at Nora for approval, who smiled and nodded. Rising, she turned to her dad. "The girl has no family outside of her mom's sister and her husband. What chance would we have going into court? We'd have to prove he's unfit, and Betty's probably afraid to testify against him." Nora choked back a tear. "I couldn't protect all the young men they brought to us missing limbs or with their insides blown apart. We lost men simply because there were so many wounded and we couldn't get to them. I'd get so frustrated, I just wanted to scream. I'm sorry, Dad, I simply could not turn my back on this child."

Her dad stood and took Nora into his arms. "Growing up, you brought home every stray dog and cat and every kid who needed a meal. I guess I can't expect you'd ever change. I'll put out some feelers; maybe this Bob character won't raise a fuss."

Nora hugged her dad. Suddenly, her knees gave out beneath her.

Nora Confronts Her Problem

Nora felt the cool wet towel on her forehead. She opened her eyes to see her mother's anxious look.

"Thank goodness you're awake. You really put a scare into us."

"I'm sorry, I don't know why that keeps happening to me." Nora tried to get up.

"You lay still; the doctor was here and thinks you're dehydrated and under nourished. We found a bottle of pills in your purse. The doctor is concerned that you might be mixing them with alcohol. You're not drinking, are you?"

Nora turned her head.

"Well, never mind," her mother said. "We're going to get you fixed up. Right now, I want you to stay in bed and rest."

"Where's Sarah Jean?"

"Sarah is fine. Right now, she's in the garden picking strawberries for supper. I don't want you worrying about her. She's a wonderful child, and we're getting along great." Harriet held out a glass of water. "Here, drink some of this. The doctor said to keep your fluid levels high."

Nora took a sip of water. "I don't mean to be causing you all this trouble."

"Nonsense," her mom said. "We have to get you strong again. I'm sorry for snooping in your purse, but the doctor wanted to know if you were on anything. I also found this."

Harriet took a folded piece of paper from her apron pocket. "It's a pencil drawing of a naked girl sitting on a beach towel."

Nora blushed.

"It's rather good. It looks a lot like you. Did you pose for it?"

"Sort of, he drew it from memory. I met this guy, Duke, when I went with Gladys to visit her folks in Pine Lake, Wisconsin. It was the Fourth of July, '42, just before I left for training camp. We danced in the street, went on a hayride, and at two in the morning we ended up skinny dipping in the lake."

Oh, my," Harriet said. "I think he might have taken advantage of the situation."

"I'm no angel, Mom. Whatever happened that night is on me. I practically seduced the pants right off him."

"You didn't, did you?"

Nora paused. "I had so much uncertainty at that time. I had poured my life into becoming a nurse. I didn't go out. I didn't date. All of a sudden, I was in the army and going to war.

"Who knew if any of us would survive?" Nora tried to read the expression on her mother's face. "It wasn't anything like I dreamed my first time would be. It was on the beach, it hurt, and I had sand everywhere." Nora ignored her mother's gasp. "To answer your question, I didn't pose for him, but I guess he saw enough of me without my clothes on to make the drawing. He sent it to me the week I shipped out."

Harriet folded the paper and handed it to Nora. "Make sure your father doesn't see this. I'm not sure he would understand."

51

"Aw, c'mon, Mom, didn't you and Dad ever do anything crazy like that?"

"Your father is not the affectionate type. I was lucky to squeeze you out of him. What happened to the boy?"

"Don't know. I broke things off, he was talking marriage. I was looking at a three-year commitment to the army; I couldn't think that far ahead."

Harriet pulled up the sheet and covered her daughter. "You get some rest. We'll get you up at suppertime."

Nora rubbed her stomach. *What's wrong with me? Why do I keep passing out? It can't be those two small bottles of gin. I drank more than that when I was overseas–a lot more. I could use a drink right now. Why did Gladys make me promise? I haven't done very well so far.*

Nora grimaced as the sharp pain in her stomach doubled her over. *Oh shit, what now?* Beads of sweat gathered on her forehead. Her lungs tightened and restricted her breathing. She felt creepy and crawly inside.

***

The next thing she knew, her mom was wiping her arm with a wet cloth. Nora's mouth was dry, her tongue crusted. "I feel awful," she said.

"You've been delirious for two days. It's the alcohol coming out of your system. It was touch and go; the doctor said you could have killed yourself mixing those pills and alcohol."

Nora rolled on her side, away from her mother's gaze. "I'm sorry," she mumbled.

"That's okay; just don't start feeling sorry for yourself. I know you. You're a strong person. You've hit a bump in the road, now you have to pick yourself up and get your life straightened out. It starts with getting plenty of rest."

"Sarah Jean?"

Harriet dipped the cloth in the pan of water, wrung it, and placed it on Nora's forehead. "She's doing great. She stayed with you while I went to the school. I talked to the principal and we're going to enroll her. She can finish out the school year and if she passes the year-end tests, she can advance to her junior year."

"I don't know if we'll be here that long."

"Don't be silly. You're not fit to go anywhere, and that girl needs to be in school. What do you intend to do, roam around the country like a couple of gypsies? School is done in three weeks. You can decide what you're going to do after that."

It was no use arguing. Nora knew full well when her mom made up her mind, discussion time was over.

"I don't want to get you and Dad in any trouble," Nora said, using the cloth to wipe the perspiration off her neck.

"Don't you worry about us; we can take care of ourselves. Are you hungry? Would you like some Campbell's Chicken Noodle?"

The soup was hot and felt soothing to her stomach. Growing up, it was the first medicine her mom gave her whenever she came down with something.

Sarah poked her head through the doorway. "Are you alright?"

Nora smiled. "Better." She put the soup on the night stand.

Sarah sat on the edge of the bed. "You were really out of it. You must have dreamed about being in the operating room. You were shouting orders and saying all sorts of crazy things. It was sort of scary."

Nora took Sarah's hand. "I'm feeling a lot better now. Mom says you're doing great. Do you like it here?"

"Your mom is really nice. She lets me help in the kitchen and I can pick anything I want from the garden. Your dad is nice, too, but I haven't had a chance to talk to him much."

"Dad isn't much for chit-chat. Mom's going to put you in school. What do you think about that?"

"I miss school. I think it will be great."

"It will be just until the end of the school year."

Harriet came into the room. "Will you be all right here by yourself? Your father's lunch is in the refrigerator. I'm going to take Sarah to buy some different clothes; everything she has is too warm for this climate."

"I'll be fine." Seeing Sarah's big smile, Nora poked her in the ribs. "New clothes, how about that?" The smile was answer enough. Nora finished her soup and lay back on the pillow. I knew Mom would do this. I may have been the one who brought home the strays, but she was the one who took care of them.

Trouble Returns

Nora woke about an hour later. She swung her legs off the bed and stood up slowly. She felt dizzy and grabbed the dresser to steady herself. She pulled her pajama bottoms up so she wouldn't trip on the pant legs. Using the walls and furniture, she made it to the kitchen. She opened the refrigerator and brought out the pitcher of lemonade. As she reached into the cupboard for a glass, she heard the screen door rattle. She turned and immediately recognized the man standing on the back step. He yanked on the door. The small hook and eye was no match for the man's strength and determination. The door swung open with such force the upper hinge came loose from the jamb and left the door hanging precariously against the house. The glass slipped from Nora's hand and shattered on the floor.

"I told you, you hadn't heard the last of me, bitch! I'm here to take my niece back to Chicago."

Nora fell back against the counter. "How did you find me?"

"You thought you were so damned smart," he said, his voice filled with hate and distaste. "Finding you was so easy, it makes me laugh." He moved toward her.

Nora quickly went to the opposite side of the table. "Stay away from me!" she yelled. He pushed the table into her stomach. "Greyhound gave me the bus driver's phone

55

number. All it took was a cock and bull story about leaving something on the bus." He over turned the chair in his way. "Oh yeah, the driver remembered you, alright, sitting in the back talking to that nigger." He feigned a move right and then laughed as Nora moved left. Drool dripped from his lower lip. "Did you know that black ass, Neil Jefferson, was some kind of a war hero? They had a big write-up about him in the newspaper, home address and everything. I told him I worked for the bus company and you were mugged in Chicago, had all your things stolen. He talked like a magpie, remembered everything about you, including your name — Nora Jensen — and your hometown...Ely, Nevada." The man pushed another chair aside. "Enough with this crap; where is she?"

"She's not here. We sent her away, she's...she's in Las Vegas."

"Don't lie to me, bitch. The lady in the drug store said you were here and brought a girl with you."

Nora opened the refrigerator door. "How about a beer? Let's talk about this."

The man slammed the door close. "Don't try to pussyfoot with me. I'm not leaving without her."

As Nora backed away, the noon fire siren went off. It startled the man and distracted him long enough for Nora to grab the butcher knife off the counter. She held it to her side. *Take one step and I swear, I'll stick this knife in you as far as I can.*

"I'm done waiting," he said. "Where is Sarah Jean?"

Nora took her free hand and yanked open her pajama top, exposing her breasts. "Why do you want that young stuff, when you can have this?"

The man stopped. "You mean, you'd let me fuck you just to keep Sarah?"

"I've been around; I know how to satisfy a big guy like you."

The man walked slowly toward her. "I don't see why I can't have both."

"Freeze, you sonofabitch!" came the voice behind him. "White County Sheriff's department. You make one move and I'll blow your stupid head off."

"Daddy," Nora sighed, pulling her pajama top closed.

The man turned his head to see a revolver leveled three inches from his nose. "Officer, I'm glad to see you," he choked. "I want to report a kidnapping."

"Put your hands behind your back," barked Officer Jensen, who quickly handcuffed the man and pushed him to his knees. "You so much as cough and I'll blow you away."

"I came here to find my niece," the man pleaded. "This woman kidnapped her."

"You shut up," John said.

Nora kept the knife pointed in the man's direction. "I'm glad you still come home for lunch."

John peeled his daughter's fingers from the knife.

"That's Sarah's Uncle Bob. He wants to take her back to Chicago. What are we going to do?"

"Well, I know a little about this Bob Cooper. I've been talking to Chicago P.D. They are quite aware of him. He was accused of sexually assaulting two minor girls in his neighborhood, got off on a technicality. He has one charge of solicitation and one charge of battery. He beat a prostitute so bad her own mother didn't recognize her.

"The bitch had it coming. She tried to cheat me," Bob said.

"Shut up. Nobody's talking to you. The way I see it, I came home to find this scumbag about to attack my daughter. Her pajamas torn, her breast exposed. A clear case of attempted rape. Good for ten plus years in prison.

"She tried to seduce me," Bob argued.

"What jury would believe this beautiful young lady, an army nurse, would be interested in a fat slob like you?"

"You're trying to railroad me." Bob attempted to get up.

"If you get up, I will take it as an attempt to escape and I will have to shoot you."

Bob returned to the kneeling position.

"I think Bob here is smart enough to know he's in big trouble and should abandon this silly quest to put a claim on Sarah Jean. If he were foolish enough to try to gain custody, I'm sure children's services would be interested in hearing what those two little girls and the prostitute would have to say. I'm sure, too, that his wife Betty would paint a gruesome picture of our Uncle Bob.

"A wife can't testify against her husband," Bob hissed.

"Wrong. She cannot be compelled to, but when offered protection and swearing on a bible, she certainly can if she wants to. I'd think about that if I were you." John helped Bob to his feet. "I have a proposition for you. I'm going to file an open charge of attempted rape against an unknown perpetrator. If you ever step foot in Nevada or try to block our attempt to gain legal guardianship of Sarah Jean, I will see to it that you spend the rest of your life behind bars."

"That's blackmail," Bob protested.

"In law enforcement, we call it a negotiated resolution. Do we have a deal?"

Bob looked at Nora. "You just met her. Sarah can't mean anything to you."

"She deserves a chance to grow, untainted by the likes of you, and able to make her mark in the world."

Probably knowing it was not a good time to continue the argument, Bob reluctantly agreed to the deal and John removed the handcuffs. He walked Bob to his car. "We have a thing here in the west, it's called the rattlesnake rule. A diamondback will rattle its tail to warn you before he strikes. Since we cannot be sure what the snake's intentions are, we preemptively shoot them. Consider this your one and only warning. If you ever come near my family again, I will shoot first and ask questions later."

Bob gave John a dirty look and drove off.

Nora was dressed by the time her dad came back in the house. She hugged him and whispered, "I would have killed him if he had taken one more step."

"I believe you would have, but it's better this way. I don't think we'll have any more trouble with Uncle Bob."

"Are you serious...we're really going to seek legal custody of Sarah?" Nora asked.

"I think that's what your mother has in mind."

Nora gave her dad another big hug as Harriet and Sarah walked in the back door.

"What happened to the screen?" Harriet asked.

John looked at Nora. "A dust devil came through and about tore it off its hinges."

Nora smiled and gave Sarah a hug.

A Letter to Gladys

Nora sat at the kitchen table, opened her spiral tablet, unscrewed the cap from her fountain pen, and began writing.

June 10, 1945, Dear Gladys, I probably should have written sooner, but things have been a little crazy around here.

She took a drink of her Kool-Aid and continued to tell her friend about everything that happened since arriving in Ely. She started with how much Sarah Jean had blossomed since enrolling in school, and how well she did on her final test.

Mom has taken her under her wing and Sarah calls her Mom. It warms my heart to hear her say that. It's like having the baby sister I never had.

Nora then wrote about passing out the night they arrived and going through a bout of detoxification.

The doctor said I was probably using alcohol to deal with the stress of the war. Shoot, I could have told him that. He also warned me it could take up to a year for the effects to completely leave my system. I'm proud to say I haven't had an alcoholic drink since.

She acknowledged that Gladys had been right about the therapeutic value of her mom's home cooking.

I'm not sure I'm happy gaining ten pounds, but I definitely feel better and stronger. I'm pretty much over blaming God for all the evil and bad things that happen in the world. Evil people are to blame.

Nora sat back in her chair and tried to choose her next words. Once she began, she didn't hold back and wrote in detail the scare she had with Robert Cooper. She praised her father for the way he handled the situation and was hopeful it would be the last time they would have to deal with that pervert. She mentioned how her mom has been on a mission, determined to become Sarah's legal guardian, describing all the paperwork they had to fill out, and how it all had to be sent to Hendricks County, Indiana where Sarah and her mom lived. The rest of the letter was about the weather, putting her resume together and being anxious to find a job and getting back to work.

Nora's dad came in the back door and tossed the mail on the table. "There's a letter from Indiana."

Pushing her tablet aside, Nora grabbed the official looking envelope and feverishly tore it open. Her frown became more intense as she read each line. "That bastard!" she shrieked. "Daddy," she said, handing her dad the letter, "Read this."

She picked up her pen and finished her letter to Gladys.

Got to go, that bastard Robert Cooper is contesting our request to become Sarah's guardian. Will write again soon. Nora.

Her dad shook his head and tossed the letter on the table. "I thought we were done with that asshole. How in hell did he find out? The county must have notified him. I should have arrested him, or better yet shot him, when I had the chance."

61

"They want us to appear for a meeting on June 26th and bring Sarah with us." Nora got up and paced around the table. "We should never have tried to go through the proper channels. I should have taken Sarah and disappeared, gone to some small town in Idaho or Wyoming. Nobody would have ever found us there."

"You can't hide forever," her dad said. "They would catch up to you sooner or later. I wouldn't worry too much; I think when we get done telling the county officials about Robert Cooper, his goose will be cooked."

Nora scooped up the letter and tried to force it back into the envelope as her mom and Sarah came in the back door.

Harriet saw the official looking envelope. "Is that from Indiana? Have they approved our request?"

Nora was about to speak, but her father interrupted her and nodded in Sarah's direction. "We should know something on the twenty-sixth. We all have to attend a meeting with social services."

"Oh dear," Harriet said. "I thought we could handle all this by mail, but if that's the case, we better start making plans to go." She looked at John. "Will you need to take some vacation time?"

"I've got plenty; that shouldn't be a problem. Sarah, why don't you and I go out to the garden and pick some berries for supper?"

Sarah nodded and took a pan from the cupboard. "The raspberries are really good right now, Daddy."

John raised his eyebrows and a smile crept across his face. He would tell his wife later it was the first time she called him 'Daddy.'

As soon as the two left, Nora handed her mom the letter. "We could have a problem. I'm sure Dad feels we don't have to concern Sarah at this point."

Her mom kept shaking her head as she read. "That man is the devil himself, but that won't matter, because we have good and right on our side. I'm sure those people will understand that Sarah would be better off with us."

Nora tapped her fingers on the table. *Right, Mom, and maybe you can call down a band of angels from the heavens to smite him.* "You never know how these things will turn out when dealing with a government bureaucracy. I told Dad I should take Sarah and find a place in some small town where no one would ever find us."

"Hide like some criminal? That's no life for you and certainly not a life for Sarah. No, we will go to Indiana and do this the right way."

Nora laid her head on the table. *God, I questioned you being all good and powerful when you stood by and let all those young men die in the war. I get the free will thing, but this is different. If you allow that man to put his hands on this innocent child, all this, 'God is good' stuff is nothing but a lot of B.S.* She pushed herself away from the table. "I've got to get out of here. I'm going for a walk." She threw the pen on the table and stormed out the back door.

***

As the date circled on the calendar drew closer, Nora became anxious. She pleaded, prayed, bartered, and demanded that God intervene on their behalf. She didn't want to believe that God would allow the county officials to give Sarah over to that man.

At first Nora and her mom kept the upcoming meeting and the fact that Uncle Robert was contesting their guardianship from Sarah. They didn't give the girl credit for piecing conversations together and arriving at the truth herself. Nora was surprised how calmly her young friend was taking the news. During supper one evening Sarah declared. "I'm almost sixteen. I'll just tell them that I want to live here with you."

Harriet fanned herself with her apron. "And we love having you here. This is just a small bump in the road. We will go to Indiana and make sure you get to stay with us."

Nora pushed her peas around on her plate. *I wish I could be that certain.*

"I've got the train reservations," John said. We pick up the City of San Francisco Streamliner in Elko on Monday the twenty-third at ten in the morning. We're in Denver the following morning and Chicago early on Wednesday. We have a three-hour layover before boarding the Hoosier State train that takes us to Indianapolis. From there, a shuttle will bring us into Danville around suppertime. We can find a hotel for Wednesday night and be ready for our eleven o'clock meeting on Thursday."

"Elko?" Harriet questioned. That's three hours from here. Who's going to take us?"

"Ben, the other deputy, said he would. We need to leave here by five to give us plenty of time."

"I can pay for Sarah Jean and me," Nora said. "I feel bad that this is costing you all this money."

"Your mother and I have never seen that part of the country. It's going to be a nice trip for everybody." John looked at Sarah. "It'll be fun, right?"

Sarah quickly agreed. "Coming out here I had my first bus ride and now this will be my first train ride. Do they have beds?"

John hesitated. "They do, but we're traveling coach. They'll give us blankets and pillows, but we'll have to sleep in our seats."

"That's the way it was on the bus. It's not so bad," Nora said.

"I can pack sandwiches and snacks to take along," Harriet said. "That will save us a little money. We'll only have to buy drinks."

A Trip to Indiana

The long-awaited day finally came. The four of them boarded the train and found seats that faced each other. Sarah sat by the window and pointed out every river and mountain peak. John and Harriet, too, were fascinated by the passing scenery. Nora was preoccupied with the upcoming meeting and wondered what problems pain-in-the-ass Uncle Bob would cause. Her consternation was the result of having to deal with imbecilic bureaucrats during three years in the army.

The train rolled into Chicago at four in the morning, right on schedule. This was the crappy part of the trip, being rousted off the train and having to spend three hours in the terminal waiting to board the one to Indianapolis. Harriet was concerned this middle-of-the-night disruption would upset Sarah, who handled it with ease; Nora was the cranky one. "I still think I should have taken Sarah and found some out of the way place where no one would find us."

By the time they got to Indianapolis and caught the shuttle to Danville, everyone was on edge. Usually the rock of Gibraltar, even Harriet was beginning to unravel. She pleaded with John to find her a shower and a bed to lie down on.

Talking to the driver, John asked, "Could you recommend a good hotel in Danville?"

The driver gave him a quizzical look. "Ain't no such thing. Best they got is Center House, they take in boarders. Mrs. Canterbury rents by the week, but she may be able to put you up for a night or two. I kin drop you off there; it's on my way."

"Is it close to the courthouse? We have a meeting there tomorrow morning," John said.

The driver smiled. "Across the street."

John went back to his seat. "I can't believe it, Danville doesn't have a hotel."

"I could have told you that," Sarah said.

"Do you know anything about the Center House?"

"Sure, it's right on Main Street."

"I guess I should have checked with you on this before we got on the shuttle," John said. "We probably could have stayed in Indianapolis."

"Is this Center House clean?" Harriet asked Sarah. "If it's clean, got a shower and a bed, it'll be good enough for me."

Sarah nodded. "Mama always said Mrs. Canterbury ran a good house. Mama cooked for Mrs. Canterbury before she took sick."

Nora was still in her foul mood. *This ought to be interesting.*

The driver stopped the bus in front of a large Victorian house. Two old gentlemen sat in rocking chairs on a front porch that stretched the full width of the building. For its age, the house appeared in good repair and sported a new coat of light-yellow paint. The deep lavender color on the shutters and gingerbread that lined the porch roof made the house look both cheerful and inviting.

"Should I go in and see what it looks like inside?" John asked.

"If they got room, we're staying," Harriet declared.

The four trudged up the steps. John led the way and Sarah brought up the rear. Mrs. Canterbury was a sweet lady in her sixties and greeted them in the foyer. "Oh dear, I have just one small room available, barely big enough for two."

Nora stepped forward. "Do you have a cot or sofa? Sarah and I can sleep on the floor if need be."

It was then that Mrs. Canterbury caught sight of the girl standing next to Nora. "Sarah Jean!" She shrieked and hugged the child as if she was one of her own. "We heard you were taken out west someplace."

Nora did not like the way the woman eyeballed each of them. "We've come over two thousand miles to get this matter resolved. We've been on a train and in these clothes for three days; do you have room for us or not?"

"Of course, two can take the room and two can sleep on the hide-a-bed in my apartment."

"You and Dad take the room," Nora said. "Sarah and I will sleep down here."

John and Harriet followed Mrs. Canterbury up the stairs. Nora and Sarah took a seat in the parlor.

"Mrs. Canterbury was happy to see you," Nora said.

"I would come here after school, do my homework, and wait for Mom to finish making supper for the boarders. We got to take home leftovers."

Mrs. Canterbury came down the stairs and ushered Nora and Sarah to her apartment in the back. "This sofa makes into a double bed. I'll get some fresh sheets. I'm sorry; I didn't catch your name."

"It's Nora."

"Pretty name; you can call me Florence," she said, opening the bed. "If you'd like to shower, the bath is through the kitchen and to the left. Dinner is at six." She finished putting the sheets on the bed. "Just make yourself at home; I'll let the kitchen know we have extra people for dinner."

"We don't mean to put you through a lot of trouble."

"No trouble," Florence said. "We're having chicken noodle soup and cornbread. The cook made a big kettle, plenty for everyone."

Nora opened the straps on her brown leather suitcase and handed Sarah some items of clothing. "Why don't you shower first? It will feel good to freshen up and put on a change of clothes." It was apparent that Sarah knew exactly where to go and was off in a flash.

Nora flopped spread eagle on the bed. *I wonder what the lady of the house meant, 'taken out west.'* Nora sat up when Florence came back into the apartment. "Mrs. Canterbury, what do you know about us?"

"I try not to stick my nose in other people's business. Sarah Jean's mom told me weeks before she passed that she was sending Sarah to her sister in Chicago. We all thought that's where she was. Then Georgina over at the courthouse got a letter saying Sarah was in Nevada. Everyone in town wondered what happened."

Nora stood and related the series of events that led to this point in time. She started with seeing Sarah and her mother at the bus depot in Indianapolis and being unable to contact her Aunt Betty by phone. That led to the confrontation with Uncle Bob. "I just couldn't let Sarah stay with that man," Nora said.

"Oh dear, I see what you mean."

"I feel bad for deceiving Mrs. Halsted. I shouldn't have done that. My mom and dad would really like to become Sarah's legal guardians. Mom has taken Sarah under her wing, and Sarah calls them Mom and Dad. She's enrolled in school and has passed all her year-end tests. She is blossoming into such a beautiful young lady."

Sarah walked into the room at the tail end of the sentence. "Who's beautiful?"

Nora smiled. "You are, and we are so proud of you."

Sarah continued to towel her hair. "I hope Mom got a shower, it really felt great."

Nora knew by the smile on Florence's face, she had heard the reference to Mom.

The chatter around the supper table began with a collective agreement that the soup was the best anyone could remember, and the corn bread complemented it nicely. The discussion then moved to the unanimous acknowledgment that a shower never felt so good. Speaking for the family, John thanked Mrs. Canterbury for taking them in.

Florence offered the family coffee in the parlor. She said she was pleased they had made the trip, happy for Sarah Jean, and hoped everything would go their way at tomorrow's meeting.

Nora noticed Sarah was unusually quiet. "Are you okay?"

"I was just wondering where Mama is buried."

Florence stood. "I can show you; would you like to go see?"

"I would." Sarah jumped up from her chair.

Nora stood, too. "I think we all would like to go."

Florence took Sarah's hand. "Let's go out back and pick a rose. You can leave it there for her."

It took Florence a little time to find the right spot. They gathered around a mound of new grass with a small metal plate that marked the burial plot. "It was a simple service," Florence said. "Pastor Wiggins had some kind words to say about her."

Sarah knelt on the grass and set the rose on the mound. "It's me, Mama," she whispered. "I'm sorry I couldn't be here for your funeral. I want you to know, I'm doing okay. I think God sent Nora and her family to take care of me. I miss you. I wish we weren't so far apart."

Nora knelt beside Sarah. "Your mom will always be at your side. Every time you see a rose it will be a sign that she is near."

Sarah turned and fell into Nora's arms. "Don't ever leave me," she sobbed. "I couldn't bear it if you leave me, too."

"I won't. I will always be there for you; Mom and Dad, too." Nora stroked Sarah's hair. "Your mom is very proud of you. She wants you to be strong, to make something of yourself, and live a life she never had."

She helped Sarah to her feet. "Are you going to be alright?"

"I'm going to get a summer job so I can make enough money to buy Mama a grave stone," Sarah said, wiping her eyes. "I want people to know where she's buried."

The Family Meets with County Officials

The smell of fresh bakery wafted through the house. John and Harriet sat fully dressed in the parlor when Sarah and Nora came out of the back apartment.

"What is that delicious smell?" Sarah asked.

"I made cinnamon rolls; would you like some?" asked Mrs. Canterbury. "What time is your meeting?"

"Eleven," Nora said, putting a roll on her plate. "Hopefully, it won't take too long, but in case we have a problem, can you put up with us for an extra night?"

"Of course," Florence said. "I hope everything works out for you. Sarah Jean seems to be very happy living with you."

"It all hinges on how much trouble this Uncle Bob stirs up," John said.

No one said a word. It was as if they all, in their own minds, wondered how things were going to play out. As they walked out the front door, Nora straightened Sarah's collar.

Danville was the size of Ely; both had about twenty-five hundred inhabitants and both were the county seat. The Hendricks County Courthouse sat directly across the street from Center House. As they climbed the courthouse steps John checked the letter. "The meeting is in room 206. I imagine we're meeting with this Georgina Watson," he said.

Sarah was the first through the door and immediately spied a familiar face. "Look!" she shouted. "There's Gladys."

Nora was flabbergasted. "What are you doing here?" She gave Gladys a big hug.

Sarah squeezed between them and hugged Gladys, too. John and Harriet closed in on the group.

"Mom, Dad, this is Gladys Iverson. She's the one I trained under at Chicago General."

Gladys shook John's hand and gave Harriet a hug. "It's so nice to finally meet you folks."

Nora pressed Gladys again. "What are you doing here?"

"I thought I would come down and give you some moral support and possibly be a character witness for you. They came to the hospital to do a background check on you and told me about the meeting. Besides, it was a nice drive, and it gave me a chance to see you again."

"That was really nice of you," Harriet said. "Nora has told us so much about you; it's nice to finally meet."

"What did they ask you? What did you tell them?" Nora asked.

"Just the usual stuff; I gave them a glowing report on you."

"You know, that weasel Uncle Bob is contesting our effort to become Sarah's legal guardian," Nora said as the group ascended the stairs to the second floor.

Gladys hesitated on the step. "I don't believe it. There is no way they would consider giving Sarah to him, would they?"

"We hope not," said John.

Room 206 was a meeting room adjacent to the courtroom. It was normally used by lawyers to confer with their clients. In the center of the room stood a long table with a chair at each end and four chairs on each side. Extra chairs were along the far wall underneath the windows and against the inside wall immediately to the right of the door.

Sarah was the first to enter. She abruptly made a U-turn.

Nora was about to ask when she looked in the room and saw the Coopers sitting on the far side of the table. She had to take a second look to make sure it was them. Bob was clean shaven, hair combed, and decked out in a suit and tie. A string of pearls and a natty hat complemented the green dress Betty wore. They looked upper middle class.

Who are they trying to kid? I can still see his black heart under that fancy suit. I just hope they can, too.

"Come in," said the lady at the head of the table. "You can sit on this side." She pointed to the chairs opposite the Coopers.

Nora took the first chair, followed by Sarah, Harriet, and John. Gladys took a seat behind them. An older lady was seated behind the Coopers. Nora rolled her eyes to Sarah and nodded in the lady's direction.

"That's Mrs. Halstad," Sarah whispered.

The woman at the head of the table got up and closed the door. Sitting down, she opened a thick manila folder. "My name is Georgina Watson. I am the Welfare Superintendent for Hendricks County. It might be good if we all introduce ourselves. Let's start with Mr. Cooper."

"I'm Robert Cooper, Sarah's uncle," he said, adjusting his tie.

Nora stared him down. *You're not fooling anybody, you, lecherous bastard.* She watched with interest as his wife introduced herself. Her eyes never left the table and the words Elizabeth Cooper spoke were barely audible, as if afraid of something. Nora studied the woman's face. *What's that all about?*

The woman sitting behind the Coopers stood. "My name is Eleanor Halstad. I was Audrey Connolly's neighbor." She gave Sarah a nod and small smile.

John and Harriet introduced themselves, as did Gladys.

"Nice to see you again, Miss Iverson," Georgina said with a smile. "I'm assuming this is Sarah Jean," she said looking at the girl. Sarah nodded.

Mrs. Watson waited for Nora to speak.

Nora said her name, took Sarah's hand, and smiled at her young friend.

"This will be an informal meeting to determine what is in the best interest of Sarah Jean Connolly." The woman pointed in Sarah's direction and continued. "As you may or may not know, Audrey Connolly passed intestate, meaning she died without leaving a will. As a minor, Sarah Jean became a ward of the county. The county also has the responsibility of distributing the estate. County Judge Roy Morton will decide of how the child will be taken care of. Since we have two parties wanting to assume legal guardianship of Sarah, it is my job to interview all of you so I can present my recommendation to the judge. Judge Morton might also have some questions for you. Any questions so far?"

"Will this be handled today? We've come two thousand miles," Nora said.

"The Coopers are also from out of town," Georgina replied. "The judge and I discussed this. He's blocking two hours of his time tomorrow. Hopefully we will be able to clear this matter then."

No one seemed pleased with that. Nora glared across the table at Bob Cooper. He returned it in kind.

"Let's get started then." The lady was surprised to see Sarah raise her hand. "Did you have a question?"

"Can't I just tell you who I want to live with?" Sarah asked.

The lady was taken aback. "It doesn't work that way. You're still a minor."

"I'm almost sixteen," Sarah protested.

"You might be able to take that up with the judge. I will have to make a report regardless. Since the Jensens made the first request, let's get a little background information on them." Mrs. Watson asked John and Harriet a ton of questions. Everything about their finances, education, and home life, practically going back to the time they met. She asked about their house and whether Sarah would have her own room. Nora thought her mom and dad offered a stable, loving environment for Sarah to thrive in.

The welfare lady asked basically the same question of the Coopers. Robert spoke and painted a similar rosy picture of what Sarah's life would be like living with them.

Nora was about to explode. Luckily, her father caught her attention and put his finger to his lips. Nora slumped in the chair. *He's lying through his teeth. Didn't you check on him? He's got a police record. To hear him, he's Mr. Goody Two Shoes.*

"Let's move to the night of May 10th. Mrs. Halstad said she drove Sarah and her mother to the bus station in Indianapolis. Is that correct?"

Mrs. Halstad stood. "It was in the middle of the night. Audrey had gotten the news from the doctor that the cancer had spread pretty much throughout her body. She really wanted to get Sarah to her sister in Chicago."

"So, you were aware that Sara was going to Chicago to live with her aunt and uncle?"

Mrs. Halstad nodded. "That's correct."

To Nora's consternation, Mrs. Watson wrote more on her tablet.

"She talked to her sister earlier in the day," Eleanor said. "Audrey didn't have a phone. She was using mine. She said Sarah would arrive about nine in the morning. I also heard her say she had sent a letter with more information."

Again, addressing Mrs. Halstad, Ms. Watson pointed her pencil toward Nora. "Did you see or talk to Ms. Jensen when you were at the bus station?"

"No. Sarah was sitting by the window, Audrey and I waved to her as the bus drove off."

Ms. Watson turned to Nora. "Let's move to how you met Sarah Jean."

Nora sat straight. "The first time I saw Sarah, she was saying good bye to her mother. When she got on the bus, we made eye contact as she came up the aisle. She sat in the seat beside me."

"Did you speak to Sarah's mother?" Georgina asked.

'No, I was on the bus. I watched them out the window." Nora waited for the woman to finish writing in her tablet before continuing. She paused at the point where they were unable to reach Sarah's aunt by phone.

"What made you decide to go to the Cooper residence?"

"I couldn't just walk away and leave this fifteen-year-old in the bus station." *What is this woman thinking?* "I am familiar with the city. As you know, I took my nurse's training at Chicago General. It was my intention to make sure Sarah got safely to her Aunt Betty's place."

"I know you and Sarah arrived at the Cooper residence. What is unclear is why you took Sarah with you when you left?"

Nora glanced across the table. Bob had a shit-eating grin on his face. "When Mrs. Cooper opened the door, I was aghast. Her face was puffy and bruised and she had a black and blue shiner under her eye. We saw battered women at the hospital all the time. I recognized the signs right away. The room looked like there had been a knock-down drag-out fight. The furniture was askew. Mr. Cooper came into the room, drinking a beer. He put his hand on Sarah and made some off-colored remark. You could see it in his eyes, his intentions were not honorable. I couldn't in good conscious leave Sarah there."

Bob raised his hand when Nora mentioned the condition of the room. Mrs. Watson called on him. "Would you like to respond to that?"

"I was nothing like that," he began. "We had an end-of-the-war party for some friends and hadn't had time to straighten up the place. As for Betty's face, she did one of those numbers where you get your foot on the wrong side of the door and then walk into the edge. She hit it pretty hard. I can see where Miss Jensen could have drawn the wrong conclusion."

"That is so much bullshit," Nora blurted. "It took repeated blows for her face to look like that. How many times did she walk into your fist...oh...excuse me, the door?"

Robert jumped to his feet and pounded his fist on the table. "You had no right to take Sarah from us."

Mrs. Watson tapped her pencil repeatedly on the table. "Please, we are not going to accomplish a thing if this becomes a shouting match. Save those arguments for Judge Morton. Moving forward, Miss Iverson, I believe you told me that Nora and Sarah came to you that day. Is that true?"

Gladys shifted in her chair. "Yes, they came to the hospital."

Mrs. Watson paused, probably expecting Gladys to provide more details. When none were forthcoming, she asked, "Did Nora or Sarah say anything about going to the Coopers?"

"Sarah told me basically the same thing Nora just told you," Gladys said.

"Did she say anything else?"

"Just that her uncle made her feel very uncomfortable."

"Did she say how?"

"The way he looked at her."

Mrs. Watson tapped her pencil and Nora wondered if it was as irritating to the others as it was her. *If she continues to do that, I'm either going to ask her to stop or snatch the pencil from her and break the damned thing in half.*

"Sarah didn't say he touched her or embraced her to make her feel that way, just the way he looked at her?" Georgina asked.

Gladys was quick to respond. "Young girls have a sense about things like that. They know when they are being leered at."

"Are you a psychologist?"

"No, but I deal with young rape victims all the time and I believe I have some knowledge of the people who commit these crimes. These victims always say, 'I saw it in his eyes,

I should have tried to get away sooner, or made more of an effort.'"

If she agreed or disagreed with Gladys' response, Georgina didn't show it. She moved to the next question. "Did Nora disclose to you her plan to take Sarah with her to her home in Ely, Nevada?"

"Yes," Gladys answered weakly.

"Did you think this was appropriate? Did you question her about doing this?"

"I suggested she should talk to social services, to work through proper channels."

Nora was about to unload on Mrs. Watson when the woman changed the subject. "I read in your final evaluation of Nora before she graduated from nurses training. You used words like 'impulsive and quick to action." Do you think these words describe Nora today?"

Gladys bristled. "I also said she was kind, caring, thorough, and sensitive. Nora Jensen was not only the best nursing student I ever had, she is also the nicest person I ever met."

Nora raised her hand. "If you are wondering why I choose to act the way I did, why don't you just ask me?"

Georgina sat back in her chair. "I would be most interested in hearing why you took the action you did."

"First of all," Nora said. "Sarah is a dear, sweet child. We became instant friends. She told me of her mother's illness and why she was going to Chicago. Here was a fifteen-year-old girl being sent away because her mother was no longer able to take care of her. It had to be crushing. She cried herself to sleep on my shoulder. My heart went out to her. I was trying to help, but when I encountered the Coopers, there was no way I was going to let this child be hurt any more than she already had been."

"But did you think it was right to take Sarah half way across the country instead of seeking help as Miss Iverson had suggested?" Georgina asked.

"I had just come back from three years in Europe. You can't imagine how many orphans this war has made. In our off-times, many of my fellow nurses and I would go to these orphanages to administer to the medical needs of these children. It would break our hearts to see their sad faces. They would hold onto our hands or cling to our legs, seeking any kind of affection. Maybe that was still fresh in my mind. I couldn't visualize putting Sarah in that kind of situation. I wanted her to know a loving family relationship. The kind she would get with my mother and dad. She deserved that."

"Although I might not agree with you taking her to Nevada, I can certainly understand your reasons for doing so." Mrs. Watson wrote quite a bit in her tablet. "I'm sure there was no malicious intent, but I wish you would have let us handle the situation."

"Her mother sent Sarah to live with us," Bob said. "She had no right to take her."

"I tend to agree with you, but that will be up to the judge to decide." Georgina placed her pencil beside the folder.

Up until now John Jensen had remained silent. "I'm a deputy Sheriff of White Pine County," he said. "When Nora related her experience with the Coopers, I did a little checking. It might be interesting if you check with the Chicago Police Department regarding Mr. Cooper."

"You're no angel," Bob snapped in reply. "You tried to shoot me when I came to Ely to pick up Sarah."

"You were about to assault my daughter."

"Whoa, wait a minute!" yelled Mrs. Watson. "You went to Nevada?"

"I tracked her down," Bob pointed his finger at Nora.

"He broke into our home," said John. "I came home for lunch and found the screen door torn from its hinges. I entered the kitchen as he was about to attack my daughter. I drew my weapon and commanded him to stand down. He's right; if he had made one wrong move, I would have shot him."

"Your daughter was offering me sex to leave Sarah there."

Georgina jumped from her chair. "That's it. This meeting is over. I am taking custody of Sarah. You people will have to argue this out in front of the judge at nine in the morning. I will now ask you all to leave this room." She came and took Sarah by the hand.

Nora saw the fear in Sarah's eyes. "Where are you taking her? Can we see her later?"

"She will be safe. You will see her in the morning in Judge Morton's courtroom."

The Ten Thousand Dollar Question

The Jensens and Gladys stood on the sidewalk outside the courthouse. "I should not have come," Gladys said. "I don't think I helped your case at all, probably made it worse."

"Don't be silly," Nora said. "If this goes bad, it's all on me. I was the one who set this whole fiasco into motion. Right now, my only regret is that I didn't take Sarah and get lost in some small town in Idaho or Wyoming."

"We shouldn't have tried to become her legal guardians," Harriet said. They might never have found us."

"If that dirtbag Robert Cooper found us," Nora said. "I'm sure Mrs. Watson would have found us, too. Our only hope is that the judge will hold off deciding until they can check on Bob's arrest record."

"I expected this to be cut and dried and be out of here today," Gladys said. "I have to get back to Chicago."

"Thank you for coming down; I'll let you know how it turns out," Nora said as everyone took turns hugging.

Mrs. Canterbury was waiting at the door. The drawn look on everyone's faces answered her immediate question. Her second question: where was Sarah?

"Mrs. Watson took her into custody," Nora said. "I guess the county will hold her until the judge makes his decision. We barely had the chance to say good bye."

Harriet put her arm around Nora. "Are you going to be alright if the judge rules against us?"

"I'll be alright as long as he doesn't give Sarah to the Coopers. Did you watch Mrs. Cooper during the meeting? She never looked at any of us. She kept her hands in her lap and seldom looked up. I think she's struggling with all of this." Nora paced the floor. "She knows good and well what I said about the situation was the gospel truth. That snake Bob has got her scared to death."

"I think you hit the nail on the head," John said. "There is an outside chance she may crack. I think in her heart, she wants to do right for her sister and for Sarah."

"I'd like to think that," Nora said. "But I'm afraid he's got her too scared to say anything. I don't know what will happen tomorrow."

Mrs. Canterbury's cook had prepared an outstanding meal. Batter-fried chicken with slaw and potato salad. Sadly, the Jensens were so distraught, they couldn't do justice to the meal. Harriet and John retired to their room soon after supper. Nora followed Florence to the back apartment.

"Would you like some hot tea?" Florence asked. "We can sit on the back porch and watch the sun go down."

"I'd love some." After settling into a rocker, Nora asked, "What was Sarah's mom like?"

"A sweet woman, hard worker, funny, full of life," Florence said. "She was devastated when her husband signed up for the navy. He was Irish and drank a little too much. Rumor had it that he was drunk when he and some of his drinking buddies joined up. He arrived in Honolulu two days before the Japanese attack on Pearl Harbor. He was aboard the Arizona and went down with the ship."

"So, Audrey was left to raise Sarah alone. And then ends up with cancer," Nora said sadly.

"The man, to his credit, did one smart thing; he signed up for the navy life insurance. Audrey got a check from the government for ten thousand dollars."

"Wow! That should have helped her a lot."

"She never spent a nickel of it. She put it all into a certificate of deposit in Sarah's name. She told me that CD was for Sarah's college education."

Nora took a sip of tea. *That snake in the grass Bob knows about that money. That's the reason he's so hell-bent on gaining guardianship of her.* "How long did her mom know she had cancer?"

"She probably ignored the early signs. By the time they caught it, she was in the advanced stages. It took her down in a matter of a few months." Florence wiped a tear on her sleeve. "She needed a chair while working in the kitchen. She had to sit a lot getting through a meal, but she wouldn't give up. She worked up until two weeks before she passed."

"I can only imagine how all of this would affect a fifteen-year-old. Which reminds me, where do you think they're keeping her?"

"We don't have any kind of facility. Georgina might have just taken her home with her. That would be my guess."

The sun set in beautiful red splendor. Pushing with her foot, Nora kept her chair moving back and forth. *Have we come all this way only to lose tomorrow? They say justice is blind. I just hope it will see through Bob Cooper's façade.* Nora stopped her chair. "There's got to be some way to stop him."

***

Breakfast was country style, with eggs, pancakes, ham, and fried potatoes. When John finished, he put his napkin on his empty plate. "My compliments to the cook; I'm going to miss all this wonderful food."

Harriet raised an eyebrow. "Maybe when we get home, you can take over the cooking," she said. Then turning to Mrs. Canterbury, "I will admit, I was a little apprehensive about staying here, but the room is comfortable, the food wonderful, and you have been a most gracious host. Thank you for everything."

Florence wiped up the crumbs as everyone got up from the table. "There is only one way to make this a great day. I wish you the best of luck at the courthouse."

Nora brushed off her dress. *Luck? Oh, yes, we're going to need lots and lots of that.*

The Judge's Ruling

Nora spied Robert Cooper as he was about to ascend the courthouse steps. She danced between cars to get across the street, leaving her mom and dad behind to wait for traffic to clear. "Robert," she yelled, "wait up."

"What do you want?" he asked, his face distorted with distrust.

"It's the ten thousand dollars, isn't it? You think you can get your hands on Sarah's money. That's what this is all about, isn't it?"

"I don't know what you're talking about." He smiled sheepishly.

"You bastard, you don't give a damn about Sarah, do you?"

"Of course, I do." His voice dripped with sarcasm.

John and Harriet caught up to Nora and watched Robert enter the courthouse. "What was that all about?" John asked.

"Sarah has a ten-thousand-dollar CD. It's from her father's insurance money. That's what he wants. He doesn't care about Sarah. We can't let him get away with this."

"Be careful," John said. "You have no proof of that."

Mrs. Watson stood outside of the courtroom. Sarah broke from her side and ran to Nora's opened arms.

"Are you okay?" Nora asked, stoking Sarah's hair away from her face.

"What's going to happen to me?" Sarah asked. "Am I going to be sent to live with the Coopers?"

"Not if I can help it."

Mrs. Watson took Sarah's hand. "Since we're just a small group, Judge Morton will see us in the conference room, same as yesterday."

Everyone followed Georgina into the room. Nora was the first to notice Robert Cooper sitting at the table, alone. Nora shot an inquisitive look at her folks. *What's the story behind this? Something is rotten in Denmark.*

Judge Morton came into the room, made eye contact with each person, introduced himself, and sat at the end of the table. He opened the folder he brought with him and studied the contents. He turned each page, spending a moment or two on each sheet. Everyone in the room sat silently, waiting for him to speak. The judge pushed the folder forward and laid his glasses on the table. "Georgina, will you keep the minutes for us — who's here and all that good stuff?"

Mrs. Watson raised her tablet and pencil.

"A rather strange set of circumstances," the judge began. "I'm assuming you are the Jensens," he said, looking in their direction.

"Yes, your honor," Nora said.

The judge then looked across the table. "And you're Robert Cooper?" The judge looked at Georgina Watson. "I was led to believe that Mrs. Cooper would also be here."

"I apologize, Judge," Robert said. "She had fish last night for supper, got sick, and was up all night. She still didn't feel well this morning."

Nora glared across the table. *That whole story is fishy.*

"Let's see if we can come to some conclusion here. I understand things got a little heated yesterday. We will not have any of that today, although I am interested in the confrontation that occurred in Ely." The judge looked again to the folder. Facing John, "I believe you are an officer of the law, am I correct?"

"Yes, I'm a deputy sheriff for White Pine County."

"Tell me in your own words what happened when you confronted Mr. Cooper."

John cleared his throat. "I came home for lunch, like I normally do. I noticed the screen door was torn half way off its hinges. Suspecting there was a problem, I drew my weapon and entered the house. This man," John said pointing to Cooper, "had a hold of my daughter."

"What did you do next?" asked the judge.

"I shouted for him to halt and identified myself as a police officer."

"Did you threaten to shoot him?"

"I told him if he made one wrong move I would shoot him."

"What did your daughter do while this was all happening?"

"Her pajama top was torn open. She covered herself."

The judge went back to the folder. "Mr. Cooper claims your daughter offered him sex."

"Nora knows I come home every day for lunch; perhaps she used that as a ploy, biding her time until I got there."

"In your mind, this was a clear case of assault?"

"Yes, your honor," John replied.

"Did you arrest Mr. Cooper?"

John bowed his head. "No," he said softly.

"You stopped what you considered a case of assault against your own daughter and you did not arrest the man? Did you file a report of the incident?"

"No, your honor," John said.

The judge hung the bows of his glasses behind his ears. "Can you tell me why you didn't take further action?"

John looked at Nora. "Looking back, I probably should have. At the time, I thought if he left peacefully, that would be the end of it."

The judge looked at Robert. "Is that what happened?"

"That screen door was off its hinges when I got there. I only went there to ask if I could take Sarah back to her aunt and me." Robert leaned back in his chair. "There was no attempted assault; it was a misunderstanding. I was the one who should have filed charges. He threatened to shoot me. I decided to work within the law and bring my fight here, confident that you would agree that they had no right to take Sarah from us."

Errr, what a liar. Nora raised her hand.

"Would you like to add something?" the judge asked.

"First, I wonder where Mrs. Cooper is. Second, has anyone checked with the Chicago Police department regarding Mr. Cooper, and third, I have reason to believe that Robert is only interested in the ten-thousand-dollar certificate of deposit that Sarah has."

Robert was about to leave his seat, but the judge motioned him to remain seated. He opened the folder. "Mrs. Watson made a trip to Chicago. Mr. Cooper was arrested for assault back in 1935. That was ten years ago, and the charge was later dropped." The judge closed the folder. "Getting sick is not a crime. I'm sure Mrs. Cooper will be present when I make my final decision." The judge waited for Robert to nod in the affirmative.

Robert, in turn, raised his hand. "Your honor, I am not aware of any certificate of deposit. As far as I can remember Audrey Connolly was as poor as a church mouse. It appears Miss Jensen knows a CD exists. Maybe she is the one who wants to get her hands on that money?"

The judge sat back in his chair and again threw his glasses on the table. "When deciding cases like this, I always try to follow the family's wishes. Audrey Connolly put Sarah on a bus to go live with her aunt and uncle. I have to take that as being her wish." He was about to continue when Sarah jumped to her feet.

"I don't want to live with them. If you send me there, I will run away. Why can't you let me live with the Jensens?" She burst into tears.

Before Mrs. Watson could make a move, Nora stood and took Sarah in her arms. The judge waited until the two sat down.

"I'm sorry," he said to Sarah. "You are a minor. In Indiana, you really don't have a say in the matter. I appreciate your wishes, but I have to decide based on my best judgment. I have always found that placing children with blood relatives has the best chance of success. I also have to ask the question, if Miss Jensen was not on that bus, would we be here today? I don't think so. As of this moment, I'm inclined to place Sarah's care in the hands of the Coopers."

"No! No! Don't do that," Sarah cried. Nora tried to console her as Mrs. Watson came and eased Sarah out of her chair. "Nora," she cried as Georgina took her from the room.

The forlorn look on Sarah's face would be forever etched in Nora mind. "You are making a big mistake," Nora shouted at the judge.

The judge glared at Nora. "No, young lady, you are the one who caused this whole commotion. You're lucky I don't have you charged with kidnapping."

John stepped between his daughter and the judge. "Come, we're done here," he whispered to Nora and ushered her toward the door.

Nora stepped aside when a man entered the room. A woman followed and walked as if in pain. Upon seeing the woman, Robert jumped to his feet. "Don't you say a thing!" he yelled and came charging toward her. John instinctively stepped between them, grabbed Cooper's arm, twisted it around his back and pushed his head down on the table. John put his forearm on the back of Robert's neck to hold him in place.

"You stupid bitch, you're going to ruin everything," Robert squealed.

The man who accompanied Elizabeth Cooper produced handcuffs. "I'll take it from here," he said, putting the cuffs on Robert. "You are under arrest for assault and battery."

Robert struggled as he was being pushed out of the room. "He was going to give her to us," he yelled at his wife. "We almost had the money."

Elizabeth grabbed her side and teetered. Nora caught her and eased her onto a chair. "What did he do to you?"

"I told him I wouldn't lie for him anymore; I was going to tell the judge to give Sarah to you. He grabbed me by the throat, said he wouldn't mess up my face where people could see it." Elizabeth grimaced in pain and put her hand to her side. "He kept punching me in the stomach until I promised not to say anything."

By now, everyone had gathered around. Nora gently ran her fingers over Elizabeth's ribs. She recoiled with each touch. "We need to get her to a doctor," Nora said. "I think she has some broken ribs."

Judge Morton nodded to Georgina.

Nora pressed on Elizabeth's belly. "Does any of this hurt?"

"I peed blood this morning," the woman sobbed. "You were right; he beat me that day you came. He was angry that 'Audrey's brat' was coming. I should have never told him about the money. He became obsessed about it. It was like you were trying to steal it from him."

"We didn't know anything about it until Mrs. Canterbury told me last night," Nora said.

"He wasn't always like that. I hoped things would get better, but I guess I was just fooling myself."

"The doctor is on his way," Georgina said.

Elizabeth wiped her hand across her eyes. "When Sarah came in the room yesterday and I saw how happy she was, I knew I had to do the right thing. My sister put her trust in me to see that Sarah had a chance in life. It was not going to be with Robert and me. I hope you can forgive me"

"There's nothing to forgive, Nora said. "Sarah will have a good home. Your sister would be very proud of you."

The doctor set his bag on the floor and rolled up his sleeves.

"Let's give the doctor some privacy to examine Mrs. Cooper," Georgina said.

Judge Morton tapped Nora on the shoulder and motioned for Georgina, John, and Harriet to follow him to his chamber. He threw the folder on his desk and asked everyone to take a seat. "Every time I think I've seen it all, something new happens. I'm thankful Mrs. Cooper had the courage to speak up." He opened the folder. "Georgina, will you keep notes. I'm going to render a decision, so this child does not have to endure anymore uncertainty in her life." He looked at John and Harriet. "I am awarding you conditional guardianship of Sarah Jean Connolly with one stipulation, that you return to my courtroom six months from now for a final review.

"If you're still happy with her and she's happy with you, I will grant you full guardianship until her eighteenth birthday."

Harriet jumped to her feet, reached across the desk, and shook the judge's hand. "Thank you so much," she said. "We will take very good care of Sarah."

"You are welcome to take Sarah with you," the judge said. "Georgina will forward legal papers for you to sign and return to us. I look forward to seeing you in six months."

Nora looked at Georgina. "Where is Sarah?"

Georgina rose. "She's across the hall in my office. I'll show you."

Sarah didn't get up until she saw everyone's smiles. She ran to Harriet. "Can I live with you?"

"The judge said we can take you home."

Sarah hugged Harriet and then hugged John. Nora felt warm, she felt relieved, and most of all, she felt vindicated. "I guess I can call you 'Sis' now," Nora said as Sarah saved the last and longest hug for her. Nora pushed Sarah to her mother. "Why don't you take Sarah over to Mrs. Canterbury's; I'm going to see if I can help Betty."

The ambulance attendants were loading Betty on a gurney. "Where are you taking her?" Nora asked.

"I want her to spend a night in the hospital," the doctor said. "We can run some tests and get an x-ray of those ribs. I think she's going to be fine; it's just precautionary."

Nora went to Betty's side. "I'll come and see you later. Is it okay if I call you Betty?"

"Of course. Wait, where's my purse?" Betty said.

"It's right here by your side," Nora said, picking it up.

Betty reached into her purse and brought out an envelope. "Give this to Sarah; it's from her mother." Nora squeezed Betty's hand. "I will. You be strong, you're going to be fine."

"I hope so." Tears filled her eyes. "I'm not sure where I go from here."

"We got to go," said one of the men.

Nora wiped her own tears as she watched them take Betty away.

Another Chicago Surprise

When Nora walked through the front door of Center House, Sarah came running and gave her a big hug. "Thank you so much, I was so afraid I was going to the Coopers."

"Your Aunt Betty did a very courageous thing for you, and she did it because she loves you." Nora reached in her purse for the envelope. "She wanted you to have this; It's from your mother."

Sarah opened the envelope and pulled out a card. She hesitated. "Look," she said and showed the card to Nora. The front was a photo of a brilliant red rose. Sarah held the card to her chest.

"It's like I told you in the cemetery, when you see a rose it means your mother is by your side." Nora said.

Sarah sat in the chair and opened the card, resting the envelope in her lap. She read what her mother had written and looked once more at the rose printed on the cover before handing the card to Nora.

In beautiful flowing script, her mother expressed sorrow for not being there to see her go to the prom, graduate from high school, and go to college. She pleaded with her daughter to use the money from her father's insurance to get an education. In closing, her mother wrote how much she loved her, and although she wouldn't be there in person, she would always be with her in spirit.

"That's a wonderful card. Your mother had beautiful penmanship. I think whenever you are lonely or miss your mother, just read her inspiring words and know she is with you," Nora said. "What else is in the envelope?"

Sarah lifted the envelope from her lap and reached inside. "My birth certificate, social security card, and this paper for ten thousand dollars," Sarah said.

"That's a Certificate of Deposit. You let the bank use your money for a specific period of time and they pay you a higher interest rate." Nora pointed to the letter. "It says you get four percent interest if you leave it until the due date, which is October 15, 1948."

"That's my birthday."

"Your eighteenth birthday," Nora added. "It will be more than enough to put you through nursing school."

John and Harriet came down the steps carrying their suitcases. "There's a train to Chicago at seven tonight. The shuttle will pick us up in thirty minutes," John said.

"You take Sarah and go," Nora said. "I'm going to make sure Betty is okay. I thought, too, I would spend a few days with Gladys. I'll call you in a week or so."

"Well, I'm anxious to get back to Ely," Harriet said. "C'mon, Sarah let's get your stuff together."

***

Nora stood on the curb as her folks and Sarah boarded the shuttle. Mrs. Canterbury ran to them, holding a large paper sack. "Here are some cold chicken sandwiches for the trip."

One last hug around and the travelers were off. Nora and Florence waved until the bus was out of view.

"They said they were taking Betty to the hospital. Is it here in town?" Nora asked.

"It's not really a hospital, more like a clinic," Florence said. "It's adjacent to Doc Blanchard's office, around the corner from the courthouse. They do blood work, take x-rays, handle fevers and sew up cuts. I think there are two beds for overnight stays. For operations and everything else, you have to go to Indianapolis."

"The doctor said he wanted to keep her overnight to make sure she was alright."

"Another way of saying I can charge a night's stay to someone's insurance. Doc is always working the system. Will you be back for supper?"

"I should be. I just want to make sure she's okay."

***

Nora walked into Betty's hospital room. "Hello, how are you doing?"

Betty was in a chair looking out the window. She turned quickly, startled by the voice. "Oh, I'm doing okay. The doctor wrapped my ribs. He thinks I might have bruised kidneys, too, but everything else seems okay."

"Sarah and my folks left. They're catching the seven o'clock train to Chicago and should be back in Ely day after tomorrow."

"Did you give the letter to Sarah?"

"I did," Nora said. "It was a brave and generous thing you did for her. When you get things straightened out in your life, I'm sure Sarah would like to have a relationship with you."

"That would be nice. Every time I look at her, I see my sister as a teenager. Sarah and I are the only ones left of the family."

After a minute of silence, Nora asked, "I don't want to be nosy, but have you decided what you are going to do?"

"I can't go back to Robert. He's gotten so much worse, I would fear for my life, but where can I go?"

"Gladys knows a lot of people. There are shelters you can go to get help. They provide a place to live, help you find a job, and will make sure Robert doesn't bother you."

"I really should get some of my things from the house, but how do I do that?" Betty said.

"I think it will take Robert a few days to get out of jail. We can take your car, drive up there, and get your stuff."

"I don't drive; Robert would never teach me."

"I can drive; do you have a key?"

"No, Robert said I never needed one."

He was probably afraid you would drive off and leave him. "That's okay; I know the bus leaves Indianapolis about three in the morning. We can be in Chicago bright and early."

"Are you going with me?" Betty asked.

"Of course, I'll see if Mrs. Canterbury can drive us to Indianapolis. Let me check with the doctor and see if he'll release you."

Nora's plan fell into place. The doctor released Betty, and Florence was more than happy to drive them to meet the bus. Once the two were safely onboard, Betty opened up about her life. Robert wasn't always so angry. They had many good years when he treated her well. That all changed when his mother passed away. Betty took a handkerchief from her purse and wiped her eyes. "His mother always had a strange hold over him. It was like he blamed me for her dying."

99

The bus slowed unexpectedly and pulled to the side of the road. Nora looked out the window. "This isn't one of our stops, something must be wrong."

The driver stood and faced the passengers. "We must have thrown a fan belt. The engine is overheating. I'll have to let it cool down before I can do anything about it."

"How far are we from Chicago?" Betty asked.

Nora looked up the road. "I'm guessing about sixty miles."

"If any of you want to get out and stretch your legs," the driver announced, "we are going to be here for a while."

Betty stood. "I'm going to have a cigarette."

Nora followed her friend off the bus. Night was trying to hang on, but the sun peeked up on the horizon, producing a reddish glow in the east. Betty took a cigarette from the pack and offered one to Nora.

Nora shook her head. "No thanks, I don't smoke."

"Smart, it's a nasty habit, I've been trying to quit." Betty took a long drag and blew out a plume of smoke. "How long do you think we'll be stuck here?"

"I don't know, let me check with the driver," Nora said.

Betty had lit up her second cig before Nora returned. The news wasn't good. The lower radiator hose had burst. The driver used the phone at a nearby farm house to report the problem. Dispatch would send a replacement bus to pick up the passengers. The driver was most apologetic.

"Maybe I should stay with Robert," Betty said. "After all of this, he may change."

"You're joking, right?" Nora couldn't believe Betty would even think that way.

"He'll be lost without me. If I stay, maybe we can get back to the way we used to be."

"I think you should get your things, go to the shelter, and if Robert wants to change, let him be the one to come to you."

"I guess you're right," Betty said, lighting her third cigarette.

By the time the replacement bus arrived to pick up the stranded passengers, the sun was high in the sky. It was close to noon before they arrived at the Chicago terminal. The cabbie jabbered about Cubs baseball all the way to the house. Nora hoped she hadn't spoken out of turn by offering Gladys' help. She wondered if she was still considering staying with Robert. Nora got out of the cab and told the cabbie to wait. "We're just picking up some things and then going to Chicago General."

Betty took a key from under the mat and unlocked the door.

Nora came up the steps with Betty's suitcase. "Gather your stuff and put it in here. I'll call Gladys to let her know we are coming."

"The phone is on the living room table." Betty disappeared down the hallway.

Nora dialed the number and waited for the switchboard to transfer the call. She turned abruptly at a coughing sound and saw the pained look on Betty's face. Her hands were holding her stomach and her lips seemed to be forming words, but no sound came out.

Nora hung up the phone. "Are you okay? What's the matter?"

Betty moved her hands, exposing the crimson stain on her dress. She looked down and watched the blood ooze through her dress. She looked at Nora. Her eyelids slowly closed, and her body unwound into a heap on the floor.

Nora took a step forward but stopped at the sight of a figure standing in the hallway.

"Who were you talking to on the phone?"

The voice was unmistakable. Robert stepped out of the shadows, holding a long knife at his side. Blood dripped from the point. "I asked you, who were you talking to?"

"The police, I called the police. They should be here any moment."

Robert smiled and wiped the knife on his pant leg. "You're lying, bitch. That's all you've ever done is lie. This is all your fault." He pointed the knife at the still body of his wife. "You turned her against me. Mother was right, you women are all a bunch of jezebels."

Nora took another step backwards, hitting the edge of the table. "Robert, Betty's hurt; we have to get her help. Please, let me call for an ambulance."

Robert looked at the body and then at Nora. "She got what she had coming and you're going to get what you deserve." He raised his arm and pointed the knife directly at Nora. He stepped over Betty and came at her.

Nora leaned back against the table. Her hand searched until her fingers tightened around the telephone. She dodged his first lunge. Taking a firm grip, and using all her strength, she brought the phone around and caught Robert on the side of the face. He stumbled backward, blood gushing from his temple. He covered his eye and gave out a blood-curdling yell. Dropping his hand, he looked in disbelief at the mucus dripping through his fingers. He seemed paralyzed by the sight of what was left of his eye. Nora reacted quickly and broke for the door. She came off the porch two steps at a time screaming for help. The cabbie bolted upright in his seat and threw open the door. Nora ran to the far side of the cab as Robert came out on the porch. Her screams brought some people to her aid. Seeing the crowd, Robert stopped, and retreated into the house, slamming the door behind him.

Nora jumped into the back seat. "Call your dispatcher! Get the police and an ambulance here. He stabbed his wife and tried to stab me. Hurry! Call now! Do it!" The cabbie grabbed his mike and relayed the message. It seemed like forever, but within minutes, cars — with lights flashing and sirens blaring — came from all directions.

Nora met the first officers on the front curb and explained the situation. "We need to get her out of there. She's bleeding badly."

Two officers had made their way to the side yard. "Someone's running out the back," one yelled. Four more officers followed in pursuit.

Nora followed the officer up the steps.

"Get out of here," he yelled. "He could still be in there."

"I'm a nurse," she said. "We need to get her help. She has a knife wound to the stomach."

The officer, with his foot in the air, hit the door at full speed. The door swung open violently. "Police!" he yelled and entered.

Nora was right on his heels and reached Betty's still body. She grabbed Betty's wrist; her pulse was weak. "Hang in there, Betty, stay with me," Nora yelled as she turned Betty on her back. "Don't give up. Help is on the way." Nora scrambled to the kitchen, grabbed a dish towel, and used it to apply pressure to the wound. "Betty, wake up." Nora patted Betty's cheeks. "Speak to me," she pleaded. "C'mon, open your eyes."

Betty's eyelids lifted ever so slowly. She looked at Nora, giving her a weak smile.

"That's it, stay with me," Nora said. "The ambulance should be here any second. We're going to get you help."

"I'm sorry, I've got to go," Betty's voice was barely audible.

"No!" Nora lifted Betty's head. "Don't go, don't leave me." Nora felt a strange tingling sensation course through her body.

***

"Nora, can you hear me? Wake up."

Nora opened her eyes and slowly looked around, not sure where she was.

"C'mon," the voice pleaded. "That's it, wake up."

Nora turned to see Gladys sitting on the edge of the bed. "Where..."

"Chicago General," Gladys said. "You've been out for eight hours."

Nora struggled to put her life in order. Robert, Betty, Sarah, was all this a dream? Was any of it real? *What happened to me?* "Betty..."

Gladys squeezed Nora's hand. "She didn't make it."

Nora turned to her side. "Dear God, it really happened."

"She lost too much blood," Gladys said. "We couldn't save her. The two of you rode side by side in the ambulance. One of the attendants said Betty reached over and put her hand on top of yours, almost if trying to comfort you."

Nora turned back to Gladys. "Robert..."

"He's down on the first floor," Gladys said, putting a glass of water to Nora's parched lips. "Police caught him hiding out in someone's shed. He lost an eye."

Nora stiffened, almost knocking the glass from Gladys' hand.

"Don't worry. They have two policemen are right outside his room. Next stop for him is the looney farm. He just lies there babbling to himself. He may have gone off the deep end."

"I don't know what happened to me. One minute I'm helping Betty and the next, I'm out like a light." Nora took another sip of water. "What do you think is wrong with me? I don't think it's the alcohol. This is different."

"Has this happened before?"

"Twice in the field hospital. I think that is why they sent me back to the states. This is the third time it's happened since I've been back."

"While we have you here, we'll run some tests to make sure it's not physiological. This seems to happen when you are in a stressful situation, so it might also be good to see a shrink. We've got a good one on staff. He's been working with some of the soldiers who are having trouble adjusting back into a normal life. I'll have him swing by."

A normal life. What is a normal life anymore? I sure as hell can't tell you. Nora tried to sit up. "Are you positive Robert can't get up here? I'm sure he'd like to finish me off."

"Those officers know the situation. I think they would love an opportunity to administer justice if he so much as blinks in the wrong direction."

Nora tried to swing her legs off the bed but was met by Gladys' hand pushing them back. "Whoa gal, you ain't going anywhere. I'll have some food sent up. Nourishment and rest will do you a world of good."

Nora felt too weak to argue.

Nora Talks to the Shrink

Nora woke to a knock on her door. An elderly man wearing a white coat peeked around the door. "Mind if I come in?"

Nora sat up in bed. "Sure, come."

"I'm Dr. Steward. Gladys asked me to have a chat with you. She said you've had fainting spells."

"She thinks it's stress related."

"You're an army nurse, right?"

"Ex-army nurse, I got out in May."

"Where were you stationed? Were you close to the fighting?"

"As close as you could get without having a rifle in your hands. I was a triage nurse at a forward medical unit. We were always just miles behind the front lines." Nora slid her legs off the bed. "Would you hand me my robe, I think I'd like to sit in the chair."

The doctor handed her the robe, turned his back, and waited for her to get settled. "I've been working with some returning vets with what the army calls battle fatigue. It is possible you might be exhibiting some of the same symptoms. The stress of war can manifest itself in many different ways. Maybe we can talk about what you encountered over there. I'd like to talk to you this afternoon."

106

"Okay," Nora said. *Re-living that experience is the last thing I want to do, but if it's connected to my passing out, let's have at it.*

"Later then; I'll see you in my office on the third floor." As the doctor prepared to leave, an attendant brought in a food tray with Gladys trailing closely behind.

"Did you get our gal fixed up?" Gladys asked.

The doctor smiled. "We're meeting this afternoon." He looked at the tray of food. "It's good that she eats. She appears worn out."

"Hear that?" Gladys said, nodding, as the doctor left the room. "I want you to eat everything on the tray." She rolled the table in front of Nora.

"I'm not eating the yogurt."

"It's probably the best thing on the whole tray." Gladys shook her head. "Stubborn as ever, but I guess that's a good sign. Thought you'd like to know, they took Robert out of here a while ago. He's on his way to Dunning for a ninety-day mental evaluation." She chuckled. "He looked like a pirate walking out of here with that black patch over his eye cavity."

"I hope they put him away for good. I don't think I'll ever forget that face, or him coming at me with the knife." Nora shivered and pulled her robe tight to her neck.

"What are your plans?" Gladys asked.

"Plans?"

"You're run down. You need proper sleep and nourishment. It wouldn't hurt you a bit to take a couple of weeks and just unwind. My folks have that big place up in Pine Lake. You could relax and find the old you."

"Do you think your folks would mind?"

"Mind?" Gladys bellowed. "They'd love it. I think that guy Duke would like it, too."

"It's been three years; he's probably married and raising a family by now."

"I doubt it. He asks about you all the time," Gladys said with a smile. "I'll call the folks and let them know we're coming. We can leave right after you talk to the doc. Now eat the damned yogurt. It's good for you."

"Here, you eat it." Nora threw the carton at her.

Gladys caught the cup, tossed it in the wastebasket and muttered, "Stubborn," as she left the room.

Nora pushed the table away and sat back. Gazing out the window, her mind drifted back to her first trip to Pine Lake. She pictured the young man she danced with in the street and wondered what he would look like today. *He probably wouldn't recognize me. I look like death warmed over. It would be fun to see him, though. After all, he was the first.*

She closed her eyes as the memory of that night flooded her mind. Suddenly her eyes popped open. She reached for her purse on the night stand. She pulled the folded piece of paper from the side pocket and unfolded it. She studied the drawing. "I don't think my breasts were ever quite that big, and they certainly never stood up like that." Nora held the picture to her chest. *It was certainly a bad idea to go skinny dipping. Things just got away from us after that.*

Nora folded the drawing and put it back in her purse. Taking out her compact, she opened it and gazed at herself in the mirror. She brushed her hair to the side. "Dear God, look at me," she said. "I feel like Dad's '37 Ford with a hundred thousand miles on it." *Maybe too many miles...for him?*

Nora breathe a big sigh. "That's all ancient history anyway," she said. "I'm going there to rest and relax. The last thing I need right now is a boyfriend."

***

Doctor Steward was waiting when Nora entered his office. After exchanging pleasantries, his questions about her military experience came in rapid succession. Many of them made her recall things she had tried her best to forget: the long hours, the endless stream of wounded, and the gruesomeness of their injuries. She struggled to explain how helpless she felt as she watched young men succumb to their wounds, some barely old enough to shave. She talked about feeling hopeless, with no chance to escape. Every day was like the day before; the names and faces would change, but the wounded kept coming.

As she talked, one moment tears streaked down her cheeks, and the next, the chords in her neck protruded as anger had her yelling at the top of her lungs. After three hours, she felt completely spent. "I don't think I can take any more of this," she said.

"I quite agree," the doctor said. "You may not have faced the fear of being shot at, like a soldier would, but I think the stress and trauma of your job was equally damaging to your psyche. This could be connected to your fainting spells. Once you've had time to decompress, they should go away. In my opinion, over time, you will be able to put this experience behind you."

I don't think I'll ever be able to erase those faces from my memory. Nora thanked the doctor and found her way back to her room.

A Weekend in Pine Lake

Gladys pulled the '39 Pontiac out of the hospital parking lot. It was a six-hour drive to Pine Lake; plenty of time to enjoy the mid-summer landscape. The sweet corn was waist high, right on schedule for a plentiful harvest. Nora wasn't very talkative. Her mind rambled through all the horrific things she had experienced but hadn't had time to tell Doctor Steward. *How do you condense three years of horror into a three-hour chat? Impossible.*

"So, what did you and Doc Steward talk about?"

"He thinks my passing out could be connected to the stress I experienced. A lot of soldiers are having trouble adjusting to civilian life; some are angry, some depressed. Families are being torn apart."

"We've seen an uptick in the number of women being battered by their returning husbands and boyfriends," Gladys said. "It's almost as if these men have become primal and decide things with force."

"I understand their anger," Nora said. "There are times I'm so angry I could jump right out of my skin. The worst part is I don't know what I'm angry about."

"That's why spending time at Mom and dad's farm in Pine Lake will be so good for you. There's nothing more relaxing than lying around in the sun."

***

110

Gladys drove through the glen leading to the house. A soft breeze gently swooshed the leaves on the trees that bordered the roadway. Gladys' mom walked out onto the porch wiping her hands on her apron as Nora came up the steps.

"It is so good to see you," she said, giving Nora a big hug. Spreading Nora's arms, she added, "Look at you, you're all grown up."

Nora smiled. *Yeah, war makes you grow up in a hurry.*

Gladys set her suitcase on the porch. "Smells good; what's cooking?"

"I'm baking some apple pies for the church social on the fourth. Are you hungry? We had fried chicken for supper; there's leftovers in the fridge."

"We drove straight through and I'm hungry." Gladys looked at Nora. "Want some cold fried chicken?"

Nora nodded. "Sounds good, let me put my suitcase away and I will be right with you."

"Take the first room at the top of the stairs," Mrs. Iverson said. "I put fresh sheets on this morning."

The kitchen smelled heavenly. Four large apple pies sat cooling on the counter, the aroma-laden heat rising visibly above them. Mary Iverson began bringing things out of the refrigerator. In a matter of minutes the table held a buffet of food that included fried chicken, potato salad, sliced cucumbers in sweetened vinegar, and canned peaches. She added a bowl of garden-fresh radishes, carrots, and string beans. "Would either of you like some whole wheat bread? I baked it this morning."

Nora was quick to raise her hand. "My grandmother baked whole wheat bread. She made me sugar sandwiches with it."

Mary laughed. "That's a new one on me."

"She'd butter the bread and sprinkle it with a mixture of cinnamon and sugar. I loved them."

"Here you go, make one for yourself," Mary said, putting a shaker on the table.

The girls filled their plates and ate until neither could eat another thing.

Where's Dad?" Gladys asked.

"I think he's down in the barn. Heaven only knows what he's doing. He went down there after supper. I'm actually surprised he hasn't come back yet; he knew you girls were coming."

"I'll go down and say hello," Gladys said, getting up from the table.

Nora thought she sensed concern in Gladys' voice. "I'll help your mom clean up here."

Within minutes, Gladys came busting through the back door, picked up the phone, and feverishly dialed.

"What is it?" Mary asked. "What happened?"

"Send the ambulance to the Iverson Farm," Gladys yelled into the receiver.

"Oh, dear God," Mary teetered, "What is it?"

"Dad had a heart attack or stroke," Gladys said. "I'm not sure which." She ran out the door.

Nora helped ease Mary into a chair. "You stay here and send the ambulance to the barn. I'm going to help Gladys." Nora ran as fast as she could to the barn. "Gladys, where are you?" she yelled.

"Here!" came the reply.

Nora found Gladys on her knees holding her dad's arms in the air. She crossed them over his chest and pressed down. "C'mon, Dad, breathe," she yelled. "Goddammit, breathe."

112

Nora dropped to her knees, pinched the man's nose, bent over and blew into his mouth. She repeated this in tandem with Gladys' compression of her dad's chest. Nora put a finger on Harry's wrist. "He's got a pulse," she said in between breaths. "It's weak, but it's there."

The siren on the ambulance broke the silence of the warm summer evening as it came screaming through the glen. Nora jumped up and directed the two men inside. Gladys moved over as one man knelt at her father's side. The second quickly attached an oxygen cup to Harry's face. The first tapped a syringe and squeezed its full contents into the farmer's arm. A third man came carrying a stretcher. Mary approached tentatively. She steadied herself against one of the barn timbers.

Gladys put her arm around her mom. "He's breathing on his own. He's going to be okay." It's hard to know if either of them believed that to be true, but it was their hope.

Nora suddenly felt woozy and eased herself down on a nearby bale of hay. *Shit, don't pass out now. These guys have enough to take care of without me taking a nose dive.* Breathing a sigh of relief, she remained conscious and was there to see Mr. Iverson smile at Gladys and his wife as they carried him out.

Gladys steadied her mom on the way back to the house. "Mom and I are going to the hospital," she said. "Why don't you stay here, make yourself at home. We'll probably be gone for quite a while."

"Go, don't worry about me; I'll be fine." Nora stood on the porch and waved as Gladys and her mom sped off. Watching the glow of the taillights evaporate into the night blackness, Nora strolled along the long porch that fronted the house. *Is it me? No matter where I go, people are getting sick, dying, or being killed. Do I bring this on? Am I being punished for something?*

Nora dropped into a rocking chair. A cool breeze carried the smell of fresh cut hay. Fireflies dancing in the air delivered a mesmerizing light show rivaling a night sky full of twinkling stars. The full moon rising added a greenish glow to the silver tin barn roof. The evening serenade included cricket chirps, an occasional owl hoot, and the soulful lament of a loon that filtered up from the lake.

She shook her head. Steward said to avoid stress. *How in hell do I do that if it follows me wherever I go?* She took a deep breath and kicked the rocker into motion. She tried to put her mind at ease, but events of the past few days came at her in rapid succession. The vision of Robert coming at her with the knife brought her out of the chair with a start. She looked out into the darkness and quickly retreated into the house. She closed the door and peeked out through an opening in the curtain. "Don't go all spooky," she said out loud. "There's no one out there." She took one more look to be sure.

In the kitchen, Nora realized that in their haste to respond to Harry's emergency, everything had been left as it was. She began by washing the dishes and putting the food items back in the refrigerator. Finding where everything else went was another matter. "Mary will just have to put the rest of these things where they belong," she said as she turned out the light.

Walking through the dark hallway, Nora pulled back the curtain and peered out the door window. Off in the distance, a light bobbed up and down. It moved too fast to be someone running or riding a bicycle, yet not enough light to be a car. As it drew closer, the beam made a sweeping pass across the front of the house. Nora ducked to the side. A man on a motorcycle made a large circle in front of the house. Stopping, the rider looked up at the dark house. Nora peeked out the corner of the window. The man kicked down the stand, threw his leg over the back of the bike, and started up the porch steps. Nora stepped aside and leaned against the wall.

She heard two knocks, more like two taps. Her heart pounded so hard she was afraid the intruder could hear it beating through the walls. The silence that followed had her gasping for air. It wasn't until she heard the engine fire that she took a normal breath. Moving the curtain just enough to see, she watched the cyclist make his way back through the glen.

By the light of the full moon, she was able to find the staircase and the first room at the top of the stairs. Safely in bed, sleep came fast.

A Surprise Awaits Nora

The knock on the door was barely audible. "Nora, are you awake?" There was no mistaking Gladys' voice. "Breakfast is on the table."

Nora rolled over. "I'll be right down." She rubbed her eyes and checked her watch. "My God, it's eight-thirty." She pulled her slacks on over her pajamas and rushed barefoot down the stairs. "Sorry, I can't believe I slept this late," she said.

"No problem," Gladys said. "Mom and I want to go back to the hospital."

"How's your dad?" Nora asked, taking a seat at the table.

"He was stable when we left at midnight," Gladys said. "I called this morning; they said he's doing better."

"That's great." Nora took some eggs from the platter and passed it to Gladys.

Mary set a plate of ham on the table. "There's bread in the toaster. You girls help yourselves; I'm going to change so I'm ready to go to the hospital."

Gladys put eggs on her plate and stabbed into a slice of ham. "Thank you for your help last night. You might have saved Dad's life by breathing into his mouth that way. Is that something you learned in the army?"

"We had just arrived south of Rome, hadn't finished unpacking our equipment, when we got hit with a slew of

116

wounded. One soldier went into cardiac arrest. This young doctor brought him out of it by using that method. Out in the field we did whatever we could to keep those boys alive."

"It was very effective; I'm going to remember that." Gladys passed a slice of toast to Nora. "Are you going to be alright here by yourself? Mom and I will probably spend the day at the hospital."

"I'll be fine, don't worry about me."

Gladys put her plate in the sink. "Did Duke come out here last night?"

"Someone came on a motorcycle."

"He came to the hospital; I told him you were here."

"It was dark," Nora said. "I got spooked. I didn't answer the door."

"That's funny; maybe you two can connect up today."

Mary came hurrying into the room. "I'm ready, can we go?"

"Go ahead, I'll clean the kitchen," Nora said.

Gladys stood. "If you want to go somewhere, take Dad's truck. It's in the machine shed. The key is on the floorboard."

"Just go," Nora said. "I'll be fine. I'm going to loaf around here."

Nora took her time and finished her breakfast. Cleaning the kitchen was easier this time, having found where some of the things belonged. Then, satisfied the kitchen was in order, Nora headed upstairs for a nice hot shower. She closed her eyes as the water splashed on her shoulders, down her back, and over her chest. All the tension she felt in her neck seemed to just melt away. Stepping out of the shower, she toweled her hair and looked at herself in the mirror. *You need some sun, girl. Look at you, you're as white as a ghost.* She ran her hand across her ribs. *You could also use a little meat on your bones.* Wrapping herself in the towel, she walked into the bedroom. Opening her suitcase, she pushed the clothes around. *I've got nothing here for sunbathing, no swimming suit, not even a pair of shorts. I'll have to do a little shopping.*

Nora went to the window. Beyond the barn was a grassy knoll overlooking the lake, a perfect place to get some sun. She dropped the towel, stepped into her underwear, slipped on a flowery cotton dress that buttoned in front, and put on socks and shoes. The towel was damp, but she folded it anyway and draped it across her arm. It took a few minutes to find her purse and retrieve her sunglasses, but soon she was out the door and on her way.

The view from the knoll was spectacular. The lake was alive with activity. Sailboats glided across the water with their white sails billowed out, resembling a flock of gulls riding on the wind. Speedboats crisscrossed each other's wake, some pulled skiers. The air was crisp and in the soft breeze the long stems of grass on the hillside danced like ballerinas. Nora spread the towel, took off her shoes and socks, and lay down. The sun warmed her face. Reaching down, she brought the hem of her dress up above her thighs, exposing the full length of her legs to the sun's rays.

Soon beads of sweat gathered on her neck. Unfastening a couple of buttons, she opened the top of her dress and let the sun warm her chest, too. She tried to remember the last time she lay in the sun. It had to be years, way before the war. Nora sat up. She looked in all directions, undid the rest of the buttons, and wiggled out of the dress. She pushed the brassiere straps off her shoulders and rolled the top of her underpants down on her hips, exposing the better part of her tummy. Stretching out her arms, she let the sun warm her entire body.

As the cumulus clouds drifted by, changing shapes, she imagined them being all sorts of things. A bird landed on a nearby bush and hopped from branch to branch as if to get a better look at her. Nora watched the bird turn his head from side to side. She pointed a finger at it. "It's a good thing birds can't talk." She giggled and took the intrusion as an opportunity to roll over. She unhooked her bra, slid the underpants down a little more and nestled her head across her arms. "There, go tell your little feathered friends about that," she said.

"Tell them what?" a voice came out of nowhere.

Nora rolled over. Her glasses hung sideways off her face as she tried desperately to cover her breasts as best she could with her loose brassiere. Pulling the dress and towel over the bottom part of her, she shrieked, "Where did you come from?" She blinked, pushed her glasses on her nose, and waited for her eyes to adjust to the sunlight. "What are you doing here?"

The man pointed back to the barn. "I've been looking for you."

"Would you please be a gentleman and turn around so a girl can get dressed?"

"Oh sorry," he said, turning. "It isn't like I haven't seen it all before."

Nora stood and hurriedly fastened her bra, pulled her underpants in place, closed her dress, and frantically buttoned the front. *I haven't seen the guy in three years and I always seem to be in some form of undress when he's around.* "You're Duke, aren't you? How did you find me?"

"I came last night, but you must have gone to bed early. Is it okay if I turn around?"

"Were you on the motorcycle?" Nora poked him in the back.

"Yeah, did you see me?"

"I watched you through the window." Nora studied the man's features. He was a head taller than she, with dark brown hair, green eyes, nice nose, and a square chin. "You look different."

"Better or worse? Why didn't you answer the door?"

"More grown up." *Better, definitely better.* "I didn't know who you were. You could have been Jack the Ripper."

Duke laughed. "What, here in Pine Lake?"

"How'd you get here? I didn't hear a motorcycle."

"I rode my bike, passed Gladys and her mom on the road. I figured you stayed behind. I knocked on the door at the house and checked the out buildings. When I couldn't find you, I climbed halfway up the silo and caught a glimpse of you out here."

"Maybe it would have been better to call first before coming out and spying on me."

"You're probably right, but I didn't expect to find you lying around half naked."

"Gladys said you've asked about me. I don't want you to get the wrong impression. What happened three years ago were two young people letting things get out of hand. A lot has happened since then. We're not the same people."

"I know, I just came to say hello and to apologize."

"For what?"

"I should never have drawn that picture of you. It might have given you the wrong impression."

"The facial likeness was pretty good, but I think you enhanced some of my features."

"You didn't pose. I had to go from memory. We only had that one night."

"It was good enough to fool my mother."

"You're kidding; you showed it to your mother?"

"It happened by accident. You want to go back to the house? There's some lemonade in the refrigerator."

"Sure. I didn't mean to spy on you. When I saw you from the silo you still had your clothes on."

"I'm sorry I accused you of spying. I left myself open to being caught like that. I didn't bring a bathing suit or anything for sunbathing. I guess I'd better do some shopping. Gladys said I could use her dad's truck, but I'm not sure how to get to town." Nora climbed the stairs. "Why don't you sit here on the porch? I'll get the lemonade."

Nora walked indoors and filled two glasses with ice and grabbed the pitcher of lemonade. *I wonder what his life has been like these past three years. It couldn't possibly compare to what I've gone through.* Nora handed him a glass and filled it.

"I can take you if you'd like," he said.

"What?" Nora took a step back.

"Shopping. "There's a variety store in town, they've got some bathing suits and clothes, but you'll find a better selection at Penney's over in Middletown."

Have I become so cynical, I think every remark has a sexual overtone? "That would be great," Nora said, filling her glass and taking a seat. "So, what have you been doing since we last...met?"

"Well, I spent two years in the army, and now I'm back down at the marina, refinishing boats."

"Were you drafted?"

"My number was called a month after you were here. They sent me to Fort Leonard Wood, Missouri."

"For basic training. Where did they send you after that?"

"I spent the whole two years right there. They assigned me to the carpentry shop, mostly building cabinets and stuff."

How did he get a job like that? He must have kissed some general's ass. "Pretty sweet deal, especially with a war going on."

"I was known as a conscientious objector."

Nora looked at him blankly. *Is he for real?*

Nora's expression was not lost on him. "It's what they call you when you fail to stab the dummy with your bayonet. I was doing great, had one of the best times going through the obstacle course, until I came to the final stage: the dummy hanging from a rope. It was made with yellow cloth, had slanted eyes painted on it and a crooked smile. I tried to run my blade into it, I really did, just couldn't do it. I ran past and finished the course."

Nora watched Duke put his fingers to his mouth and pinch his lips. He swallowed before continuing. "The drill sergeant dressed me down in front of the men, called me a bunch of choice names, and said he'd give me one more chance to complete the course the proper way. I told him not to bother; I wouldn't be able to do that to a real person anyway." Duke took a sip of his lemonade.

Nora studied the ice in her glass. "Did they throw you in the brig?"

"Nah, they moved me to another barracks. We had to wear fatigues with a big 'CO' printed on the back. For the next three months, my head hardly ever came out of a garbage can. If they weren't clean enough, and they never were, I had to scrub them all over again. I swear, I mopped every wood floor on the entire base. When my class shipped out, I was sent to the cabinet shop."

"Why are you telling me this?"

"I didn't want you to hear it from someone in town."

"Does the whole town know about it?"

"Oh yeah, I've been raked over the coals pretty good. The gossip in this town can be pretty brutal. The town lost a couple of guys in the war; I understand their anger."

"Why did you come back here? Why wouldn't you go someplace where nobody knew you?"

"If I did, I'd be running away and hiding all my life. I'm not a coward; I just don't think I can kill anyone."

"Even if they're trying to kill you?"

"The army teaches you to trust and rely on your buddies. That was my overriding fear. If I didn't act, I could put a fellow soldier in danger, maybe even cause his death. I certainly didn't want that to happen."

"Maybe if you had to kill or be killed, you would be able to do it?"

"I was more worried I could get someone else killed."

"I wonder if some of the young boys they brought to the hospital had the same fear and hesitated long enough to catch a bullet."

"I think a person pretty much knows who he is. Before I moved here, some buddies of mine were going pheasant hunting and asked me along. We were all about fifteen years old. I'd never hunted before, never even shot a gun. One of the guys took a 20-gauge shotgun out of the case, loaded some shells, and showed me how the pump-action worked. We walked through this corn field and I kicked up a jackrabbit. He was bounding this way and that. I leveled the gun, took aim, and pulled the trigger. The rabbit tumbled in the air. When I got to him, his hind legs were bloodied and motionless. He made this mournful sound and tried to pull itself forward with its front paws. The poor creature was trying to live, to get away. My stomach turned upside down. I stomped on its head, trying to put it out of its misery, which only brought out a more heart wrenching sound. Finally, in desperation, I used the gun to blow its head off. Falling to my knees, I cried like a baby. I dug a hole with my hands and buried him right there."

"That had to have been terrible."

"I never hunted again. And after that, I knew I could never kill another living being."

"A lot of GIs are having a difficult time dealing with that very thing. They're having trouble adjusting to life away from the battlefield. Many of them need psychiatric help."

"Cliff Nelson at the marina was good enough to give me my job back. I guess my woodworking skills trump public sentiment; besides, I had to come back here, it was my only chance of ever seeing you again."

"You're joking, right?"

"They say a person always returns to the scene of the crime." He broke out in a wide grin.

"Listen, smarty, we're going to have a big problem if you keep bringing that up. I told you I'm not that same person, and you..." *Good grief, I lost my cherry to this guy and I'm not sure if I know his last name."*

"And me...?"

"Listen, I've had my own battles with the army, this war, and life in general. I see nothing wrong with standing up for your convictions. I've had to do it myself. Someday I'll tell you about Sarah Jean Connolly. Would you like some more lemonade?"

"No, I should be going. Even though Cliff lets me set my own hours, I don't want to take advantage."

"I'd love a ride on your motorcycle. I had a ride on one in Sicily and loved it."

"Sure thing, I'll come over about seven."

An Evening Ride

Gladys and her mom came home while Nora was taking an afternoon nap. The chatter and laughter from downstairs woke her. By the jovial tone, Nora figured Gladys' father was out of the woods. She fussed a little bit with her hair and shifted her dress before descending the stairs.

"Is your dad doing better?" she asked, walking into the kitchen.

"He's doing great," Gladys said.

"Yes," Mary added. "He's sitting up, talking, and has good color."

"I told the doctor about you blowing into Dad's mouth that way; he thinks it may be the reason Dad is doing so well. If you ever see that young doctor again, the one who showed you that method, be sure to thank him for us. By the way, we passed Duke on his bicycle this morning. Did you guys get to see one another?"

"He got to see a bit more of me than I of him."

Gladys looked bewildered.

"Never mind; yes, we had a nice visit. He's coming back after work. We're going for a motorcycle ride."

Mary opened the refrigerator. "A lot of people were upset with that Duke Brady, he wouldn't go fight with the rest of the boys. Is anyone hungry?"

That's it, his name is Brady. "Looking another man in the face and pulling the trigger is not an easy thing to do. He told me about his army experience."

"The war is over, Mother," said Gladys. "It's time for the gossip ladies to move on."

Amen. "Don't bother fixing anything for me," Nora said. "I made myself a sandwich with the leftover ham. Duke and I may catch something later."

"In that case, Mom," Gladys said, closing the refrigerator door, "let's you and I go to Teddy's and get a hamburger. I think I'm ready for a beer. What time is Duke coming?"

"He said around seven. You guys go. I'll putter around here until he comes."

"We'll probably be asleep when you get back; neither of us slept very well last night," Gladys said. "The back door is always open."

Nora took her time getting ready. She felt good, more relaxed than she'd felt in a long time. *I guess I didn't realize how tense I had become. I still can't believe Betty is gone. I hope they lock up Robert and throw away the key.*

Standing in front of the mirror, she straightened the collar on her shirt. The top button was open, but she unbuttoned the next one down. She frowned and buttoned it back up. *Let's not give him the wrong impression.*

She straightened her slacks, brushed her military style hair into a duck tail, applied lipstick, and gave herself an approving nod in the mirror.

Nora was sitting on the porch when Duke rode up on his cycle. He put down the stand, turned off the engine, swung his leg over the seat, and stood to the side. "Well, what do you think of it?"

Nora strolled to the bike. "It looks like a Cadillac compared to the bike I rode on in Sicily. I love the royal blue paint and all the white pin striping." She put her leg over the back of the bike and sat in the seat. Gripping the handlebars, "Will you show me how to drive it sometime? I'd love to take it for a ride."

Duke climbed on behind her. "The first thing is to know where everything is. The switch is on top of the gas tank," he said, reaching around her and placing her hand on the silver control.

She felt his chest press against her back as he put his chin on her shoulder. "The throttle is the right-hand grip. You give it the gas by twisting it toward you. The lever on the left grip is your hand brake. You also have a foot brake on the right and the clutch is under your left foot." He moved her hand from the switch to the knob on the left side of the gas tank. "This is the shifting lever. First gear is all the way forward. Each notch back is the next gear.

Nora felt the warmth of his breath on her neck and took in the musk of his cologne. "It's beautiful; it must have cost a fortune."

"I got it for practically nothing, compliments of the army."

"You didn't steal it, did you?"

"I think the army term is 'procured.' I built an oak desk for the sergeant in charge of the motor pool. He was so happy with it, he wanted to do something nice for me. I asked him about this cycle sitting in the corner. They had cannibalized it for parts to fix other bikes. It was missing a front wheel, the gas tank, the rear fender, and a bunch of little stuff. Luckily, the engine was still intact. He not only let me have it, but he dug up a title for it, too."

"Can he do that?"

"Sergeants run the army; they can do anything," Duke said, getting up off the bike. "A buddy helped me get it to the cabinet shop. I completely dismantled it, cleaned and sanded every part; spent most of my free time and weekends working on it. Sarge let me pick anything I wanted off the scrap heap. That's where I found a dented gas tank and fender as well as the few miscellaneous parts I was missing. I bet you can't even tell where the tank was dented."

Nora rubbed her hand up and down both sides of the tank. "You really did a nice job."

"But," he said, "the coup de grace — one day we got a shipment of paint, gallons and gallons of black, brown, and olive drab. Lo and behold, among the dull and dreary was a gallon marked royal blue. It was probably meant for the navy. I painted the frame black and the rest, this majestic blue."

"Who did all the fancy pin stripping?" she asked.

"Yours truly. That was a challenge of its own. A stripping brush is made from horse hair. It took a weekend pass and some scouting around to find a farmer who would let me cut some hairs off his horse's tail. The guy thought I was nuts, but it made a dandy brush."

Nora laughed. "So how did you get it home?"

"I hid the pieces and parts all over the cabinet shop. The night before my discharge, my buddy and I stayed up all night and put it together. The next day I drove up to the gate. I reached in my jacket for my discharge papers and the sentry said, 'Nice cycle, who makes it?'

"I said, 'It's a Harley Duke Davidson.' He checked my papers and never questioned a thing about the bike. I rode it out of there and all the way here." He patted the cushion behind the driver's seat. "The bike was designed for one person. I added this padding to the rear carrier for an extra rider. Those bars on either side are where you put your feet."

"So, where are you taking me?"

"There's a fourth of July dance and corn roast in the park by the band shell. Would you like to check it out?"

"Do they still do the hay ride?"

"They haven't had one since that time in '42." He smiled.

"Well, I'm not sure about dancing, but a corn roast sounds interesting."

"Dancing is how we met; don't you remember?" Duke teased.

"I haven't danced since; I'm probably pretty rusty."

"I've never been good, but I'd like to give it a whirl."

Nora slipped off and climbed back on behind Duke, putting her arms around his waist. He kicked down the starter and the engine sprang to life with a low deep-throated rumble. "Just keep your feet on those rests. Be careful of the muffler, it gets plenty hot." He revved the engine a few times and then slowly powered down the driveway.

Nora immediately felt at ease and leaned with him as they motored through the glen. She relaxed and felt comfortable putting her hands on her knees. The wind blowing through her hair brought back memories of Sicily and the ride she and Antonio took through the countryside. It seemed like a very long time ago.

130

Main Street was crowded. People stood in clusters, laughing and talking, while a number of couples strolled along on the sidewalk. A group of children ran and danced in the street as a string of firecrackers exploded in rapid succession. People stepped out of his way as Duke cruised slowly down the street.

Duke turned his head. "I think everyone man, woman, and child in the county is here tonight." He drove the cycle on the grass near the entrance to the park.

Nora slid off the back even before he had come to a complete stop. Rolling forward another ten feet, he turned off the engine, just as two women ran up to him.

"I was hoping you'd come," shrieked one girl. "Remember, you promised me the first dance." She put her arm around Duke's neck.

"You have to dance with me, too," squealed the second one.

Duke took the girl's hand from around his neck. "Maybe later, okay?" He looked back at Nora and shrugged. The two girls followed his glance and gave Nora the evil eye.

Nora smiled and the girls retreated back toward the band shell.

"You've got quite an entourage," Nora said as Duke walked to her.

"I didn't promise…"

"Oh?" Nora took a step toward the band shell.

Duke stepped in front of her. "It wasn't really a promise. I saw her the other day and she asked if I was going to the dance. I said no, but if I did, she could have the first dance."

"Sounds like a promise to me."

"But don't you see, I was never coming to the dance…until you came back."

"It would be a shame to waste this beautiful music."

"Would you like to dance?"

"Are you sure you have enough room on your dance card?"

"Very funny." Duke took her hand and led her to an open grassy area in front of the band. Dancing on grass camouflaged most of their missed steps, and soon they just rocked back and forth to the music. She closed her eyes and nestled her head on Duke's shoulder. If looks could kill, Nora saw the daggers the two girls threw at her.

The band switched to a polka and couples immediately yelled and hooted as they twirled to the music. Duke backed off. "Not for me," he said.

Nora quickly agreed. "I never got the hang of that."

Duke led her to the side of the shell, away from the dancing throng, and turned to her. "I'm really glad you came back. I've never stopped thinking about you or hoping I would see you again." He leaned forward, kissed her cheek, and moved to kiss her on the lips.

Nora drew back. "No, not here; come, let's go for a ride." She took his hand and literally pulled him to the bike. She waited for him to kick-start the engine before climbing on. In the corner of her eye she spied the two girls running toward them and saw the anger on their faces as Duke throttled off.

"Where would you like to go?" he asked.

"Surprise me," she said, tightening her grip on his waist.

The deep roar of the engine and the wind blowing through her hair were exciting and adrenalin-charged. The ride took them down tree-lined country roads, past fields of sweet corn, and along the edge of Pine Lake. Duke slowed the bike and navigated the cycle up a grassy hill until they were high on a bluff overlooking the lake. With daylight savings time still in effect, the late day sun was just now slipping below the tree line. The sky was painted in broad strokes from a pallet of reds and oranges. The lake was calm and mirrored the sky.

"What a beautiful sight," Nora said, sitting on a large out-cropping of stone. "Where did you live before coming here?"

"I grew up in a one-horse town in upstate New York. Everyone worked in the local furniture factory. Mom did payroll and time cards, and Dad worked in the shop. He ran a side business doing furniture refinishing. I was about thirteen when he got me involved. Soon he was running the business and I was doing all the work."

"What brought you to Pine Lake?"

"When I got out of school, the furniture factory was already in decline. I didn't see much of a future in sticking around. I'd saved up a couple thousand dollars working for my dad. A buddy of mine talked me into hitchhiking to California, you know, maybe get into the movies. I figured it would be a chance to see some different parts of America. We got as far as Chicago and he decided we should make a detour into Wisconsin. He had an uncle who lived here. Long story short, after a few days, he got homesick and hopped a bus back home. I fell in love with the lake and the town from the moment I got here. I decided to stay. My buddy's uncle worked as a mechanic at the Boat Works and talked Cliff Nelson into giving me a job. Refinishing boats is pretty much the same as doing furniture." Duke picked up a stone and tossed it over the bluff. "People say I'm very good at it."

"Have you given up your dream of being a movie star?" Nora too, picked up a stone from her perch and threw it over the bluff.

Duke laughed. "That was my buddy's dream, I just wanted to get out and see what the world had to offer."

"That's what I said, but seeing the world is not what it's cracked up to be."

Duke sat on the grass. "You said you had problems in the army; what did you mean by that?"

"I was so naïve when I enlisted. Like you, I came from a small town — in Nevada. I never paid much attention to what was going on in the world. Even when I got to Chicago, all I wanted to do was get my nursing certificate. I had this glamorous vision of being an army nurse, this Wonder Woman, taking care of our brave men."

"And it wasn't like that?"

"You have to understand, when I enlisted, nurses were given the rank of 2nd Lieutenant. They called it a 'relative rank,' which meant zilch in the army's chain of command. A private first class had more authority than we did; practically every GI in the entire army outranked us and thought we were open game. I had my butt slapped or pinched and my breasts squeezed more often than you could shake a stick at, and there was nothing I could do about it. It wasn't until the head of our corps, Flo Branchfield, petitioned Congress in '44 to give us full officer status that things changed. It didn't stop the male officers from taking liberties, but at least we weren't being pawed by the enlisted men."

"Couldn't you go to your company commander?"

"I blew the whistle on one doctor. He caught me alone in the supply tent and tore the buttons off my shirt, trying to get his hands on me. He grabbed my hair, pulled my head back, and tried to see how far he could stick his tongue down my throat. He howled like a castrated pig when I bit it as hard as I could. Spitting blood, he doubled over when I planted a knee in his crotch."

"Geez, what happened then?" Duke asked.

"My written complaint to the CO ended up in the wastebasket and netted me a lecture on how to conduct myself to keep from provoking such advances. The captain was slapped with a three-day pass in Rome, probably to meditate on his evil ways or maybe to rest the family jewels."

Duke tried to conceal his smile. "I suppose I'd better be careful if I try to kiss you again."

Nora ignored his attempt at humor. "For the next few weeks, I pulled extra duty and caught a lot of flak from some of the other doctors. Hell, even a bunch of the nurses gave me a bad time about it. The lesson I learned — defend yourself and keep your mouth shut."

"A lesson I learned rather quickly myself," he said.

Nora jumped off the rock perch and tossed another stone over the bluff. "I also got myself into hot water when I complained too loudly about army brass engaging in battles without regards to having sufficient medical services to handle the wounded. We'd get overrun with wounded. We were working in tents on makeshift operating tables out in the middle of nowhere, and the wounded would just keep coming. There was no way to give them the care and treatment they deserved." Nora paused and looked out at the fading orange sky. "I spouted off and got my butt chewed big time."

"I can see where that might have rankled a few generals," Duke said.

"Sad to say, at times, some of the wounded were due to some gung-ho 2nd Louie, still wet behind the ears, forcing his men into situations where they'd get their asses kicked. I have a feeling some of those jackasses went down from friendly fire."

"There have been a lot of horror stories coming out about the war," Duke said. "I guess we have to be thankful it's over. Would you like something to eat? There's a tavern up on the west end that has pretty good food." He reached down and gently took her hand.

She turned to him. "I don't know if I will ever be able to rid my mind of the things I've seen."

He kissed her tear-streaked cheek and drew her close as the last glow of sunlight disappeared.

"I'm starved," she said softly resisting his attempt to kiss her on the lips.

Duke Feels the Scorn

Harvey's Tavern was bustling. Walking to the front door, Duke peered through the glass. "Want to sit out here on the porch? It's pretty crowded inside."

"I'd prefer to, it's such a beautiful night." Nora pulled a chair out from one of the tables and sat.

"What would you like to drink?" Duke asked, laying his gloves on the table.

Nora rolled her tongue around in her mouth. *Do I dare? A gin and tonic sounds good; hell, a gin and anything sounds good.* "Just a coke," she finally said. The evening air was warm and moist. She opened another button on her blouse and leaned back in the chair. Her mind wandered back to their first meeting. That July night, before she went off to war, before her world was pushed to the brink between heaven and hell, between life and death. She smiled as she recalled, him trying to jitterbug in cowboy boots and the two of them kissing under the hay on the wagon ride. She smiled, remembering how innocent and naive she was back then.

The tavern door opened violently. Duke came out and grabbed his gloves. "C'mon, let's get out of here."

"What...why?" Nora leaped from her chair, knocking it over backwards.

Before Duke could explain, a man came through the door, shouting at Duke.

"You're nothing but a stinkin' coward," the man yelled.

Duke lowered his head, walked past the man, and descended the steps without saying a word. He turned to see if Nora was following.

Nora walked past as the man shook his fist and shouted again, "Why don't you come back here and fight like a man. What's the matter, you some kind of pussy?"

Nora stopped midway down the steps. She turned and walked back, getting into the man's face. "You need to watch your language. Haven't we had enough fighting?" She pushed the man backward. "Why don't you go back inside and drown your anger in a beer."

The man shook his fist over Nora's shoulder. "Just stay out of this end of the lake."

As soon as Nora climbed on, Duke gave it the gas. The ride back to Pine Lake went fast. Duke slowed the cycle as they approached town. Turning his head, "you want to go back to the farm?"

"Not really," Nora said. "Could we go someplace peaceful, maybe where there are no people?"

Duke nodded. He made a few turns and then sped up a long street. He drove the cycle up the drive of a large two-story house. The place looked tired and neglected. The paint was dull and peeling in many places. He pulled up to the back door of the dark house.

"Whose place is this?" Nora said, casting a wary look.

"Mine," he said, lifting the mat and picking up a key.

"Good place to hide the key, no thief would ever think to look under the mat."

"Nothing in there to steal." Duke opened the door. "Wait here while I find a lamp." He soon returned carrying a kerosene lamp with the flame dancing around in the glass chimney. "Watch your step; there are a lot of loose boards on the floor."

The lamp threw an eerie glow around the room as Duke led the way. The smell of old wet lumber clogged her nostrils. Nora strained to see her surroundings. The walls were just stands of two by fours and the floor was covered with broken lath and chunks of plaster.

"Are you fixing it up or tearing it down?" she asked, stepping over a stack of lumber.

Duke laughed. "Sort of in between."

Nora wiped across her face. "Pfsuth," she spit. "I think I just swallowed a spider," she said, brushing cobwebs from her hair.

Duke swung around. "Oops, sorry about that...here give me your hand...stay close to me."

"Can't we turn on the lights? It's spooky in here."

"No electricity. I'm still tearing out the old plaster; I haven't started re-wiring yet."

"You doing this all yourself?" Nora stepped over some tools.

"In my spare time." Duke set the lamp on what appeared to be a table covered with a large cloth. He moved forward to the front window. "Look at this," he said. "Isn't that a beautiful sight?"

Nora steadied herself on his arm and came around to the window. The lights from town lay before her. In the distance, the moon cast the scene in multiple shades of grays, its shimmering white light dancing across the black ripples on the Lake. Lights speckled the distant shore.

Nora tried to get her bearings. "We must be on the hill north of town?"

"Yep, it's the old Lawson Place. She lived to ninety but spent the last fifteen years in a nursing home. In the meantime, this place sort of fell apart. She had no heirs, so I bought the house from the trustee for three thousand dollars."

"And you think you got a good deal?"

Duke looked around. "It will be when I get it done. Would you like a coke? I've got some out in the garage. Stay right here, I'll be back in a jiffy."

"Wait…" Duke was gone before she could stop him. "… Don't leave…me."

Nora looked around. She never was fond of the dark, and surely not being alone in the dark…in a dilapidated house that could be…with very little stretch of the imagination…haunted. She moved closer to the lamp. It flickered. "Don't you dare go out," she commanded. Then straining to see through the darkness, "If you don't get back here this minute, I'm going to kill you." Her voice trailed off.

"Kill who?" Duke asked, setting the cokes on the table.

"You!" she shouted. "Don't you leave me here again!"

Duke pulled the cloth off a large turn-of-the-century sofa. "You had the lamp; I wasn't gone more than three minutes. C'mon, let's sit here."

Nora picked up the soda and eyed the couch. *Okay, Buster, just what do you have in mind?* "I told you, we're not the same people, what happened three years ago was just a point in time when two people…"

"You said someplace peaceful, with not a lot of people…"

"I didn't mean…"

140

"No problem, if you're not comfortable, we can go. I just wanted to show you the place, but I guess it would be better during the day."

"Do you think?" Nora said. Then pausing for a second, she shifted her tact and sat on the sofa. "I'm curious, what was that all about at the tavern? Why was that guy so angry?"

Duke sat, leaving plenty of space between them. "First of all, thank you for coming to my defense. It wasn't necessary, but thanks, anyway."

"That guy was pretty upset."

Duke chuckled. "Between the two of you, going one on one, my money would have been on you."

Nora forced a smile. "He called you some pretty bad things. Do you just walk away from any confrontation?"

"When the situation calls for it."

Nora started to get up. "Hey, you don't have to tell..."

Duke grabbed her arm and pulled her back. "His name is John Kruchinski. His kid brother and I were drafted at the same time. Dave was killed in the Normandy invasion. A mortar dropped into their landing craft just as they hit the beach. Twenty-seven men were blown to bits. John hasn't gotten over Dave's death."

"Does this guy think you should have died, too?"

"People deal with grief in different ways. He's angry at the world and fighting him won't accomplish a thing. We all have to handle the pain this war has thrust on us in our own way."

Nora thought of her own situation. "This war has caused so much pain. I'm afraid we'll be dealing with it for a long time." She watched Duke stare at his soda.

"I would gladly give my life if it would bring Dave back," he said solemnly. "But that's not going to happen, so in that situation, yeah, I'll walk away every time."

"Doesn't it bother you that people think you're a coward?" she asked, then realized how callous that sounded.

"I can't help what people think and fighting every man in town will not change how they feel. All I can do is be myself and hope, over time, these wounds will heal." Duke took a drink of coke. "What about you, do you think I'm a coward?"

"I…no…I don't know," Nora searched her mind for the right words. "Coward is such an ugly word, but no, I think it takes courage to follow what you believe in your heart. It probably would have been far easier for you to just stab the dummy, finish your training, and hope you'd never have to kill anyone."

"But that's what soldiers are supposed to do, and failure to do it, could put the man next to you in harm's way."

Both Duke and Nora seemed lost in thought as they gazed at the flickering flame of the lamp.

Duke rose. "C'mon, I'll get you back to the farm."

A Surprise Visitor Awaits

Nora leaned back and took in the splendor of a star-studded night sky, with the full moon at center stage, as Duke drove through the glen leading to the Iverson farmhouse. The tall rock formations that rose on either side of the gravel road, along with the large oaks, whose limbs spread out over the roadway, created a tunnel-like entry into the property. The delicate fragrance of the blooming foxgloves and other wildflowers filled the night air, moist from the spring water that trickled through the crevasses in the stone.

Looking ahead, Nora saw the house was dark save for a single light on the front porch. She squeezed Duke's ribs. "Stop here," she said. "They're asleep. I don't want to wake them."

Duke throttled down the engine and coasted to a stop.

"I can walk from here," she said, sliding off the back of the cycle.

Duke switched off the ignition and kicked down the stand. "I'll walk you to the door."

"That's alright, I'll be fine."

"There have been some black bears roaming around here recently; are you sure you don't want me to walk you to the door?"

Nora stopped and took a half step backward. "Bears?" she peered into the woods.

143

"C'mon, I'll make sure you get to the door safely." Duke grabbed Nora's hand and started up the road.

Pressing herself close to him, "I didn't know there were bears around here."

"Well, the last confirmed sighting was about twenty years ago, but you never know."

"There are no bears here." She pushed him away. "You just said that to scare me, so you could walk me to the house."

"It worked, didn't it?" He reached out his hand.

Nora made no attempt to extend hers.

"I get the feeling you're upset with me for some reason."

"I just don't want this to get out of hand. I'll be leaving here in a few days. I've got a lot of things going on, things I need to get straightened out. I'll be going back to Ely."

"Any chance, you'd be coming back?"

"That's it, I don't know. It's a long story, but I have sort of taken on the responsibility of raising a fifteen-year-old girl. She's with my folks now, and I know they are willing to help, but I was the one who brought this about and I can't just dump her on them." Nora saw the disappointment on his face. "It probably wasn't a good idea for me to come here."

"I always hoped you would," he said, then quickly added, "Bring the girl back here, I'll help."

"Duke." She reached for his hand. "You live here in this resort paradise, you swing wherever the wind blows you. I can see myself living here...with you, but ..."

Nora was startled when a figure appeared from around the corner of the house. The moon and porch light silhouetted the man, but his walk, his shape, and size were all too familiar. Still forty to fifty feet away, she didn't need to see the black eye patch to know who it was. Her heart sank. "Oh my God, it's Robert!"

"Robert?" Duke asked.

"Cooper."

Before Nora could explain, the man stopped and reached into his pocket. "How do you like that," he said with obvious delight. "Miss Nora Jensen, being delivered right to me."

"What are you doing here?" Nora shouted. "What do you want?"

"What do I want?" He snarled. "I want you." Grinning wide, saliva rolled from his mouth and onto his chin. He brushed the glob away as his other hand came out of his pocket, bringing with it a shiny metal object. The silver revolver glistened in the moonlight. "Mother was right. She warned me about the evil whores in this world. And you, bitch, have fucked me over for the last time."

"Hey, you can't talk to her that..." Duke took a step forward.

Nora grabbed Duke's arm and pulled him back. "He's got a gun!"

Duke stepped in front of Nora and extended his hand. "Just stay calm," he said in a soft tone. "Let's talk about this."

"This will do my talking," Robert said, waving the weapon. "Step out of the way; I don't have a bone to pick with you."

"I'm sure we can settle this without anyone getting hurt." Duke took a step backward, forcing Nora to do the same.

"Be careful," Nora whispered. "He's already killed his wife."

"That money was rightfully mine. Now Betty's dead, and it's all your fault." Bob waved the gun. "Get away from her or I'll shoot you, too. If this bitch hadn't stuck her nose in our business, none of this would have happened. She brought this on herself and now she's gotta die."

As if the whole world suddenly shifted into slow motion, she felt Duke push her aside. Falling to one knee, she saw the flash and heard the shot as warm blood splattered across her face. Duke twisted, looking bewildered, he gave out a long groan. Grabbing his arm, he tumbled to the ground, sending dirt and dust into the air.

Nora righted herself and reached back for him. "Duke, are…"

"Run!" he yelled. "Get away from him."

Nora froze for a second. "Duke…"

"Go! Run, Dammit, get the hell out of here."

Nora frantically looked in all directions. The closest shelter was the barn. Running as fast as she could, she zagged as a second shot rang out, splashing dirt up at her feet. She grabbed the handle on the barn door as another bullet slammed into the wood, just inches above her hand. Wood splinters flew everywhere as she ducked into the barn.

"That's it, run bitch!" Robert shouted. "I'll get you. You have to pay. You're gonna die."

Nora's eyes were slow to adjust to the pitch black. She reached out into the darkness and found a wall; frantically she went, hand over hand, searching for a place to take cover. She turned back long enough to see the moonlit silhouette of Robert, standing in the doorway.

"Come out and take your medicine," he yelled. "You can't hide forever."

Nora's hand came to the end of the wall. Feeling around the corner, her hand landed on a board that swung away from her. It was a gate to some kind of stall. She went in and closed the gate slowly, trying not to make any noise. She felt hay or straw under her feet. Finding the corner, she sunk to her backside and brought her knees to her chest. *Please God, don't let him find me.*

She heard Robert moving along the other side of the wall. She heard the huff of air that shot from his nostrils as his breathing came in short bursts.

"I'm going to find you, bitch. You're going to pay for everything: the money, Betty... I know you can hear me. You might as well come out and get this over with."

Nora curled tighter and tried to control her breathing. A gasp could give away her position. She heard him getting close to the end of the wall, then rounding the corner, he stopped. She hoped he wouldn't come into her stall. He stood still, no doubt, listening for her to betray her whereabouts.

"Heh, heh," he chuckled playfully. "You're probably wondering how I found you up here in this podunk town."

He took a step forward. "It was so easy. I remembered your dear friend, Miss Iverson, from our little meeting in Danville. Oh yeah, the big-time nurse from Chicago General."

Nora put her hand over her mouth, trying to mask her breathing as much as possible.

"One call, that's all it took. They were so helpful." He giggled again. "A little chit-chat and the hospital operator was only too happy to divulge that their head nurse and friend Nora had gone to Pine Lake for the weekend. That had to be little ole you; how many Noras could there be?"

147

This time he laughed heartily. "And now, I'm going to watch you die."

Just then, lights flooded the barn. Nora gasped and blinked at the sudden brightness.

Robert turned at the sound of her outburst. He, too, blinked and pushed the stall door open, sending it crashing into the wall. "Ah, there you are, my little meddling fool, cowering in the corner like a dog who knows he's done wrong."

She saw the scorn in his eyes as he raised the revolver. Closing her eyes, she felt her heart in her throat. *What is it going to feel like to be shot?* Her eyes flew open at the sound of a loud masculine yell. Duke, with a pitchfork under his arm like a jousting pole, came charging at Robert.

Reality returned to slow motion. Robert swung the gun around, but never finished his turn before Duke ran the fork into Robert's mid-section. Robert gave out a blood curdling howl. His hand fell to his side, quivering as his finger pulled the trigger, emptying a shell into the floor. Straw and a cloud of dust mushroomed into the air. Nora grimaced seeing the pitchfork tines protruding from Robert's back, showering her with another round of blood droplets.

Continuing his battle cry, Duke didn't stop until he had pushed Robert all the way to the back of the stall, pinning the stunned man to the wall. Robert's eyes bulged; blood oozed from the corner of his mouth. He coughed twice, his body shook, and his chin slowly dropped to his chest. The gun slipped from his hand and fell into the straw. Nora instinctively grabbed the weapon and flung it into the far corner.

Duke stood. Dazed, he began weaving back and forth. He let go of the handle and stumbled forward. Righting himself, he closed his eyes and slumped to the floor.

Nora crawled to his side. "Duke, speak to me." She patted his cheek. "Duke, stay with me." She put her head to his chest. He was breathing, but barely.

His sleeve was soaked in blood. She leaned down and bit the cloth, opening a small hole. With her fingers, she tore the material from shoulder to wrist. Blood continued to pump from a small hole in the upper part of his arm. "Duke! Listen to me. Stay with me," she tore open her blouse. "Don't you leave me." She wrapped the blouse around his arm below his shoulder, tied a knot, and continued to twist it until the blood stopped squirting from his wound. She pushed her finger into the bullet hole to further restrict the loss of blood. She kept releasing and tightening the tourniquet, pleading with him to stay awake.

"Help!" she yelled. "Please, somebody help me." She looked at Duke, though in her mind, she saw the faces of the many soldiers whose lives slipped away from them.

"My God, what happened?" Gladys screamed as she ran into the stall. She was momentarily startled at the sight of the man pinned against the wall before dropping to her knees next to Nora. "We heard the gunshots but didn't know what was happening. Mom called the police."

"Duke's been shot. The bullet must have hit an artery; he's lost a lot of blood," Nora said. "Call for an ambulance. He needs helps right now."

Gladys quickly got to her feet. "Stay with him, I'll be right back." She hurried off.

Nora loosened the knot and re-tightened it. Leaning down she kissed Duke on the lips. "Don't leave me," she whispered.

"Leave you; where am I?" His voice was weak and barely audible.

"Duke, talk to me," she said. "Stay awake. Help is on the way."

"I...I...I don't feel so good."

"Don't try to talk, just listen. You've been shot, you've lost a lot of blood, but you're going to be alright. Just stay awake...don't go to sleep

"I'm so tired...I don't..."

"Listen to me, you have to stay awake. Don't you dare nod off!" She wanted to slap his face but couldn't. Her hands were busy holding the tourniquet and keeping a finger in the wound. "Oh Duke, I'm so sorry for getting you mixed up in this," she cried. "This wasn't your fight."

His eyes opened halfway. "It's what soldiers do."

Nora glanced at Robert. "What...kill?"

"Protect their buddy," he said, as his eyelids slowly sagged.

"Duke!" she yelled. "Don't you leave me! Duke!"

Sirens came from all directions as the ambulance and police arrived at the same time. Two young police officers stepped to the side, turning away from the sight of the man hanging against the wall, and out of the way of the attendants who came carrying a stretcher. One eased Nora's hand from her make-do tourniquet, while the other one withdrew her finger and applied pressure to the wound with a large gauze pad. The first guy unwound her blouse, tossed it aside and applied a tourniquet of his own, locking it in place.

Nora scooted back to the wall. She brought her knees to her chest and began rocking back and forth.

"Adrenalin, quick, his pulse is really weak," the older attendant said. "We don't want to lose him." Then looking back at Nora, "We'll have to check on her, too. She's probably in shock." The younger attendant tapped the syringe, pushed out a small amount, and handed it to his partner.

"Check the guy on the wall," the attendant said, emptying the syringe into Duke's right arm. "By his color, I doubt if he needs our help."

The young attendant put his fingers on Robert's neck. "No pulse." He knelt beside Nora. "How are you feeling, can I help you up?"

Nora pushed his hand away, then returned her arms across her knees. "Please don't lose him," she murmured. Then biting her lip, "Please God, don't take him. None of this was his fault he doesn't deserve to die."

"Let's get him on the stretcher and to the hospital," the older one said. "You stay here, help the woman, and get that guy off the wall...I'll try to get back or send someone to help."

Nora tried to get up. "Wait, I'm going with you."

One of the officers helped her up. "Maybe you need to stay here and tell us what happened. I don't think that fellow with the pitchfork in his stomach got in that predicament by himself."

Nora tried to break free. "His name is Robert Cooper. He tried to kill us. Please, let me go, I've got to make sure Duke is alright."

151

Again, the siren blared as the ambulance sped away from the barn. Nora broke free from the officer and slumped to her knees. "Oh, please, God, don't let him die."

The attendant brought a blanket and put it over Nora's shoulders. "Here, ma'am, cover up with this."

Nora pulled the blanket tight across her chest, realizing her bra was the only thing covering her chest. "Please," she pleaded. "Take me to the hospital, I've got to see if Duke is okay."

"Is this Robert Cooper related to you?" the officer asked. "Why was he trying to kill you?"

Gladys pushed the officer aside. "Get your ass away from her. Look at her color; can't you see she's in shock?"

"But..." the officer pleaded.

"Don't 'but' me," Gladys shot back. "I'm taking her up to the house." Gladys put her arm around Nora as she was about to collapse. "You can wait with your stupid questions." Then, seeing the attendant pull the pitchfork from the wall and Robert's limp body crumble to the floor, Gladys pointed to the heap. "He's the guy doing the shooting. Check on him, he's killed before. They had him locked up. How did he get free?"

Nora began to shake uncontrollably.

"C'mon, officer, make yourself useful," Gladys said. "Help me get her to the house."

Nora Visits Duke in the Hospital

Nora woke with a jerk, blinking from the sunlight. Moving her head side to side, she focused on each item in the room, trying to determine where she was. She was warm but felt clammy. She pushed back the heavy covers before realizing she was only in her panties and bra. Pulling the sheet back up under her chin, she continued to survey the room, trying to sort out whether the thoughts and visions that raced through her mind were real or imagined. Recognizing Gladys' upstairs bedroom gave her comfort, but also sent a shiver down her spine, knowing the ordeal with Robert really happened.

Nora bolted upright as Gladys came into the room.

"Good, you're awake," Gladys said. "How do you feel?"

"Okay, I guess." Nora held the sheet in place as she slid her legs off the bed.

"Whoa, you stay right there. You're in no shape to go anywhere."

"But...Duke...is he okay?"

"Stable. I talked to the hospital just a bit ago. He's weak, lost a lot of blood, but they're keeping a close eye on him." Gladys reached down and searched through Nora's tattered suitcase. "Have you got a shirt or a blouse in here?"

"Grab anything, I really want to go to the hospital."

Gladys tossed a tan shirt and brown skirt in Nora's direction. "You listen to me, young lady, you were in pretty bad shape when we got you up here last night, and you weren't in very good shape to begin with. If you don't slow down and start taking care of yourself, you'll be the next one in a hospital bed."

"Yes, Mother," Nora said, buttoning her shirt.

"Don't 'yes, Mother' me. I mean it. They're doing everything they can for Duke; you being there is not going to make a difference."

"Will you take me, or do I have to walk?" Nora asked, looking at herself in the mirror.

Gladys shook her head. "Stubborn, just plain stubborn," she muttered and walked out of the room.

Nora ran a comb through her hair. *Gladys is right. I look like shit, but I'm the reason he's lying in that bed and I should be there with him.* She ran a stream of lipstick across her lips, pinched her cheeks to bring up some color, and headed downstairs.

Nora came into the kitchen as Gladys was pouring orange juice in a glass. "I made you a couple pieces of toast. You're not going anywhere until you eat and drink this juice."

Nora was about to protest when Gladys raised her hand. "If you try to fight me, I'll tie you to the chair." Gladys pulled out the chair. "Now sit."

Nora knew it was useless to argue any further. She sat, took a bite of toast, and washed it down with a swallow of the juice.

Mary walked into the room fumbling in her purse. "Are we leaving right now?"

"As soon as Miss Stubborn finishes her breakfast," Gladys replied.

"I'm sorry, how is Mister Iverson doing?" Nora hated the fact she had completely forgotten about Gladys' dad being in the hospital.

"He's doing much better," Mary said. "He's been up walking the hallways."

Nora put the last piece of bread in her mouth. She stood and gulped the juice in one big swallow. "We're ready," she said, taking Mary under the arm and ushering her to the door.

Gladys brought up the rear, shaking her head.

"Duke is probably still in the emergency room," Gladys said as the three walked up to the hospital door. "Mom and I will go to see Dad and then I'll come find you to check on Duke."

Nora followed the signs and began poking her head into rooms along the way. A nurse intercepted her. "May I help you?" she asked curtly.

"I'm looking for Duke Brady."

"Are you family?"

Nora had to think about how to answer the question. *No, I'm not family, but almost being killed together, should account for something.* "No, but..."

"The doctor is with him now," the nurse said, stepping in front of a door. "You can wait in the lobby. I'll see if he can have visitors."

"I'm not waiting anywhere." Nora brushed past the woman and pushed open the door.

"I'm sorry, Doctor, this woman..." the nurse tried to step in front of Nora.

"...is a battlefield nurse," Nora said, finishing the woman's sentence. "With lots of experience treating bullet wounds."

The young doctor grabbed the hospital nurse's arm. "It's alright, let her come in."

Nora immediately stepped to Duke's side. Instinctively, she checked the label on the pouch hanging on the metal stand and the plastic tubes leading to his arm. She felt his head and began taking a pulse reading on his wrist. "When was the dressing changed on the wound?" Without asking, she began removing the tape and gauze from his arm.

"Here...wait, you can't do that," the doctor said, stepping forward.

Nora quickly sized up the young man with the stethoscope hanging over his shoulder. Late twenties, fuzz for whiskers, squeaky voice, a newbie for sure. "I've treated a thousand bullet wounds; how many have you?"

The doctor stepped back. "Just this..."

Nora stopped unwrapping the bandage. "May I have a look?"

The doctor appeared to ignore the menacing look the nurse gave him and nodded to Nora. "Old Doc Bachuber patched him up. He's had two transfusions and we've been pumping him full of antibiotics."

"Morphine?"

"Yeah, that, too."

"Ease up on the morphine until he asks for it. To guard against infection, it's better if you let his body put up a fight." She carefully rolled back the dressing. Leaning over, she sniffed at the wound. "It looks good, no infection that I can tell. Let's change the dressing while we're at it."

The doctor tapped the nurse, who immediately understood and rushed off to get the necessary materials.

"I take it you were in the war?" he asked. "The ambulance guy said you probably saved this guy's life by applying the tourniquet as quickly as you did. I never heard of putting a finger in the wound, but I guess it makes sense."

"Improvisation. We had to do a lot of that in the war." Nora stepped aside as the nurse returned and began wrapping the wound.

Nora went to the other side of the bed and raised one of Duke's eyelids. "Has he been awake yet?"

"A little bit; the morphine has kept him pretty much out of it."

"It would probably be best for him to wake up." Nora leaned, put her head to his nose, and listened to his breathing.

"Hi," Duke whispered weakly.

Nora came up quickly.

Duke blinked as if it took all his might to hold his lids from falling.

Nora picked up his hand. "How are you doing?"

"Okay, a little groggy." He glanced around the room. "Hospital?"

"Yes, but you're doing fine," Nora said.

Duke studied Nora's face, and then slowly turned to the side. "Is he?"

"Robert? Dead? Yes."

Duke stared into space. "If I hadn't...he was going to kill you."

"I know...it was a very courageous thing you did." She leaned down and kissed him on the lips.

"What's that for?"

"Call it a down payment on a thank-you for saving my life."

The nurse finished dressing the wound and stepped aside as Gladys and a uniformed officer came into the room. Nora backed away and Gladys walked to the foot of the bed. "You're some kind of a hero," she said, patting Duke's foot. "You've got the whole town talking."

Duke glanced at Nora before steadying his eyes on the officer.

Nora reached for Duke's hand as the officer came to the side of the bed.

"This is Ben Davis from the sheriff's department," Gladys said. "I met him in the hallway. He's in charge of the investigation."

"Investigation?" Nora felt a chill.

"That's right, ma'am," the man said. "We've got a man here with a bullet hole and another dead on the end of a pitchfork. We're not sure what happened, but we have to get to the bottom of this."

"Robert almost killed me!" Nora shrieked. "Duke was shot protecting me. Haven't you checked on that guy?"

The officer held up his hand. "We're in the process...why was he trying to kill you?"

Nora wondered where to start. "I...he...it was a child custody thing. He was trying to get his hands on a ten-thousand-dollar life insurance payment. He stabbed his wife. The man is crazy."

"His name is Robert Cooper," Gladys said. "The last we heard, they had him locked up at Dunning. It's a mental institution outside of Chicago."

"We haven't confirmed this is him, but a man by that name and description did kill a security guard in Chicago, stole his weapon and his car. If this is the same guy, there's no doubt he's a bad actor, but we still have to make sure his death was justified. Are you up to talking to me?" he asked Duke.

Duke nodded.

"Good." Ben turned to the women. "I would like to interview him in private. Can I ask you gals to leave the room?" Seeing Nora about to protest, he caught her by the arm. "Could you wait in the lounge; I'd like to get a statement from you, too."

"I can give it to you right now. The man shot Duke and he was about to shoot me."

"Please do not say anymore." The officer escorted her to the door.

Nora turned her head to Duke. "I'll be back, okay?" she said with a smile.

She yanked her arm from Ben's grip. "What is it with all this secrecy?" she shrieked.

Gladys pushed Nora the rest of the way out the door and part way down the hall. "Ben's a good guy, just doing his job. C'mon, let's see if Mom wants to get something to eat."

"Why did we have to leave? Does he think I'm lying?"

"Since you and Duke are the only ones who know what happened, I imagine he's going to compare your stories to make sure they match."

"Why wouldn't they match?"

"I didn't say they wouldn't," Gladys said. "Everything is going to be okay. This police thing is a mere formality."

Nora rolled her tongue around inside a dry mouth, and for the second time in as many days, she wished for an alcoholic lift.

An Open and Shut Case?

Gladys kept her eye on Nora. She had witnessed Nora crumble under the stress of Sarah's encounter with Robert and again when Betty was murdered. This was supposed to be a relaxing weekend. A chance to unwind and plant her feet on solid ground. "Are you going to be all right?"

Nora stopped and leaned against the wall. "What is that guy after? You were there. You saw what happened."

"I didn't really see anything," Gladys said. "It was pretty much all over when I got to the barn." She put her arm around Nora's shoulder. "I'm sure this is all just routine. I've known Ben since high school; he's good people."

Nora pulled away. "He knows Robert killed that guard. Why is this so hard to understand that he was trying to kill me...us?"

"Like I said, it's a routine investigation. Do you want to go with Mom and me to get something to eat?"

"I'm going to the lounge. Just bring me a coke or some orange juice. I'll have a little talk with "nice guy Ben."

"You won't help yourself if you go in with that shitty-ass attitude. Please, relax and answer his questions." Gladys watched Nora walk toward the lounge. "Remember what I said...and for God's sake, put a smile on your face."

Nora turned and stuck her tongue out at Gladys.

"Stubborn," Gladys mumbled and went on her way.

Nora took a seat by the window. Crossing one leg over the other, she kicked her foot in a steady rhythm. As if her leg and hand were attached by a single string, she tapped her fingers on the arm of the chair. Then all movement slowed as she felt the warning signs that had precluded her passing out before. She swallowed hard and tried to breathe in long drawn-out breaths. *Don't do it. Not here. Not now.*

"Nora, Nora, can you hear me?"

Nora opened her eyes to see Gladys's concerned look. Other people with the same worried look stood by.

"Here, take a sip of this juice." Gladys brought the glass to Nora's lips.

"What happened?" Nora tried to raise her head.

"Ben found you passed out in the chair. You put a scare into everyone."

Damn, here I go again. What the hell is the matter with me? Where is my Grenadier in a bottle when I really need him? Nora took the glass and sat upright. "I'm sorry...I just don't know what...there's just been so much going on...I...

"It's okay," Ben said. "I'm just glad you're okay."

Nora's mouth felt as dry as the Nevada desert. She took a sip of juice. "I'm fine; just give me a minute to get my bearings."

Gladys stood. "Okay, folks, the party's over, let's get back to work. These two have some business to discuss."

The room cleared. Gladys nodded and smiled as she ushered the last of the people out.

Nora finished the juice, set the glass on the table, and watched as the officer dragged a chair next to hers. "I'm sorry."

"No need to be sorry, you've been through a lot."

"No, I'm sorry for getting so upset with you."

Ben turned a few pages in his notepad. "This won't take long. I think Duke pretty much filled me in on what happened. We found the car Mr. Cooper is alleged to have stolen and I'm sure the gun we found at the scene belonged to the guard who was killed. I just need you to clear up why he intended to kill you?"

Nora started at the very beginning and methodically laid out how the chance meeting with Sarah Jean brought about the saga of her and Robert Cooper. It seemed to her they were on a collision course to a fiery end, but she never imagined it would be anything like this. She lay back in the chair. "Do you need anything else?"

Ben finished writing in his pad. "I guess that takes care of it. I'll hand this over to the District Attorney, but I'm sure no charges will be filed."

"Against who? Me? Duke?

"It's up to the DA, but I think he will see that Duke's actions were justified."

"Would it be better if I were dead? I would be if Duke hadn't acted the way he did."

"I agree, I was just saying…"

"I don't want to hear another word." Nora climbed to her feet. "I'm going to see Duke. I'm done talking." She turned on her heels and left.

Time for a Life Change

The nurse came out of Duke's room and tried to block the doorway. "Maybe you should let him rest," she said.

"Just get out of the way, I'm in no mood to…"

"Don't be silly," Duke yelled. "Let her come in."

The two women brushed past each other and exchanged menacing glances.

Duke was sitting up in the bed and gave Nora a big smile.

"How are you doing? You look much better," she said.

"The stuff they were giving me made me loopy. I think it's finally wearing off."

Nora came to the edge of the bed. "Morphine can send you into orbit. Do you still have a lot of pain?"

Duke touched the bandage. "Nothing I can't handle. Did you talk to Ben?"

"We talked. Why do I get the feeling he doesn't believe what we are telling him?"

"A man is dead. They have to make sure it was justified."

Nora walked to the window. "What, shooting you and almost shooting me isn't justification enough?"

"Extenuating circumstances. I'm sure the DA will do the right thing. It doesn't matter, I would do the same thing in a similar situation."

Nora sat on the bed. "I'm sorry you got the raw end of the deal. You were very brave and I'm alive today because of what you did."

"I'll take the final payment of that kiss you promised me."

Nora hesitated. "I shouldn't. It will just make things harder."

"Harder? For what?"

"To say good bye. It's what I was telling you when we were walking up to the house. I have to go back to Ely. My folks have been wonderful, but I can't just dump Sarah on them. I'm the one who caused the whole affair."

"Can't you bring her here? I told you, I'd love to help."

"That's sweet." Nora turned away. "It's more than that. We had a chance encounter three years ago, but things are different now. I've had a great time with you these past few days, but you don't know me. I'm not that innocent girl from back then. I've had…"

"I don't care. I'm not lily white either. I just know I've loved you from the moment I saw you back in '42. It's the reason I came back to Pine Lake. I felt it was the only way I would ever have the chance of seeing you again. I don't want to lose you a second time."

"I should have never come back here; look at all the trouble I've caused."

"Don't say that. Can't we work something out?"

Nora pulled the wrinkles out of the bed sheets. Picking up his hand, "I wish I could figure out how to make it all work out…here…with you. But look at me; I'm a wreck. I need time to get my life in order."

"Let me help you," he said. "Can't you stay a little bit longer?"

Nora put her finger to his lips. "It would be wonderful if we had more time to get to know one another...but..."

Duke took her hand and held it tight. "I don't need more time, I've had three years to think about you. I'll marry you right now."

Nora pulled free and ran to the door. "I can't," she said softly. Then, without looking back, she left the room.

***

Gladys found Nora sitting on the outside steps. "How's Duke?"

Nora stood. "Better. When were you planning to go back to Chicago?"

"I'm staying an extra week. I called the hospital this morning to let them know. You're welcome to stay as long as you want."

"I've got to get going; my folks are probably wondering what happened to me. Is there a bus that comes through here?"

"Greyhound, but I don't know their schedule. They stop by the drug store."

"Same as Ely. Is the store far from here?"

Gladys pointed down the street. "Five blocks. Do you want me to drive you?"

"No, the walk will do me good." Nora brushed off her skirt. "I wanted to scout around the town anyway. I'll catch up to you and your mom later."

Nora walked briskly. The warm morning air and bright sun lifted her spirit. She encountered children playing in the street and folks on the sidewalk. People were friendly and greeted her as she passed by. Main Street was busy with tourists lingering after the Fourth of July holiday. The drug store stood on the corner across from the court house and was easy to find.

The clerk handed Nora a schedule. "The bus comes through around four-thirty. It goes north one day and south the next. Today it's southbound."

"Southbound...today...four-thirty?"

"Yep," said the clerk.

Nora checked the clock over the clerk's shoulder. The hands were straight up. "How much to Chicago?"

"Two seventy-five."

Nora paid, started to leave, and came back to the counter. "Do you have a taxi?"

The clerk nodded. "Would you like me to call him?"

"Please."

Nora waited at the curb. Her stomach burned and bubbled up in her throat. She felt guilty to be running off like this, but what could she do? "Why did I ever consent to come here?" she muttered to herself. "Look at the mess I've created. Robert is dead, Duke's been shot, and I could have been killed, too."

A nondescript car pulled to the curb. Nora bent. "Are you the taxi?"

"Yes, ma'am, where to?" he asked.

"Could you take me to the Iverson farm?" She opened the door and settled into the back seat.

"Lots of excitement up there. You heard about the shooting?" the driver asked, putting the car in gear. "And the guy being stabbed with a pitchfork?"

Heard? No. Experienced. Nora smiled but chose to remain silent.

"Seems a guy was trying to kill this woman but shot her boyfriend instead. The boyfriend, with a bullet in his arm, ends up harpooning the guy with a pitchfork. We've never had anything like that happen before. Normally things are pretty quiet around here."

Nora shifted in her seat. *Things will get back to normal as soon as I leave.*

Standing on the steps, she watched the taxi turn and head back through the glen. Someone had pushed Duke's cycle up by the barn, reminding her of their carefree ride before Robert showed up and all hell broke loose. She didn't feel right about leaving but couldn't rationalize any other course to take. She went upstairs and gathered her things.

Leaving? Not so Fast.

Nora set her beat-up suitcase next to the front door, walked into the kitchen, and tossed her purse on the table. She took a loaf of bread from the box, opened the refrigerator and found the makings for a sandwich. Setting her plate on the table and pouring herself a glass of lemonade, she began searching through drawers for pencil and paper.

She took a small bite of the sandwich before picking up the pencil. She tapped it on the paper trying to mentally compose some kind of thank-you letter to Gladys and her mom. It was supposed to have been a quiet restful weekend. How could she have predicted something like Gladys' dad having a heart attack or Robert showing up? Worse, how could she have known that seeing Duke would stir such emotion and further complicate her life? Surely none of this, except for Gladys' dad, would have happened if she had just said her "hellos" to Gladys in Chicago and continued on to Ely. If she could, she'd be the first person to turn back the hands of time.

Nora had been so deep in thought she never heard the car pull into the yard and was only aware of Gladys and Mary's presence when they were standing beside her.

"What's going on? We've been looking all over town for you."

"I'm leaving."

"We gathered that; the gal at the drugstore said you bought a ticket. Why?"

"I should never have come here. I've caused problems for everybody," Nora said.

"Don't be silly," Gladys said. "You probably saved Dad's life."

"But look at the thing with Robert and Duke getting shot."

"Thank goodness it happened here where Duke could save you. Who knows what would have happened if he had caught up to you somewhere else?" Mary said.

"Mom's right," Gladys said, pulling out a chair. "Were you going to just run off without a word?"

"I was writing you a letter." Nora pushed the blank paper in Gladys' direction.

"This isn't like you. What are you running away from? Is it Duke?"

Nora took a hanky from her purse and wiped the corners of her eyes. "I can't stay, I've got Sarah Jean to think about. Ever since I got out of the army my life has been one big squirrel's nest. Everywhere I go people end up dead or getting shot."

"What, you think you're some kind of voodoo doll? That you're responsible for the bad things other people do? Don't be silly and running off like a thief in the night is not going to solve anything. What Duke did shows how much he cares for you. Were you going to run out on him, too?"

"He wants to marry me."

"So," Gladys snorted. "Is there some reason you can't marry him?

"I've got Sarah Jean. She's my responsibility. I brought that whole thing about and I am not going to let...her..."

Nora stopped mid-sentence at the sound of a knock on the door.

Mary scurried to see who it was. "It's Ben," she said, leading the way into the kitchen.

"Ladies," he said, taking off his cap. Looking at Nora, "I'm happy I was able to catch up to you."

"What, more questions?"

"Not mine. The DA would like to talk to you."

"Is there a problem?" Gladys asked.

"I told you everything I knew." Nora showed her defiance. "What more can I say? Besides, I 'm leaving on the bus in a little more than an hour."

"This is not a request. You will accompany me to talk to the District Attorney."

"And if I don't?"

"I'll have to take you into custody as a material witness in the death of one Robert Cooper. It will be your choice," he said with a puzzling smile, "whether we do it with or without handcuffs."

Gladys pulled out Nora's chair. "She'll be more than happy to accompany you."

Nora switched her angry look from Gladys to the officer. "I don't know what more I can say, but if I miss my bus, I'm going to be PO'ed."

***

The DA's office was on the second floor of the courthouse. A scruffy man in a rumpled suit sat behind the desk. He stood when Nora entered. "Miss Jensen, thank you for coming in."

"I was told I didn't have a choice."

"I know this has been very upsetting for you, but we have an obligation to review all the evidence in a case like

170

this, especially when it involves a death. We have one little issue left to resolve."

"I told him everything." She pointed to Ben.

The DA picked up the silver pistol from his desk. "Do you recognize this gun?"

"I think it's the one Robert had."

"It was found at the scene. In your statement, you said that the deceased is the one who shot Mr. Brady. Is that correct?"

"Yes."

"At any time was this gun in your possession?"

"What! No! Of course not."

"We've found two sets of prints on the gun, one we assume belongs to the deceased. The other is a smaller one, more the size a woman would make." The DA looked over the top of his glasses. "Could those prints be yours? Are you sure you didn't shoot Mr. Brady and are using his arm wound to cover up some reason you wanted Mister Cooper dead?"

Nora couldn't believe what she was hearing. "Wait, everything happened just like I said. Why would I shoot...let me think?" Nora rubbed her temples. "I saw the tines poke through Robert's back. I felt the blood splatter on my face." She closed her eyes and searched through a memory she was trying so hard to forget. "Robert hit the wall. His one eye bulged out. He stiffened...like an electrical shock coursed through his body. I saw his hand tighten around the gun and he fired it into the floor. Then...then..."

"Then what?" the DA asked, coming forward in his chair.

"The gun fell in the straw...I picked it up and threw it in the far corner."

"That's where we found it," said Ben. "We wondered how it got way over there."

"If you look in the floor and find the bullet, you'll know I'm telling the truth," Nora said.

"That would also account for the spent shells," Ben said, getting up. "I will personally go and search the stall."

"It all sounds reasonable enough to me," said the DA. "Let's hold this in abeyance until we see if Ben is able to recover the missing slug. We'll meet in my office at nine in the morning."

"I have a bus ticket to Chicago. It leaves at four-thirty," Nora said.

"Without you, I'm afraid," said the DA. "I'll see you in the morning."

172

Nora Becomes the Driver

Nora walked out of the courthouse wondering what to do next. She slapped on her sunglasses and closed her purse in a huff. She thought about defying the DA's order and hopping on the bus, but that could get her in a lot of trouble. *I guess I'm stuck here until the day after tomorrow.*

Starting down the steps, she was greeted by a horn beep and recognized Gladys' car. She hurriedly opened the passenger-side door.

"What was that all about?" Gladys asked before Nora had settled in the seat.

"They found my fingerprints on the gun and think I shot Duke to cover up some cockamamie scheme to kill Robert."

"Are you kidding? How did your fingerprints get on the gun?

"I forgot, when Duke..." Nora swallowed hard as the visual of Duke charging Robert with the pitchfork and pinning him to the wall filled her mind. "...that Robert fired a shot into the floor and dropped the gun. Instinctively, I grabbed it and threw it in the far corner to get it away from him."

"Were you going to leave without saying good bye?" The voice came from the back seat.

Nora swung around to see Duke sitting there with his arm in a sling. He didn't have to say another word, disappointment was written all over his face. "Were you?"

"I...I..." Nora slumped in her seat.

"I'm sorry if I pressured you to stay," he said. "Maybe I just assumed too much, or maybe I thought you felt the same about me as I do about you."

"I do care...it's just...I don't see..."

Gladys put the car in gear. "I told Duke what you were planning. He insisted I bring him here. I think you two need some time to work this out."

"Hold up, Gladys," Duke said. "I'll get out here." He opened the back door and slid out. "Nora is the one who has to decide what she's going to do. I'll walk home from here."

"Are you sure you're all right to walk that far? I can drive..." Gladys' words trailed off as she watched the man walk away. Letting out the clutch, she pulled away from the curb.

"Why can't I do anything right?" Nora said just above a whisper.

"Feeling sorry for yourself is not going to fix a thing," Gladys said, holding out a hanky. "If you feel you have to leave, then you need to do that, but that man deserves to know where he stands. Even if you don't love him, he saved your life; you owe him the decency to let him know that."

"But I do," Nora said quietly. "I just don't know how to make it all work."

"Okay, I understand about Sarah. That is something you and your family will have to work out. She's got two years of high school left, after that she's married or off to college. Two years is not a long time." Gladys looked over to her friend. "Are you listening to me?"

Nora nodded and blew her nose.

"It's a fact, women in America outnumber the men and those killed in the war is only going to make things worse. Here you have a guy who is ass-over-teakettle in love with you and you him, and you're going to walk away without so much as a 'howdy-do' or 'see you later?' That's just nuts. Talk to him. I'm sure there is some way to work things out."

Gladys pulled into the yard and shut off the engine. "The next bus to Chicago isn't until Tuesday. That should give you guys plenty of time to get your act together." The women got out of the car and started to the house. "Well?" Gladys put her arm around Nora's shoulders.

Nora forced a smile and nodded.

Mary Iverson came out of the kitchen wiping her hands on her apron. "Are you hungry? I made some chicken salad, you…"

Nora shook her head, grabbed her suitcase, sitting by the front door, and headed upstairs. Putting the case on the bed, she paced the floor wondering what her next move would be. Brushing back the curtain, she saw the royal blue motorcycle parked next to the barn. Unbuckling the straps, she flopped open her suitcase and rummaged to find a pair of slacks.

Moments later she stood by the bike and mentally walked through what Duke had told her. "I should be able to do this." She tried to visualize what both he and Antonio did to start their cycles. She put her leg over the back of the bike and settled in the seat. As if going through a checklist, she squeezed the lever on the left handle bar. Hand brake. Twisting the right grip, throttle. She pressed down on the right foot pedal. Brake, and clutch is on the left.

She was leery of the next step. Did she have enough weight and leg strength to kick start the engine? "Okay," she said with contrived courage. "I have to do this in order." She rocked the bike back and forth. "That's good we're in neutral." She leaned a little and kicked up the stand. Taking a deep breath, she turned the switch, adjusted her foot on the starter pedal, and with a leap, came down with all her weight on the starter. The engine sputtered and died.

"Damn...wait...give it a little gas." She gave the throttle a slight twist and again kicked down on the starter. The engine came alive with a roar before slowing to a smooth idle. Nora revved the engine a couple of times.

"What the hell are you doing?" Gladys yelled as she came running across the yard. "You'll break your neck on that darned thing."

"I'm going to see Duke."

"Take my car."

"I can't."

"Why not?"

"I don't have a driver's license."

"You need more than a license to drive that thing; you need your head examined."

Nora stepped down on the clutch and pulled the shifting knob back a notch. "I think I can do this," she said, easing up on the clutch. The bike moved ahead slowly. She gave it a little more gas and steadied it across the yard. Making a wide swooping turn she passed Gladys with a big smile. Nora made a few more laps around the yard before stopping next to Gladys.

"You're right," Nora said. "I need to get things worked out with Duke. Don't wait up for me, okay?"

"Be careful," Gladys said. "It won't do either of you any good if you break your neck on the fool thing."

"I'll be fine." Nora accelerated down the drive.

Pine Lake is not that big, but Nora still made a few wrong turns before finding Duke's place on the hill. Pulling up to the back door, she waited for him to come out. She revved the engine a few times, wondering if maybe he hadn't heard her. Still no sign of him. She kicked down the stand and turned off the engine. The back door stood half open. She pushed it wide and stepped inside. "Duke," she yelled. "Are you here?" She stepped over the pile of boards in the kitchen and yelled again.

"What?" came a muffled voice.

Nora proceeded into the living room and found Duke sitting on the couch with a bottle of beer in his hand.

"It's probably not a good idea to drink alcohol on top of all the medication you've had," she said.

"Oh yeah? It seemed like a good idea to me." He took a swallow from the bottle.

"I know you're upset, but can we talk about it?"

"What's there to talk about, you're leaving." He took another swallow of beer.

"Did you see me? I rode the motorcycle over here."

"I heard you...didn't know you knew how." He studied the label on the bottle.

"The shifting took a while to get used to, but I'm getting better.

"You could have gotten hurt."

"Are you angry I rode it over here?"

Without acknowledging the question, Duke took another drink.

177

"Listen to me," she said, making him move over and taking a seat next to him. "I'm sorry, I guess I just panicked." She took the bottle from his hand and set it on the floor. "I've got so much going on in my life and then you started talking marriage, I couldn't process everything."

"I suppose it's my fault, too. You're all I've thought about for three years. I lost you once. I don't want to lose you again. But I should have never pressured you like that."

"I wish you would understand, I have to go back to Ely. I have to get things worked out with Sarah. She has been through so much. I want her to have a stable environment and I don't think I can do that on my own. My mom and dad love her and can give her the nurturing she needs, but I want to be there, too."

"So, you're leaving."

"Yes, but it doesn't have to be forever. She's got two years of high school and then who knows. College? Marriage?" Nora took his hand. "It wouldn't be that long, maybe she and I could come and visit you at Christmas time?"

"Would you?" he asked, coming upright. "I mean, that would be great. You could also spend time in the summer. Hell, you could spend the entire summer here if you'd like."

"Let's not get carried away, but yes, I'm sure there would be many ways we could see one another. Maybe you could visit us in Ely?"

"You bet." His voice rose with excitement. "I'd love to meet Sarah and your folks."

Nora smiled. "I never meant to hurt you. I guess I just felt I needed to escape."

"I'll try my best to never make you feel that way again."

Nora cradled his head in her hands and slowly touched her lips to his, first lightly, then with force and full of passion. Opening her eyes and drawing back, she saw his surprised look. "That's for saving my life," she said softly. "I always pay my debts."

"I hope you don't have to leave right now; I'd sure like to have some more of that."

"I'm here until Tuesday."

He turned her and lay her supine on the couch. "I suggest we don't waste a minute." Moving his wounded arm and sling to the side, he leaned forward and kissed her. First gently, letting his lips wipe the moisture from hers, before pressing his tongue into the far recesses of her mouth. As day moved into darkness, they became lost in the magic of each other's embrace.

Then Came Morning

Nora woke and pulled the blanket to her chin. Feeling the silky fabric slide over her breast, she was instantly aware, but peeked to confirm, she was naked. She sat up. Holding the blanket in place, she visually searched the room. The flickering kerosene lamp put the room in motion as shadows danced up and down the walls. Duke was nowhere in sight. The air was filled with the sweet smell of bacon frying. She flopped back on the pillow. Stretching, she smiled, thinking how passionate and satisfying their lovemaking had been. So different from the first time, three years ago.

Reaching from under the covers her fingers danced along the floor until she found her clothes, lying in a heap. Suddenly, Duke's rich baritone voice rolled out from the kitchen in a chorus of "Mademoiselle from Armentieres." She dressed quickly. Carrying her shoes into the kitchen, she was greeted with a smile and a big finish to the song, "Hinky Dinky Parlez-vous." Nora shook her head as she sat on the stack of lumber and laced up her shoes.

"How do you like your eggs?" he said, turning away from the fold-out camp stove sitting on a rickety table. Bare chested and wearing nothing but a pair of boxers, he gave her a big smile.

"What time is it?" Nora looked out the window. The first light of morning was still not bright enough to put color in the gray countryside.

"Ten to five."

"Oh geez, I've got to go. What is Gladys and her mom going to think when I come strolling in at this hour?"

"Don't you want something to eat? The bacon's done. I can fix you a couple of eggs."

Nora stuck a piece of bacon in her mouth. "Do you cook all your meals on that little stove?"

"It's for camping, but it works great. I promise I'll have cupboards and a stove by the time you get here at Christmas.

She leaned and gave him a kiss on the cheek. "I really have to go before my reputation ends up in the toilet."

He followed her out the back door and watched as she settled on the cycle. As if everything was second nature, she turned the switch, kicked over the engine, and with a fluid motion, shifted it into first gear. "I'll come by later," she said as she made a slow turn and went down the driveway. She turned to see him wave and then sped up the street.

Nora coasted into the yard, trying to use the engine as little as possible. She hoped not to wake Gladys and especially not her mother. The war had brought about a new wave of social freedom, but Nora was sure Mary Iverson still held onto a set of high moral values. Kicking down the stand, she turned the switch and slid off the seat. Running to the house, she kicked off her shoes and tiptoed up the porch steps. The front door made a squeak as she opened it and another when she eased it closed. She almost made it to the stairs when Gladys walked out of the kitchen.

"Good morning, are you sneaking in or sneaking out?"

Nora's face reddened. "I didn't think you'd be up already."

"Farmers are up at this time every day. Mom's in the bathroom doing her hair. I suggest you git upstairs and change your clothes before coming down. It will save a lot of explaining."

Nora gave her a big smile and scampered up the stairs.

The shower felt wonderful. The water warmed her on the outside as the memories of last night warmed her to her core. She brushed through her hair numerous times and spent a few extra moments to add a little makeup and lipstick before descending the stairs.

"Good morning," she exclaimed as she entered the kitchen.

Mary put down her fork and jumped to her feet. "Oh good, the food is still hot. We have scrambled eggs and bacon."

Nora took a seat at the table. "Sounds great."

Mary set the plate in front of Nora. "What time did you get in last night? I never heard a thing."

"It was late," Gladys said. "I'm sure she and Duke had a lot to talk about."

"We did," Nora added. "And I think we got things straightened out."

Gladys choked on the eggs.

"That's wonderful," Mary said. "So, what are your plans?"

"I'm leaving Tuesday on the bus, going back to Ely. Hopefully Sarah Jean and I will be back for a visit at Christmas time."

"That will be nice. You're welcome to stay with us."
Nora smiled and nodded.

Mary looked at Gladys. "You'll be here, won't you?"

"Wouldn't miss it," Gladys said as she gathered up her dishes. Turning to Nora, "Mom and I are going to spend some time at the hospital. What are you going to do?"

Nora swallowed the last mouthful of eggs. "I told Duke I'd come over today.

"More talking?"

Nora knew what Gladys was inferring and gave her a cross look.

"Maybe we can meet up at Teddy's for supper?" Gladys said. "Invite Duke, too."

"I'll see what he says." Nora put her dishes in the sink.

Duke walked out the back door as soon as she rode up on the cycle. "You're getting pretty good at that."

She turned the switch and kicked down the stand. "Driving it is a blast. Hey, where's your sling?"

Duke extended his hand to help her off the bike. "It feels fine," he said, moving it up and down. "The sling kept getting in my way." He pulled the cloth from behind his back and rested his arm in the fold. "Come in, I want to show you something."

Nora stepped over the stack of lumber and made her way to the couch in the living room.

Duke dragged a steamer trunk into the room and used a key to open the lock. Letting the top rest against the back he took out a large tablet. He sat next to her and put the pad on her lap.

"What's this?" she asked, turning over the cover.

The first page contained a pencil drawing of a large rock out-cropping overlooking a lake. "We stopped there," she shrieked. "There–on that high bluff." The next page was a drawing of the courthouse. She glanced at the initials in the lower right-hand corner. "Did you draw these? They are very good. My mother thought the drawing you did of me was very good, although she wasn't too enthused about me sitting there with no clothes on."

Duke's eyebrows raised. He put his hand on the tablet. "Maybe you shouldn't see the rest of these."

"Why?" She brushed his hand away. "What else do you have in here?" She turned the page and paused. It was a drawing of a young girl lying on her side in a pile of hay. Her skirt was raised to a point her underpants peeked out on her hip. The girl's blouse was splayed open, exposing all but the nipples of her breast. She studied the face. "Is this me?" she gasped. "I never posed for that."

"Didn't have to, it's what I saw in my head."

Nora turned the page. This was of a girl in short shorts and a halter top lying invitingly on the front deck of newly varnished Chris-Craft. She flipped back to the previous page, comparing it to the girl on the speedboat. "Is this supposed to be the same girl? This one looks more like Betty Grable."

"It's still you. My memory must have faded a bit at that point."

"Were you trying to turn me into a pin-up girl? I don't know if I…"

"It's the two loves of my life — you and mahogany boats." He reached for the tablet. "Maybe you should stop right there."

Nora took no heed and quickly turned the page. She had to catch her breath as she scanned the drawing.

184

"Wow," she said, the words barely audible. "You do have quite an imagination. I hope this wasn't done in winter, that poor girl would have caught a death of cold with no clothes on."

"Winters were pretty lonely."

"So, you just sat around drawing dirty pictures." Nora was trying to be funny but saw the dejected look on Duke's face. "I'm sorry," she said. "It's just a shock to see a naked picture of yourself, although I wish I looked that good."

"I never had a picture of you, I had to draw you to keep you fresh in my mind."

Nora continued to look at the drawing and wondered if she could even get into a pose like that with all her private parts so cleverly concealed. She could see the fullness of her breast, but one nipple was covered by an arm and the other by the swirl of the blanket she was lying on. One leg was also propped in a way that everything two inches below her belly button didn't show. "You're very talented. This is very good, but couldn't you draw me with clothes on?"

"It was my picture. So I got to choose the setting."

"You haven't shown these to anyone, have you?"

"Never would, and maybe I shouldn't have shown them to you."

"I'm very flattered, maybe a little shocked, but then I guess I don't know what goes on in that pretty little head of yours."

Duke tried to take the pad from her hands. "I'm not some kind of pervert. I drew them to keep you near me, to feel your presence around me. You came into my life back then and were gone so abruptly, it left a big hole in my heart. And now I'm faced with you leaving again."

Nora held the pad tight. "These are beautiful. I am overwhelmed by your talent and honored to be a part of your work. Maybe we need to find a camera and take some actual photographs. I'd like some of you, too."

"I have a Brownie. We'll have to get some film."

"Let's go up on Sandstone bluff. We can take some shots of the lake, too."

Duke waved his sling. "That might be a problem."

"I can drive the cycle as long as you don't mind riding behind me." She watched as Duke appeared to process the offer. "Do I detect some hesitation; do you have a problem taking a back seat to a girl?"

"Are you sure you...oh, what the heck, I'll give it a shot."

Duke shouldn't have given it a second thought. Nora quickly adjusted to having a rider behind her. She was more concerned with him keeping his hands on her waist and not exploring anywhere else. After a brief stop at the drug store to pick up two boxes of 127 film, they were on their way. The ride to Sandstone was fun. Duke relaxed as Nora maneuvered the cycle along the country roads. Only once did his hands come up and cup the lower part of her breast. An elbow to his gut sent a strong message that molesting the driver was not allowed.

It was a fun day for the two as they stopped at various points around the lake. Nora playfully posed, moving her head side to side and changing facial expressions from bright and smiling to solemn with her lips turned down at the corners. She sat on rocks, waded knee deep in the water, and leaned against a half dozen different trees. She did manage to snap a few shots of him in unguarded moments. Late in the afternoon, they ended up at the dock where Duke brought out a Chris-Craft runabout and had Nora lie across the front deck. The setting sun illuminated Nora's slender body in contrasting highlights and shadows. Duke didn't stop until he had shot up the last of the film.

He rewound the film. "I can't wait to get these developed. These last shots should be spectacular." He helped Nora off the boat. "Are you getting hungry?"

"I've been having so much fun, I haven't thought about food."

"Teddy's got some pretty good home cooking."

Nora looked at her watch. "Gladys suggested we get together there for supper. She told me to invite you."

"I'd rather it would be just you and me."

"Do this for me," she pleaded. "I haven't spent much time with Gladys and her mom, and they have been so good to me."

Doug put his arm around her shoulder. "That's fine with me."

Dinner with Gladys

Nora brought the cycle to a stop in front of Teddy's Tavern. The building was old and tired; most of the paint had peeled off the clapboards. Around the turn of the century, it served as the family home. In 1904 Teddy's grandfather turned it into a tavern, and it soon became a local favorite. After the First World War, Ted added a large room onto the front and gutted the rest of the first floor to give the place more room. He added a kitchen and began serving fish on Friday nights and chicken on Saturday. His half-pound hamburgers were well known. Returning GIs from this war quickly made Teddy's their favorite watering hole.

The story goes that during prohibition in the 30s, Teddy made it into an ice cream shop. His wife was selling cones and sundaes out the front door while Ted sold moonshine out the back. The revenuers had Ted in their sights, raiding the place while Ted was out cooking up a new batch. Finding his stash in the wall behind the icebox, they threatened to charge his wife as an accessory unless he pleaded guilty to possession. That landed him six months in the pokey, but they never did find his still.

"I was wondering if you guys would show up," Gladys said as she stood and pulled out a chair for Nora.

Duke shook hands with Mrs. Iverson. "Hello, I'm Duke Brady."

"I know who you are," Mary acknowledged sharply. "How's your arm?"

Duke pulled it out of the sling and waved it around. "It's doing fine."

"I wouldn't be too frisky," Gladys said. "You don't want to open the wound."

Duke smiled, nodded, and sat next to Nora.

"I think his bruised ego hurts more than the wound," Nora giggled. "He's had to let me drive the cycle and ride in back."

Duke's face flushed. He shook his head. "That's no lie."

"We just put in our order," Gladys said. "Mom and I are having hamburgers."

"That's good for me." Nora turned to see what Duke had in mind.

"Fries, too," he added.

Gladys signaled the waitress and ordered the additional food. "So, what did you guys do today?"

Nora put her hand on top of Duke's. "We cruised around the lake. Took a bunch of photographs."

"Are you still planning on leaving tomorrow?" Mary asked.

"I have to," Nora smiled at Duke.

"I promised Nora I would have a room ready for her when she comes at Christmas," Duke said. "I'll even put up a tree."

Mary looked at Gladys and then at Nora. "Do you think that would be wise? What would people think?"

"I don't really care..." Duke never completed his sentence before Gladys spoke up.

"Mother, this is 1945. The war has changed everything. Women have been liberated. They've had to put on pants

189

and work right alongside men. They've worked in factories, built tanks and airplanes. They weld, drive trucks, and can swing a hammer or wrench as well as the guys. We should let Duke and Nora decide where she's going to stay."

Mary's pursed lips signaled her strong disagreement with the new world order. "Are women going to smoke, drink, and spit tobacco, too?" she asked curtly.

Nora clasped a hand across her mouth to keep from laughing. She turned her head so her big smile would not mock the older woman.

Duke, too, must have thought better of pressing the issue any further. He bowed his head and choked back a snicker.

Mercifully, the waitress brought their food and provided a welcomed break to a contentious conversation. Each became more concerned with passing the mustard and catsup than reaching a decision about where Nora and Sarah Jean would be spending Christmas Eve.

The four of them stood on the sidewalk outside of Teddy's. Nora swung a leg over the cycle seat. In a fluid motion, she turned the switch and kicked down the starter. The engine sprang to life with a roar. She gunned it a few times. Mary stepped back to get away from the smoke and noise.

"What are you guys gonna do?" Gladys asked. "Do you want to come over to the house? I think there is still some pie left."

Nora looked at Duke as he settled in behind her. She was sure she read a 'no' in his facial expression. "It's my last night," she said. "Let me take him home, spend a little time, and then I'll come back to the farm."

"More talking?" Gladys asked with a sly smile.

Nora knew what Gladys meant, but just shook her head. She clicked the cycle into first gear and roared off.

"Thanks," he said as he opened the back door of his place. "I was hoping we'd have a chance to be by ourselves for a while."

She poked him in the ribs. "Well, don't get any silly ideas, there's not going to be a repeat of last night."

He raised his eyebrows and gave her a cheesy smile. In the blink of an eye, his expression turned sober. "Just so you know, Christmas is a long six months away."

"Well, I agree with Gladys, the war has changed a lot of things, but I don't think I'm quite as liberated as Wanda the welder. Maybe we can get back to the way things used to be. Maybe Mary Iverson's world is not all that bad."

"I'm sorry, but I can't undo the feelings I have for you." He put his hands on her shoulders. "I need you. I want you...all of you...but I'll take any part...anything you give me."

She put her finger to his lips. "Just give me time. Let me get things worked out with Sarah Jean. I promise, I'll come back in December."

"For how long?"

"I don't know, maybe over Christmas and New Year's."

"Two weeks," he pleaded. "Make it two weeks."

"I'll try."

Duke lit the kerosene lamp and placed it on the table next to the couch. "Can you stay a while?"

"I should be going. What are we going to do about the bike? Do you want me to leave it at the farm?"

"Why don't I drop you off, then you won't have to worry about it."

191

"Are you sure? What about your arm?"

Duke raised the sling. "The arm's fine. I'm sure I can handle it. What time is your bus?"

"Four-thirty. Are you going to come and see me off?"

"I've got to check in at work and I want to run over to Middletown, but yeah, I'll be there," he said, his voice trailing off.

Nora used both hands to lift his chin off his chest. Looking into his eyes, she pressed her lips to his. She watched as he slowly closed his eyes and drew her tight in a warm embrace. Her fingers threaded through his thick hair and she inhaled the musk that was his alone. It was as if time stood still and neither wanted the moment to end.

Duke spoke first. "I'm really going to miss you." He blinked to hold back the water gathering in the corners of his eyes.

Nora wiped away his tears. "I'll miss you, too."

They were both quiet on the ride to the farm. Nora slid off the back of the seat. "Are you coming in?

"Nah, this is yours and Gladys' time. I'll see you tomorrow." He put the bike in gear and slowly accelerated down the drive.

***

Nora took her suitcase from the trunk and placed it on the sidewalk. She gave Mary a hug first and then extended her arms to Gladys. "Thank you for everything."

"We should be thanking you," Gladys said. "If it weren't for you, Dad…"

"I'm happy I was there to help. Really, these few days in Pine Lake were just what I needed. Even with everything that has gone on, I've learned a lot about myself. Hopefully,

192

I can get myself on the straight and narrow and get on with life."

The greyhound tooted its horn as it drove up to the curb. Nora stepped back and looked up and down the street.

Gladys saw the concern on Nora's face. "Was Duke coming to see you off?"

"He said he would." Nora slowly reached for her bag. "Maybe he got held up at work."

The bus door swung open and the driver descended the steps. "Leaving in two minutes. Are you carrying your bag on or do you want me to stow it below?"

"I'll take it on." Nora turned and gave Gladys a warm smile. "Tell Duke I'll write when I get home."

Nora put her bag in the bin above and took a seat by the window. She waved as Gladys and her mom began walking to their car. *Why didn't he come to see me off?* She fumbled in her purse to find a hanky. The driver came on board and pulled the door closed behind him. Sitting in his seat, he shuffled through some papers. "We'll be on our way in a minute; can't let the paperwork slide."

Nora wiped her eyes and was startled when Duke pounded on the window. "Sorry," he yelled, placing his hand flat against the window. She placed her hand against the glass to match his. The engine came alive and the bus began pulling from the curb. Duke ran alongside as far as he could, mouthing the words, "I love you, I love you." Nora whispered the words back to him.

On the Way Home

Nora looked back, her vision of him clouded by the swirling blue exhaust smoke. She continued to wave even though she knew he couldn't see her. She settled back in her seat as the bus circled through town. She studied each building and looked for any familiar faces on the sidewalk. Within minutes, they passed the welcome sign and the town gave way to fields of corn and pastured animals. The trip to Chicago, considering the many stops along the way, would take the better part of eight hours.

It was hard to believe that less than two weeks ago she had accompanied Betty back to Chicago. She searched her mind wondering if there was anything she could have done to prevent her death. It seemed once fate put Sarah Jean on that bus, her life, Sarah's and the lives of the Coopers were destined to collide. Even so, she couldn't see herself doing anything different, except maybe being more mindful of how dangerous Robert Cooper was. No one could have predicted how this had turned out, just as no one knows what Sarah's life would have been like if Nora had left her with the Coopers in the first place. That was the one thing Nora was sure of. She was not going to leave Sarah Jean where Robert could get his hands on her money or her body. Yet sometimes knowing you're right still can't erase the guilt that comes when you've had a part in someone's death.

Nora gazed out as the sun tinted the wispy clouds in red and orange. The rolling hills of southern Wisconsin made it feel like the bus was on a lazy roller coaster track. The up and down and side to side motion was very relaxing and she soon drifted off to sleep.

***

The bus terminal in Chicago was busy. Even at eleven o'clock at night a lot of people seemed to be on the go. Having had a number of recent excursions through the place, Nora needed little time navigating through the crowds. The bus west would depart at six-fifteen. Nora bought an apple, a bottle of soda, and a newspaper just before the gift shop closed at midnight. She found a spot near the departure gate, tucked her trusted case under her legs and settled down for her six-hour wait.

She took a bite of the apple and opened the paper. She skimmed through the front section, which chronicled the aftermath of the war and how the government would try to get America back to a peacetime economy. Halfway through the second section a small article, titled "Hospital Guard Murderer Meets End in Wisconsin" caught her eye. She folded the paper in half and began reading. Sure enough, in black and white, was the whole saga of Robert Cooper. Nora quickly scanned the article looking for her name. The guard was named and so was Duke, for being the one shot protecting 'an unnamed woman.' Quoting a local source, the reporter pretty much gave all the details as if he had read the statement she gave Ben. Nora was happy she was not named in the story. She figured Ben might have protected her as a way to make amends for causing the uproar over her fingerprints being found on the gun. The article also listed Robert Cooper's other run-ins with the police. Along with a charge of murdering both the guard and his wife, it included a charge of child molestation of a twelve-year-old neighborhood girl. Nora crumbled the paper and threw it in a nearby trashcan. "I knew it," she said. "That guy would have preyed on Sarah for sure. He deserves what he got." Nora felt her blood pressure rising. She took a swig of soda.

A Long Bus Ride Home

The eight-hour bus ride to Chicago and the two-and-a-half-day trip to Ely gave Nora plenty of time to sort out her feelings. Her first vow was to conquer her dependence on alcohol. She hadn't had a drink in over two months, but knew the cravings were still there. The lingering feelings of guilt and anger left from the war would certainly add to the difficulty, as would the deaths of Robert and Betty Cooper. The lump in her throat made it difficult to swallow. Her tongue searched for saliva in a dry mouth. She rolled her tongue across her lips and could almost taste the juniper-laced flavor of gin. *Stop it!* Nora sat up and stared out the window. *I can't let myself think that way. I've got way too much going on, too much responsibility. I've got Sarah Jean to think about...and Duke.* A smile erased the frown line on her forehead. The mere thought of each of them brought a warmth in her chest. *I wonder how this is going to work out with Sarah, and what about Duke?*

Nora relaxed and rested her head on the back of the seat. Recalling that night in Indianapolis, watching Sarah and her mother in that final embrace and the young girl's frightened look as she walked up the aisle on the bus, she closed her eyes.

***

Bus schedules go strictly by the clock and stops come at all hours of the day and night. The stop in Ely came in the latter. Nora stepped off the bus a little past one in the morning. The driver barely waited for her to step away from the bus before closing the door and driving off. Main Street was dark and deserted, save for two parked cars. The moon was full, nullifying the puny glow of the lonely street light suspended over the intersection. It swung lazily in the warm breeze. A car drove past, barely slowing down before continuing its way out of town. Nora watched the taillights disappear into the night. She smiled. Just another person passing through this dot on the map. She set her suitcase on the sidewalk and contemplated her next move. She really didn't want to wake up the whole household by calling her folks. They kept a key under the welcome mat, and after spending umpteen hours on the bus, she felt the half-mile walk would feel good. She picked up her bag and started walking.

The lights of one of the parked cars came on and she heard the engine fire up. Looking back over her shoulder, she watched the vehicle make a U-turn and come her way. She stepped back as the car pulled up. Nora breathed a quick sigh of relief when she recognized the sheriff's department logo on the door. Andy Werfel, one of her dad's deputy friends rolled down his window.

"Can I help you, ma'am?" he said.

She leaned. "Hello, Andy, it's me, Nora."

"Well, I'll be," he said. "What a pleasant surprise. Your dad's been wonderin' when you'd be coming home. Hop in, I'll give you a ride."

Nora set her suitcase in the back seat and climbed in the passenger side. "I didn't want to wake the folks. I could have walked."

"Don't be silly. I ain't got nothing better to do. 'Sides, your daddy would have my hide if I let you walk out here by yourself."

Nora looked out the window. "This town never changes, does it?"

"Not much," Andy said. "People come and go, but everything else stays the same. Speaking of people, a guy was looking for you earlier."

"Who, someone from town?"

"I didn't actually see him. Julie at the Dairy Bar Grill was tellin' me about him. I stopped in for a piece of pie at 'bout eight; she said it was a guy on a motorcycle." Andy pulled up in front of the Jensen house.

"What color was the cycle?"

"Julie didn't say." Andy jumped out of the car and fetched her case. "Are you gonna be able to git in the house, or do you want me to hit the siren a few times?"

"Don't you dare," Nora scolded. There's a key under the mat."

"Your mom and dad have had a wonderful time with that Sarah. She's made quite an impression on people around here."

Nora wanted to hear more about Sarah, but a light came on in the kitchen. "There's Mom, she hears everything. I better get in there. Thanks for the ride."

"No problem," Andy said. "Welcome home."

A Surprise for Nora

Harriet opened the back door. Recognizing her daughter, she could barely contain her excitement. "I'm so glad...when did you...why didn't you call?" Harriet put her arms around her daughter.

Nora held for a few extra moments. "Just got off the bus. Andy Werfel gave me a ride."

Her mom grabbed the suitcase from Nora's hand as her dad entered the room. "Look," she said. "Nora's home."

John gave his daughter a hug. "We were getting a little worried about you."

"I'm fine. I probably should have called. A lot was going on. How's Sarah? I've missed her."

Harriet shushed her daughter. "She's doing great. Let's not wake her or none of us will get any sleep tonight. She's sort of taken over your room. I can get my sewing crap out of the spare room and move her in there tomorrow."

"Don't worry about it," Nora said. "Just give me a pillow and a blanket. I'll sack out on the couch."

"I'll get that for you right now." Harriet scurried off.

Nora turned to her dad. "Has anyone come to the house asking for me? Someone on a royal blue motorcycle?"

"Not that I know of. Are you expecting someone?"

"It could be Duke. A fellow I met in Pine Lake. We had sort of a mix-up saying good bye. I have a feeling he jumped on his bike and came out here."

"On a motorcycle?" John looked down his nose at her.

"It's not like that; he's a good clean guy," Nora said. "He restored an old army motorcycle."

"Okay, then, all I could picture was a guy with long hair and tattoos riding a Harley."

"You'll like him; he's real sweet."

"So you think?"

Harriet thrust the bedding in Nora's arms. "C'mon, let's get back to bed. We can hash all this stuff out in the morning." She pushed John out of the room.

Nora tossed the blanket over the sofa and dropped the pillow at one end. She stripped to her panties and bra, settled down onto the sofa and took a deep breath. The smell was familiar, one she grew up with; it smelled like home. She pulled the blanket over her, nestled her head against the pillow, and smiled. *That crazy Duke. Why in the world would he come all the way out here?*

***

Nora came out of a deep sleep and immediately sensed someone was watching her. She opened one eye just enough to see a cherub face looking straight at her. Sarah Jean pounced on her. "I'm so glad you're home. I missed you terribly," she squealed.

Nora brought her arms out from under the covers and squeezed the excited girl. "I missed you, too."

"Why didn't you let us know you were coming?" Sarah stammered. "I was worried about you."

"What? Were you worried that I wouldn't come back?"

201

From the look on Sarah's face, Nora realized that's exactly what she meant. She immediately hugged her again, pulling her close. "Don't you ever worry about that." Then holding Sarah at arm's length, "We're a team, you and I, we're sisters and nothing or no one will ever come between us."

Harriet entered. "Better get some clothes on, there's a fellow pulling up to the house on a motorcycle."

Nora gave Sarah one more squeeze. "Occupy him for a few minutes, Mom." Nora took hold of a few strands of hair. "I can't let him see me like this." She grabbed her clothes and high-tailed it off to the bathroom. After almost four days on a bus, even "presentable" was going to take more than a few minutes. She needed to start with a shower and work her way forward from there. She finally finished up with a splash of Mom's perfume behind each ear.

Nora glanced at the hall mirror for one final look before entering the kitchen. "Ooh!" Nora stumbled backward. "Oh my God, Antonio...how did...I thought you were..." Nora used the back of a chair to steady herself.

Harriet stood. "Antonio was telling me all about how you two met in Sicily."

"All," Nora said feebly.

The man stood. "I haven't been able to get you out of my mind," he said in a thick Italian accent.

"I thought...we all thought you were...shot...for desertion."

"My family paid a large..." Antonio searched for the word... "corrompere. One hundred twenty thousand Lira. That's a thousand American dollars."

"A bribe?" Nora asked.

"The Italian army was very corrupt. In the middle of the night, I was put on a ship going to Canada. And now that the war is over, I can go back to Sicily. I remembered you talking about Ely, Nevada, so I came to see if I could find you."

"I don't know what to say." Nora sank down into the chair.

John walked into the kitchen buttoning the cuff on his uniform. "Is this the young man you were waiting for?"

"Not exactly," Nora said, barely audible.

John straightened his collar. "Well, are you going to introduce me?"

Nora quickly rose. "Daddy, this is Antonio Giuseppe Garibaldi. We met in Sicily."

"His family has vineyards. They grow grapes and make their own wine," Harriet said, handing John a cup of coffee. "They've been doing that for over a hundred years."

"So, what brings you to America?" John asked, taking a sip of coffee.

"He's been in Canada," Nora said. "He had to leave Sicily to escape Mussolini. He's planning on going back to his home."

"And I want Nora to come with me," Antonio added.

John spit the coffee back into his cup. Father, mother, and daughter all said a collective, "What?"

"We can be married. I will take very good care of her," Antonio said.

Nora grabbed him under the arm and led him out the back door. Turning to her folks, she blurted, "Loverboy and I need to have a private talk."

Sarah joined John and Harriet by the window. "We can't let her go," Sarah said.

John looked at Harriet. "Did you know about any of this? I thought she was expecting some guy on a blue motorcycle...from Pine Lake. Who the hell is this guy?"

Harriet let go of the curtain. "I don't think she was expecting this fellow."

***

"Are you nuts?" Nora screamed. "You can't just waltz in here and think I will drop everything and go to Sicily with you. I hardly know you. We had one long weekend together. That's all."

"But we..." he interrupted.

Nora scratched her forehead and lowered her voice. "I know...things got carried away. But that doesn't change anything. We barely said ten words to each other the whole time." Nora watched Antonio's shoulders sag. "I'm sorry you made the trip all the way down here, but my life is here. My family is here. I have responsibilities. There is no way I'm going to Sicily with you."

***

"I've got to get to work," John said. "But you tell that girl there will be no decision on anything or anyone going anywhere until I get home."

Harriet pushed John. "I'm sure Nora can take care of the situation. Go out the front door; you don't want to interrupt them." Harriet pulled Sarah away from the window. "And you, young lady, I believe your room could use a good cleaning." Harriet patted the girl on the butt and sent her out of the kitchen. Although she tried, Harriet couldn't tear herself away from watching the goings-on. She did, however, stand to the side so the couple was not aware they were being watched. "Oh, oh," she said, moving forward and pushing back the curtain. "Dear God, what's going to happen now?"

Double Trouble

Sarah squeezed in next to Harriet to get a look out the window. "Are they still arguing?"

"Yeah, and it's about to get more interesting," Harriet said. "Look up the street. Here comes a guy on a blue motorcycle."

Nora had stopped yelling and returned to speaking in normal tones, trying to make her Italian suitor understand they had no future. "What happened in Sicily," she said, looking him straight in the face, "were two people trying to survive another day in a world torn apart by war and death. I'm sorry if my actions back then misled you in any way." She was unaware of the approaching rider on the royal blue motorcycle when she took Antonio's hand. "There is no way I can go with you to Sicily. Life has moved on, I have a teenager I am responsible for and a family I'm very close to. I couldn't leave either one of them."

Antonio responded by taking her into his arms. "You're all I thought about for the past two years. Won't you give me a chance? I could make you very happy."

One would call this the most inopportune time — for all parties involved — for the man on the blue motorcycle to ride up. A photo of the shocked look on Nora's face would have been priceless.

Nora tried to break free of Antonio's embrace. "Duke! What are you doing here?"

"Interrupting a tender moment, I suspect," Duke said, sitting back on the seat and taking off his gloves. Throwing a leg over the gas tank and walking toward the couple, "I don't want to cause an ugly scene," he said, staring down the dark-haired man. "But would you mind taking your hands off my girl."

"I know what this looks like," Nora stammered. "But let me explain."

"Nothing to explain." Duke extended his hand to the man. "Hello, I'm Duke."

"Antonio." The man shook Duke's hand.

"Antonio is from Canada," Nora said. "We met in Sicily."

"A world traveler, no doubt." Duke made no effort to conceal his sarcasm.

"His home is in Sicily," Nora said. "He fled to Canada during the war."

"Fled?"

"They were going to shoot me for desertion," Antonio said. "The Allies were advancing fast. Our army was in disarray, my whole battalion surrendered not more than 30 kilometers from the village where I lived. I hid and when everyone was gone, I walked home. A Mussolini sympathizer turned me in."

"I thought he was dead. We had met the week before and when I returned the following week, I found out he had been arrested."

Antonio looked at Nora. "It was a beautiful three days."

"It was a chance meeting." Nora certainly didn't want any of the intimate details to come out at this time. "My bicycle threw the chain. Antonio was kind enough to fix it."

"How long have you been here?" Duke asked.

"He showed up a little bit before you." Nora felt the tension as the two men sized up one another.

"I came here to find her," Antonio said. "I want her to come with me to Sicily to get married."

"Hold your horses; no one's getting married," Nora blurted. "Let's all calm down and take a deep breath."

As if on cue, Harriet walked up. "Why don't you all come in the house and have a cup of coffee. I'm sure you have a lot to talk about. And we don't want to have a spectacle out here on the grass for the whole neighborhood to see."

Duke was quick to step forward. "Very perceptive of you," he said, taking Harriet by the arm and walking toward the house. "Are you Nora's sister?"

"No, I'm her mot..." Harriet realized by Duke's smile that he was complimenting her. She pushed him away. "You're a rascal, aren't you?"

As they gathered around the table, the silence was deafening. Harriet worked as fast as she could to fetch and fill a cup of the steaming liquid for each of them. Sarah walked behind with cream and sugar. The men eyed each other. Everyone waited for someone to speak.

"Antonio's family has vineyards," Harriet offered. "They make their own wine."

"It is the best in all of Italy," Antonio added. "The Garibaldi wines are famous for more than one hundred years."

"I'm a beer man," Duke said, taking a drink of coffee. "That's a pretty fancy bike you've got out there."

"It is a 500cc Benelli, made in Italy. My family sent it to me. I do not recognize the one you are riding."

"GI Surplus, government issue. Custom made. One of a kind."

Nora had enough. "Listen, let's stop playing cat and mouse. Duke, why don't you and Sarah go outside and get acquainted. Mom, could you give Antonio and me a little privacy?"

Harriet jumped up from her chair. "Absolutely. I've got a ton of wash to take care of."

Nora waited for the room to clear before going over all the reasons why there was no way she would be accompanying him back to Sicily. She repeated her apology if their weekend tryst had misled him in any way. It took a while, but she was finally able to convince him there was no maybe, if only, or perhaps to her decision.

Sarah was sitting on Duke's bike pretending to be riding when Nora and Antonio emerged from the house. Duke watched intently as she walked the foreigner to his cycle. He and Sarah leaned to hear what was being said.

"You know, I will never forget you," Antonio said, his voice cracking with emotion. "If you ever come to Sicily, please look for me." He turned the switch and kicked the starter. "It was nice to meet you," he yelled to Duke. "Maybe we'll meet again sometime." Duke waved and smiled. Antonio pushed himself backward, put the cycle in gear, and sped off.

"Duke's going to teach me how to ride as soon as I get my license," Sarah said as Nora approached.

"Young ladies do not drive motorcycles," Nora said, giving Duke a dirty look.

"He said you drove it when you were in Wisconsin."

Nora rolled her eyes and shook her head. "Mr. Brady suffers from a loose tongue. Besides I only did it because he...his arm...oh never mind, just get your butt off of that bike."

"Is he coming back?" Duke steadied the cycle while Sarah dismounted.

"I hope not."

"Seemed like a really nice fellow."

"Meaning?"

"Vineyards, family wine business, a pretty good catch for some lucky girl."

"Whose side are you on?"

"Yours. Don't forget you could get your hands on that fancy 500cc Bella Guzzy.

"Benelli," Nora corrected. "And now will you stop it and tell me why you're here?"

"You obviously made quite an impression...over one long weekend? That must have been a pretty special three days."

Whether he knew it or not, Duke was pressing the wrong button. "That was two years ago, in the middle of a war," Nora huffed. "Listen, I don't have to explain a thing to you. If you don't like it, lump it." She turned on her heels. "C'mon, Sarah we're going inside."

Duke picked up his gloves. "I guess you have a choice between a deserter and a conscientious objector," he shouted.

Without stopping, Nora turned her head and said, "You both can go to hell."

Harriet met the girls at the door. "What happened? What did I miss?"

"Antonio's gone and Duke will be leaving shortly," Nora said as she circled the table.

Sarah said nothing. She simply raised her eyebrows.

"Oh dear, what did you say to them?" Harriet asked.

Nora huffed. "I don't want to talk about it, Mom. I'm going to my room. I need time to think."

Harriet hugged Sarah as Nora brushed past.

Nora shut the door and sank onto the bed. Her hands trembled and her only thought was how much she needed a drink. Her mouth was dry. She rubbed her temples. Looking around the room she caught sight of a large poster. *Where did that come from?* Cutout paper hearts in red and blue encircled the words "I Love My New Home" written in large, flowing, cursive lettering. Continuing to survey her surroundings, Nora saw other pieces of unfamiliar memorabilia adorning the walls. Tears gathered in the corners of her eyes. *This isn't my room anymore. It's Sarah Jean's.*

Nora stood and wiped the last little bit of water from her eyes. Her back stiffened. *This is no time to give in or give up. I'm stronger than that.* She opened the door and was surprised to find Sarah standing there. She hugged the girl. "Forgive me," Nora said. "It's like I said, we're sisters and nothing and no one is ever going to come between us."

Harriet came wiping her hands in her apron. "That Duke came to the door. Said he wanted to apologize. I told him it would be best to come back later."

"That's good," Nora said, giving her mom a hug. "I'm going to need some time to figure things out."

"Will you talk to him if he comes back?" her mom asked.

"I have to. I'm not sure why he's even here. It probably would have been better if he had missed the whole thing with Antonio. Goodness sakes, they talk about women being jealous."

"Sarah, why don't you go to the garden and pick us some strawberries for supper?" Harriet suggested.

"You're going to talk about what happened in Sicily, aren't you?" Sarah protested.

"Don't be silly," Harriet began. "We…"

"It's okay, Mom," Nora said. "I think Sarah is mature enough to handle the situation." Nora sat at the table. "Is there any of that coffee left?"

Harriet set the pot in front of Nora and left the room. Sarah moved her chair close.

Nora held out her pinky finger to the young girl. "Sister, I want you to swear you will keep my secret." Sarah locked her pinky to Nora's and nodded solemnly. Nora didn't hold back. She related how during the time she met Antonio, she had witnessed some of the worst wounds she had ever encountered. Limbs completely blown away, young men with their insides full of shrapnel, their bodies shot full of holes. Not only the severity of wounds, but also the sky-rocketing number of wounded the unit had to care for. She spoke of how pleased she was for each young man they were able to save, but how deep her feelings of despair were, for each soldier who succumbed to his wounds. Sometimes reality was just too hard to deal with. Meeting Antonio caught her during one of those times when she was looking to escape the brutality of war. Yes, they were three special days and she admitted they both allowed their emotions to overrule reason. Even now, Nora couldn't be sure there was any love involved. It was more like being reduced to a basic need for human touch.

Nora took Sarah's hand. "I'm not proud of what happened back then, but I hope you understand the circumstances of what I was going through."

Sarah nodded. "All those wounded men, it must have been awful."

"I hope you never have to go through anything like that yourself. Now remember, all of that is our secret; no one ever has to know anything about it."

"Heavens no," Harriet said, catching the tail-end of the conversation. "Especially not your father; I'm not sure he would understand." She went to the window. "In case anyone cares, that Duke fellow is sitting under the tree."

Nora joined her mom at the window and watched Duke toss pebbles against the tire of his cycle. "I guess I'd better go out there. I'll have to face him sooner or later."

Sarah tugged Nora's arm. "What are you going to say to him? I really like him."

"I'm not sure; it depends." Nora walked to the door.

A Future in Doubt

Duke sprang to his feet when Nora came out of the house. He took a stutter-step forward before standing his ground.

Nora stopped, leaving plenty of space between them. "What are you doing here? I told you when I left Pine Lake, I have responsibilities, I have Sarah, and I've got to get my life in order."

"I'm sorry, but I had to…"

"And another thing, what did or didn't happen with Antonio is none of your business."

"You're right. I'm sorry, I wasn't very nice."

"Why did you come? And why were you late when I got on the bus?"

Duke reached in his pocket. "I went to Middletown to get you this." He opened his hand to show her a small blue velour box. "When I got back, the bus was already leaving, I didn't know what to do."

"So, you jumped on the bike and road 1500 miles to…?" Nora choked on her words.

He'd opened the box. "I had to…Will you…?"

Nora squeezed his hand closed. "Don't…"

"But I want…"

"No, please, don't say it. I can't…I…There's Sarah; I'm not ready…"

Duke squeezed the box closed in his hand, looked at the ground, and shook his head. "I guess the joke's on me?"

"I don't mean to hurt you. But you have to understand, my life is hanging by a thread. I can't make a long-term decision when I'm fighting every minute just to keep myself sober. That's right, I can't go two minutes without wanting a drink. You have to give me time to get my head screwed on straight."

"I'm sorry, I didn't know..."

"No, I'm the one who should be saying that. I should have been up front with you." Nora held out a trembling hand. "Look at this. I've got the shakes so bad, I'm ready to fall apart."

Duke took hold of her hand. "Is there anything I can...?"

"No, I've got to lick this on my own. I just need time. Can't we leave things like we said...for Christmas time?"

"Sure," Duke said, backing away. "But why won't you let me help you? I could..."

"The help I need is for you to trust me. To give me time to get my life in order. Unless I can lick this addiction, I won't be any good to anyone."

Duke put on his gloves, threw a leg over the bike, and settled in the seat. "If that's what you want. I guess you don't know how much I love you?"

Nora straddled the front wheel and grabbed the handlebars. "I'm sorry, I didn't mean to upset you. I know you love me, but I need...time."

Duke turned the switch and kick over the engine. He looked at Nora as if waiting for her to move. When she released her grip on the handlebar, he pushed the cycle backward, bringing the wheel out from between her legs. Swinging the bike around, he clicked it into gear. "I'll see you around."

Nora waved the dust away from her face as he sped up the street.

Harriet and Sarah were waiting by the door when Nora came in. Neither wanted to be the first to speak. Nora befuddled them by walking to the sink. Gripping the porcelain, she gazed out the window. "Well, that went badly," she said.

Sarah was about to step forward. Harriet held her back. "It was probably just a little spat. He'll be back."

"No, I hurt him pretty good," Nora said. "That might be the last we see of Mr. Duke Brady."

"That's silly," Harriet scoffed. "Why would he come all the way from Wisconsin?"

Nora turned to face her mom. "He had a ring, he wanted to propose."

"He asked you to marry him?" Sarah blurted. "What did you tell him?"

The long pause felt awkward for everyone.

Harriet released some nervous energy by straightening the doily under the fruit bowl on the table. "I guess his leaving is answer enough."

"Why did you say no?" Sarah asked. "Don't you love him?"

"I don't know him that well. We've only known each other for a short time. Besides, I've got you to think about. I've got to help raise my baby sister." Nora patted Sarah on the head.

Sarah pushed her hand away. "I'm not a baby, I'm practically sixteen." Then in a playful way, she poked Nora

216

in the ribs. "If he'd be willing to wait a couple of years, I'll marry him."

The chase was on. Sarah took off for the living room with Nora in hot pursuit. "So, that's the kind of sister you're going to be," Nora said. "A boyfriend stealer."

Sarah danced behind the couch. "You said you didn't want him."

"I said no such thing, you little vixen. I just told him it wasn't the right time."

Sarah stopped the ruse and came to Nora's side. "You mean you still might marry him?"

"We will have to wait and see."

"Good gravy," Harriet said, straightening the rug that had gotten strewn about in the fracas. "Who would have thought when we got up this morning that we would have a day like today? We had one guy flashing a diamond ring and another wanting to haul you off to Italy, Sicily, or some faraway place. I'm just happy your father wasn't here to witness it all."

Nora put an arm around her mom's shoulders. "I hope this hasn't upset you too much."

"It's no big deal to me," Harriet said. "You're the one who blew off two proposals in one day. Maybe you should be hoping you'll get another one someday."

Sarah hugged them both. "What's a vixen?"

"Someone who will use her beauty and charm to get her way," Nora said, tickling Sarah's ribs. "And you've got a wagon load of both."

Sarah returned the tickle. 'Maybe you need to be a vixen when it comes to Duke."

Life's Little Twist

Nora felt uneasy. Sarah was probably right. It's one thing to want time to get your life in order, but even if she wasn't ready to accept the ring right now, she could have left the option open if she decided to change her mind. A burnt bridge is hard to cross. He proved his affection for her by buying the ring and riding all the way from Wisconsin to give it to her. *Another of my not-so-smart moves,* Nora shrugged. *Oh well, what's done is done.*

She did wonder if he made it back to Pine Lake. She wrote a thank-you note to Gladys that turned into a three-page chronicle of events involving Duke, Antonio, and the contents of the blue velour box. At the bottom of the letter, she added a postscript, asking if she had seen Duke lately.

Gladys probably saw through Nora's veiled inquiry, but nonetheless, kept her friend updated on his sightings. Since her dad's heart attack, Gladys had spent most of her weekends in Pine Lake and had plenty of opportunity to report on Duke's whereabouts. She made sure she included the ones where Duke was in the company of one of the local jezebels.

Nora was sure it had to be one of the "dancers" who waited for him at the band shell. Although she looked forward to receiving Gladys' letters, they only made her question her decision of not accepting Duke's proposal. She thought about writing to him, even calling, but wasn't sure what she would say. And then there was the possibility he no longer had an interest in talking to her.

***

Those first three to four weeks at home were hard. Multiple times each day her stomach ached for alcohol and her mind tried to seduce her into having a drink. It took all the strength and willpower she could muster to resist. As hard as it was, she felt things were getting a little better each day. At first, she attributed the nauseous feeling she kept waking up with to be part of the withdrawal process. It wasn't until she realized she had missed her period that her fears were confirmed. *Dear God, what next?*

Nora sat on the edge of the bed and wondered how she could be both elated and depressed over the thought of having a baby. She wanted to shout about it from the rooftops but knew her circumstance was not something to broadcast. Having a baby out of wedlock would surely bring shame to her and the baby. Nora didn't give a damn about what people would think of her; it was the child she wanted to protect. That would have been so easy if she had accepted Duke's proposal. A quick wedding and the ruse of a premature birth would satisfy a lot of inquiring minds and wagging tongues.

Nora stepped in front of the mirror. She lifted her pajama top and rubbed her hand across her stomach. She smiled at not seeing any sign of her hidden treasure. Her smile soon faded and tears collected in the corner of her eyes. This was not something she was going to be able to fix on her own. She had gone days without having so much as a thought of wanting a drink, but at this moment, that's all she was thinking about. *That's nuts, what would that solve?* "No more cop-outs," she said, looking at herself in the mirror and brushing the tears aside. "I'm having this baby with or without a daddy. Damn what's right and proper, damn gossiping women, and damn Duke Brady if he backs away."

Harriet was at the table peeling carrots when Nora walked into the kitchen. "Morning," she said, pouring herself a cup of coffee.

Harriet set down the peeler and started to get up. "Can I fix you some toast or something?"

"No, Mom, just sit. I've got something to tell you." Nora set her cup on the table. "Where's Sarah?"

"I gave her five dollars. She and her friend Dee rode their bikes into town to shop for school supplies. She's sort of taken over your old bicycle. What is it you wanted to tell me?"

"I don't want to alarm you…"

"Oh dear," Harriet said. "Alarm me?"

"I think I'm pregnant."

"Pregnant!" The word exploded into the room before Harriet could cover her mouth with her hand. "How, who?"

"Duke."

Harriet sat back in her chair. She searched the room as if the answers to all her questions were written on the walls. "How could…?"

"It was one night. Poor judgment on my part."

"How far along are you?"

"A month, maybe two; you know, I've never been regular."

"What are you going to do? Call Duke?"

220

"This isn't the kind of news to spring on him over the phone. Besides, after the way he left here, I'm not sure what his reaction is going to be."

"If he's the father, he has a right to know."

There is no "if," Mother. It was one night. I haven't slept with anyone else...except for Antonio and that was over two years ago."

"We had these talks when you were in high school; don't you remember?"

"Mom, I remember, but we're beyond that now. I have to go back to Pine Lake and deal with Duke face to face."

"Do you think there will be a problem? He will marry you, won't he?"

"I don't know. Will it be all right if Sarah stays here with you?"

"Of course," Harriet said, getting up from the table. "She's already enrolled in school. There is no need to include a fifteen-year-old in all of this." Then wiping her eyes with her apron, "I don't know what I'm going to tell your father."

Nora got up and put her arm around her mom. "I know I've disappointed you. I'm sorry. I'll tell Daddy at lunchtime, but right now I have to pack if I'm going to catch the afternoon bus."

"No," Harriet said. "We'll tell your father you're going back to work things out with Duke, nothing more. And that's enough for Sarah, too. I'll find the right time, if there ever is one, to fill in the details." Harriet tossed the peeler in the sink and threw the carrots in the wastebasket. "Nobody likes cooked carrots anyway."

***

Nora sat on the bench outside of the drugstore and slid her old brown suitcase between her legs. She wondered if her dad bought the yarn her mother had told him and Sarah. She hated the deception and worse, that either of them would be disappointed in her. She would deal with that at a later time. Right now, her unborn child was the one needing help, a chance for legitimacy. How would she break the news to him? She mouthed a few opening sentences. "Guess what? You're going to be a daddy." She nixed that one. too flippant. Her second and third tries were no better. "How do you feel about children? We're having one." Or "I'm pregnant. What are we going to do about it?" As the bus rolled up, she finally gave up. "I just hope he won't be too upset." She boarded, stowed her case, and settled back into her seat. She rubbed her hand across her stomach and smiled. "I just want a healthy child."

A Return to Pine Lake

No one looks forward to a two-and-a-half-day bus ride, and Nora had reason to dislike this one even more. A single thought, one that haunted her the whole way, was how Duke would take the news she was about to bring him. He freely spoke of his love for her, but would having a baby change all that? She couldn't be sure. Doing something to halt the pregnancy never entered her mind. If Duke was not going to man up, she would stay in Chicago, have the baby, and raise it herself. For a few fleeting moments, she even flirted with the idea of contacting Antonio. After all, Europeans were much more understanding of this sort of thing, especially since the war. Who knew how many French and Italian girls were carrying babies fathered by departed GIs?

Arriving in Chicago, she still had no concrete plan of what to do. It would all depend on Duke.

***

Gladys was surprised when Nora showed up at her Chicago General office door and for a moment was at a loss for words.

Surprised?" Nora asked.

"Shocked." Gladys took the suitcase from Nora's hand.

"What's this about? Why didn't you let me know you were coming? What's wrong?"

"That's what I like about you." Nora mimicked her friend. "Let's get straight to the point. Mind?" she said, pointing to a nearby chair.

Gladys followed close behind. "Are you okay? Are you in some kind of trouble?"

"I guess you could call it trouble. I'm going to have a baby."

"What!" Gladys took a step back. "That's…great…a baby? That's wonderful. Duke?"

Nora nodded. "He doesn't know yet."

"Are you sure? Have you been checked?"

Nora hesitated. "I missed my period, but I've never had a regular cycle. Oh God, do you suppose I'm not?"

"Let's have one of our doctors' take a look…take a few tests. Sit tight; I'll see who I can scare up."

The doctor was a grandfatherly man with a fine sense of humor. "In my preliminary assessment of your situation, I would say you can tell your husband it's okay to start buying the cigars." He laughed out loud and then added, "I think you would have definitely killed the rabbit."

Nora bit her lip and forced a smile.

"Just to be on the safe side, though, let's take some blood and urine and I'll have it sent over to the lab."

Nora dressed and returned to Gladys' office, plopping in the chair. "It's not a false alarm. I'm a woman with child. Correction, an unwed woman with child."

"Maybe you should have accepted Duke's proposal."

"I won't hold this over his head," Nora said, slapping her hand on the desk, "but, if he so much as looks cross-eyed at me, I'll leave and have this baby on my own."

"Before you get yourself all worked up, my suggestion would be to wait and see what Duke has to say. You might be surprised."

Nora slumped in the chair. "Right." Her answer lacked conviction.

"To tell you the truth I hadn't planned on going to Pine Lake this weekend, but knowing you, you'd probably walk there if I didn't take you. Give me a couple of hours to get things squared away here and we'll drive up together. If we leave by four, we can be there by ten. I'll call Mom and let her know we're coming."

***

Main Street was deserted when the girls rolled into Pine Lake. Gladys watched Nora study the clock on the courthouse lawn. "You're not going to confront him tonight, are you?"

"I guess not." Nora held her hands in a ball to keep them from shaking. "I'm too tired and too emotional right now." Her dry throat was always the precursor to the feeling of wanting a drink. "Let's get a good night's sleep and see what happens in the morning."

"Good idea." Gladys drove in the direction of the farm.

Gladys' folks had left the light on in the kitchen and an apple pie on the table. The note listed all the things to eat in the refrigerator. "Are you hungry? How about a ham sandwich?" Gladys said, peering in the refrigerator.

"I'll just have a piece of this apple pie," Nora said. "And a glass of milk to wash it down."

Gladys poured the milk and also set a ham sandwich in front of her friend. "Here, eat this; remember you're eating for two now."

Nora returned a dirty look.

Gladys opened a beer and sat down to her sandwich. "So, what's you plan for tomorrow?"

"I'd like to catch Duke early, before he takes off for work or wherever," Nora said. "Can I use your car?"

"Sure. Do you have a license?"

Nora remembered her wise-crack from when she rode Duke's motorcycle. "From Nevada; Dad got it for me."

"I'd sure like to be a fly on the wall when you tell him," Gladys said. "I guess that's none of my business...but still...if you need some moral support?"

"I'll be all right. I think it's best if I go alone."

Gladys reached into her purse. "I'll leave the keys here on the counter." Then, picking up the dishes and putting them in the sink, she said, "I'm sure Mom has you set up in the first bedroom at the top of the stairs."

"You didn't tell your mom about...you know...?"

"No, but in this town, it ain't going to take long for the word to get out. Prepare yourself."

Nora nodded her head in agreement. She picked up her suitcase and headed for the stairs. "I guess we'll ALL know more by tomorrow."

Duke Gets the News

Nora felt like she hadn't slept a wink. She rolled over and peeked at the clock on the nightstand. Ten after five. The sun was just coming up. Staring at the ceiling, she immediately began questioning how she should proceed. Would it be better to catch Duke this morning or meet him later in the day, maybe this evening, like after supper? Swinging her legs from under the covers, she rubbed the sleep from her eyes. *Stop the waffling, already. Just get dressed and get over there.*

Nora closed her door quietly and tiptoed down the stairs, hoping not to disturb anyone. She was about to open the front door when Mary came out of the kitchen. "Good morning," she said brightly. "My goodness, you're up early."

Nora did her best to smile.

"I was just getting ready to make a spinach soufflé. Are you hungry?"

"I was...I thought I'd...I was hoping to catch Duke before he went to work. I have some important news to tell him."

"Important news?" Mary stepped forward. "What news is that?"

It's...I'm...I wanted to let him know...I will definitely be coming for Christmas." Nora caught her breath and searched Mary's face for a reaction.

"Will you be staying with us? I really don't think it would be wise to stay at his place. You know how people in this town love to talk."

"I certainly know that," Nora said under her breath.

"Why don't you come in the kitchen and have something to eat. That news can wait. Besides, you don't want to be prowling around his place at this hour of the morning. You might run into someone unexpectedly."

Nora followed Mary into the kitchen and caught the drift of what Mary was saying. "Has he been...?"

"I'm not one to spread gossip about anybody, but I've heard he's been keeping company with that waitress at the coffee shop, Natalie something." Mary poured a cup of coffee and set it on the table. "Here, I'll put down a piece of toast for you. Do you like spinach soufflé?"

Nora pulled out a chair and sat. "Yeah, I like spinach soufflé." She stirred the coffee and peered at the swirls in the dark brown liquid. *What next? He's already got a girlfriend? It must be that ditzy blond who tried to corral him at the Fourth of July dance. Maybe I should just get out of here, find a place in Chicago, and have this baby on my own.* She let out a huge sigh.

Mary spun around. "Did you say something, dear?" She handed Nora the toast on a dish.

"Nah, I just choked a little on the coffee."

"Is it too strong? Harry likes it that way; I usually water it down."

"It's fine, I took too big of a swallow."

Nora was happy to see a pajama-clad Gladys enter the room. "If anyone cares, my room is right above the kitchen and it's pretty hard to get any sleep with you two magpies yakking it up down here."

"Oh hush," Mary said. Then turning to Nora, "She's always grumpy when she gets up on the wrong side of the bed." She handed Gladys a cup of coffee. "Here, this should put you in a better mood."

Gladys took the cup, waited for her mother to turn away, and gave Nora a questioning glance. "What's up?" she mouthed without sound.

Nora put her finger to her lips and shook her head. "Your mom is making us a spinach soufflé."

Gladys smiled. "Nice." Her raised eyebrows seemed to be begging for more information.

Without turning away from the counter, Mary said, "Nora has some big news to tell that Duke Brady."

Gladys choked on her coffee.

Nora kept shaking her head, her eyes pleading for Gladys not to say anything more.

Mary continued her story. "Nora is going to come back to Pine Lake at Christmastime. I think she should stay here with us, don't you? No sense giving our local busybodies something to talk about."

"Oh yeah, we wouldn't want to give them anything to talk about," Gladys said. Then turning to Nora, "Come out on the porch, you have to see this beautiful sunrise." Nora followed quickly and was ready for Gladys' first question. "The big news is you're coming at Christmas?"

"She caught me by surprise. I didn't know what to say." Nora let out a burst of air. "That's all I could think of."

"That's okay, as soon as she gets that soufflé in the oven, she'll be off to get dressed. You can take off then, I'll cover for you."

"You aren't going to tell her, are you?"

"Don't worry, I'll think of something."

"Let's hope you can come up with something better than I did." Nora led the way back inside.

Mary was going up the stairs when the girls came back into the house. "Will you keep an eye on that soufflé? I'm going to wake your father and get myself dressed."

"I'll watch it, Mom," Gladys said, as she pushed Nora to the kitchen. Plucking her car keys off the counter, she tossed them to Nora. "Here you go, now get over there and get this over with." Nora blew Gladys a kiss.

Pine Lake had not yet come alive; the streets were empty. Nora figured the few men she saw going into the coffee shop were fisherman, filling up before a big day on the lake. Everything looked quiet as she approached Duke's place. Getting out of the car, she noticed his motorcycle parked by the back door. *I guess he's still here.*

Coming around to the back of the house, she looked in the window. "Oh!" she jumped back. Staring out at her was Duke, bare chested and a face full of shaving cream. He beat her to the back door and frantically toweled the cream off his face.

"Nora! What are you doing here? I can't believe it." He ran his fingers through his ruffled hair and straightened his pajama bottoms. "Come in. Oh my God, it's so good to see you." Duke led the way. "Be careful of the cupboards, the varnish may still be a little tacky."

Nora stepped gingerly around each piece of cabinetry and couldn't help but admire the beautiful wood grain and fancy pin striping. "You've been busy."

Duke picked up some lumber and tossed it aside, clearing a path for Nora to walk. "I was up until two this morning putting on the last coat. I was going to set them in place when I got done working today." Moving into the living room he used the towel to swat dust off the couch. "Sorry, everything's a little dusty." He stood to the side. "What brings you...?"

Nora walked to the front window.

"Is everything all right?" He waited. Then gently put his hand around her forearm and turned her.

Nora quickly wiped the tears off her cheeks.

"What is it? What's wrong?"

Nora fell into his arms, rested her head on his chest and sobbed.

His arms tightened around her and she felt safe in his embrace. "I'm sorry," she whispered.

Duke put his hand under her chin and raised it. "For what?" He looked deep into her tear-filled eyes.

Nora saw the concern on his face and turned away. "You're going to hate me."

"Hate you? I could never..."

"I'm pregnant," she said, breaking free. She stepped back and searched his face for any clue to what he was thinking. The long moment of silence seemed like an eternity. Overcome with panic, she bolted for the back door.

"Wait...wait...Nora, stop!" He caught up to her in the back yard. "I'm sorry...no, I'm not sorry...I think it's wonderful."

She wasn't smiling and tried to pull away.

"No, wait, I know this has to be very upsetting to you. How do you feel about it?"

Nora stopped. "Do you really think it's wonderful?"

Duke took her into his arms. There was no hiding his excitement. "I think it's beyond wonderful...it's..." His demeanor changed and his tone became serious. "What are we going to do about it?"

"I guess that depends on you," she said. "What do you think we should do?"

"Get married!" He hugged her and raised her in the air. "That's what I think we should do." He danced around holding her off the ground.

Nora was the first to see the neighbor lady watching from across the yard. She whispered to Duke. "Put me down, we've got an audience."

Duke let Nora down slowly, waved at the woman and gave her a broad smile. "A beautiful day, don't you think?" he shouted, as Nora made straight for the house.

Once inside, he took her in his arms and kissed her, first on her lips, then on each cheek, and finally on her neck. Coming back around, he pressed his lips hard onto hers. Nora felt his chest heave, his heart beating in unison with hers. He drew back. "You do want to get married, don't you?"

"Yes," she said softly.

Duke straightened. His smile was gone, and a serious look took its place. "Holy crap! The ring." Duke pounded his fist on one of the cupboards.

"What about it?"

"I threw it in the lake."

"You what...?"

"I thought I had lost you. I was so upset when I got back here, I threw the dumb thing in the lake." He turned away. It took Duke a few moments to bring himself to look at Nora. Her facial expression was as blank as his. Then slowly the corners of her mouth turned up. At first it was just a giggle; soon she was doubled over laughing, and he was doing the same.

232

Regaining her composure, she asked, "Seriously, are you sure this is what you want, with the baby and everything?"

"Never been more serious about anything in my whole life."

"You know people are going to talk. There's no way that this won't come out somehow."

"Let them, it won't bother me. What about you? You'll probably take the brunt of it."

"I think I can handle it."

"Okay then," Duke said. "Let's get this show on the road. What do we need to do first?"

"Gladys said we could get married the same day in Iowa. It's a three-day waiting time here in Wisconsin."

Duke scoffed. "We're not sneaking off in the dead of night, running here or there. We're going to get married right here. We'll have old Judge Willard marry us on the court house lawn."

"Do you really think...?"

"Damn betcha." His voice was full of excitement. "And if anyone has a problem with that, they can kiss my royal pitoot. Give me a few minutes to get dressed and we can go down to the courthouse and get a marriage license."

"Duke, wait a minute. This is all going too fast."

Duke stopped. "You're not changing your mind, are you?"

"A few more days is not going to make a big difference."

"What do you have in mind?"

"My folks. Sarah. My dad doesn't know anything about this. Maybe we could go to Ely. People come to Nevada to get married all the time."

Duke gave her a big hug. "I think that's a splendid idea. It would be great to have your folks there." Duke began fumbling in a coffee can. He picked out a ten-penny finish nail. Using a pair of vice grips and needle-nose pliers, he bent it into a circle. After a few adjustments, he dropped to a knee. Taking her left hand, he looked at her and smiled. "Before we leave Pine Lake, I want to make this official." He slid the curved piece of steel onto her third finger. "Nora Jensen, will you marry me?"

Nora gazed at the crude ring. "I will," she said softly.

The Wedding is On

Gladys met the couple at the door. "I guess by the smiles, you two love birds got things worked out?"

"We're getting married…next week in Ely," Duke said. "Nora wants to go back by her folks."

"Come in, Gladys said. "This calls for a celebration."

Mary came from the kitchen. "What are we celebrating?"

"Duke and Nora are getting married," Gladys announced.

"Married?" Mary jolted upright and took a step back. "When?"

"Next week," Duke said, with a broad smile.

"My goodness, this is so sudden," Mary said, looking from person to person, trying to glean more information.

"The sooner the better, right?" Gladys nodded to Nora.

Nora blushed and held out her hand. "Duke made me an engagement ring."

"I thought he bought you…?"

Mary brushed past Gladys to see. "What is that? It looks like a nail."

"Just temporary," said Duke.

"I would hope so," Mary said. "I don't understand why all the hurry up. You'll hardly have time to get out invitations, order a wedding cake, or shop for a dress."

"Right now, the important thing is for them to get married," Gladys said.

"Oh," Mary said, looking puzzled. "Oooooh!" she said again, as it dawned on her what Gladys meant. "I see…dear me…" Mary turned and headed for the kitchen.

"I'm afraid we shocked her," said Nora.

"Pennsylvania Dutch upbringing," Gladys said. "She'll be all right. So, what are you going to do now?"

Nora looked at Duke and shrugged her shoulders.

Duke was all smiles. "I think we should drive to Middletown and buy you a proper wedding dress."

"There's a bridal shop next door to Penney's," Gladys added.

Nora felt uneasy. She grabbed onto Duke's arm to steady herself.

"Whoa, are you okay?" Duke eased her down as she sat on the second step of the stairs.

"I think so; let me sit here a minute. I guess all the excitement…I feel a little fluttery inside."

"I'll get you some water," Gladys hurried to the kitchen

Duke knelt in front of Nora. "Is it a pregnant thing?"

"No, I've had those nauseous feelings. This is different. Just let me sit here a while. I think I'll be okay."

Gladys came from the kitchen with Mary close behind. "Here's some water."

Nora took the glass. "I didn't sleep much last night." She took a small sip of the water. "Maybe I need to lie down for a while."

"That's a good idea," Gladys said, helping Nora to her feet. "Mom, grab her other arm; let's help her up to bed."

Duke got to his feet. "Is there anything I can do?"

"I think you did enough," Mary said, leaving no doubt about what she meant.

Once they helped Nora into her pajamas and under the covers, Gladys pulled down the shade. "I'll leave the water on the night table. If you need anything just yell; we'll be right downstairs."

Nora managed a brief smile. "Tell Duke I'll talk to him later."

"You just get some rest," Gladys said. "That's an order."

The women were surprised that Duke was nowhere around. Gladys went to the window and saw him walking briskly down through the glen. "Why would he leave? I would have given him a ride."

"I never did like that guy," Mary said, walking to the kitchen. "Now look at the trouble he's put that poor girl in."

"It takes two to tango," Gladys said. "You can't blame it all on him."

Mary pushed a chair violently to the table and grabbed a pan off the stove. "Men!" The pan landed in the sink with a loud crash.

"You're right, we ought to get rid of them all." Gladys took a seat at the table. "What do you think we should do about Dad?"

"Your father is not..."

"C'mon, Mom, Nora isn't the first girl to find herself in this position. The war has changed everything. At the hospital, we've had lots of unmarried girls having babies from guys who went off to war and even some married ones who had babies when their husbands have been gone for more than a year. This *is* 1945."

"That may be true in Chicago, but not here in Pine Lake."

"What about the Jefferson girl? Everyone's been saying she was three months along when they got married."

"Her mother told me it was a preemie."

"The baby was eight pounds. She went full term," Gladys said, getting up to answer the phone. "Duke and Nora will get married and will deal with the questions as they arise." Taking the receiver from the wall phone, she put it to her ear and spoke into the extended tube. "Hello."

Gladys put her hand over the speaking tube. "It's the hospital switchboard; I wonder what they want?"

"They probably want you to come down there and deliver another illegitimate baby."

"Mother, will you hush." Gladys took her hand away. "Yes, doctor, I see…yes…I'll be sure to tell her…thank you for calling." Gladys placed the receiver on the hook on the side of the wooden phone box. "That was Doctor Gardener; he's concerned about one of Nora's test results. He wants to see her as soon as possible."

"That sounds serious," Mary said, the edge in her voice turning compassionate.

"I'm going to check with Nora to see what tests he did. He really sounded concerned." Gladys hurried up the stairs.

She knew something was dreadfully wrong the minute she entered the room. Nora looked pale and was curled in the fetal position. Gladys pulled back the covers. The bed was a deep crimson. Gladys dropped to her knees and cradled Nora's head in her hands. "Oh my God! Nora, Nora, can you hear me?"

Nora barely opened her eyes.

"Stay with me now. Stay with me." Gladys jumped up, ran to the bathroom and grabbed every towel she could find. Running back to Nora's room she yelled down the stairs. "Mother! call the hospital. Get an ambulance over here. Right now."

Mary ran from the kitchen. "What is it? What happened?"

"Nora's hemorrhaging. Call the hospital. Do it...and bring some ice...as much as you can carry."

It seemed like a very long time, but the ambulance was there in a matter of minutes. Gladys used the ice and towels to slow the flow, but Nora had lost a great deal of blood. The one attendant, probably a new recruit, made an abrupt turn at seeing all the blood. He stumbled down the stairs, hand over his mouth, trying to keep from upchucking. Gladys helped the other man put Nora on the stretcher. Then going to the top of the stairs, she yelled at the young man. "Get your ass up here and help get this girl into that ambulance."

The guy wiped his mouth with his sleeve, having lost his stomach on the porch. "I can't," he said.

"You get up here right now or I'll come down there and kick your butt all the way up here."

Gladys had years of nurses-in-training give her that "I can't" wimp out. She never took it from them and she sure as hell was not going to take it from this lad. The boy, too, must have thought better of defying her. He scrambled up the stairs and grabbed the lead edge of the stretcher. Gladys helped guide them down the stairs and into the ambulance. Jumping inside, she made sure to keep the towels and ice between Nora's legs. "I've got things under control back here. Get up front and get this buggy to the hospital. NOW!"

239

Gladys stayed at Nora's side even as they wheeled her into the operating room. She kept talking, telling Nora to stay awake, that everything would be all right. From Nora's color and her years of nursing experience, Gladys knew her friend was in grave danger. The doctors would have to get the bleeding stopped right away or...Gladys didn't even want to think about the "or." She fell into the nearest chair and tried to rest her hands in a way so not to smear blood on her pants. The ambulance driver brought her a wet towel and she was able to wipe most of the blood from her arms and hands. She looked at the younger fellow. "Your first trip?"

The guy nodded his head.

"Sorry for being so hard on you...too many years in the business. I just hope we got her here in time."

"Me, too," the young man said.

Something is Dreadfully Wrong

Harry and Mary arrived and were as concerned about their own daughter as they were about Nora. "My God. Look at you. You've got blood all over you," Mary said.

Gladys looked at her blouse and slacks. "Yeah, but it's not mine."

"Have you heard anything? How's she doing?" Mary looked around. "Where do they have her?"

"OR" Gladys pointed down the hall. "Haven't heard a thing yet." Gladys wiped the moisture from the corner of her eyes. "I'm scared. She's lost a lot of blood. Something must have ruptured. They might be having a hard time getting it stopped."

"The baby?" Mary asked.

Gladys shook her head before her chin lowered. "I doubt...there's a chance...of..."

Harry eased himself onto a couch across the hallway from Gladys. Mary joined him. They all moved forward in their seats when a nurse came out of the operating room and ran past. She talked to the nurse at the nearby station and then hurried back to the OR.

"I'll see what that was about." Gladys walked to the station. "They're calling in a surgeon from Middletown," she said, returning to her seat. "I don't like the sound of that." Gladys checked her watch and figured it had been over an hour since they had brought in Nora. "The longer this goes, the more serious it becomes."

"She's not going to die, is she?" Mary asked.

Gladys could only shrug her shoulders.

Time dragged on. Staff hurried into and out of the operating room. A man in a fresh gown, rubber gloves, and face mask entered the OR from a room across the hall. Gladys assumed it was the surgeon from Middletown. A few minutes later, Duke bolted through the front door. He came running up the hallway carrying a large box under his arm.

"What happened? Where's Nora?" He bent over to catch his breath.

Gladys stood and put an arm around Duke. She felt his body tremble. "I think she had a miscarriage; she was hemorrhaging badly."

She's going to be all right, isn't she?" The box slipped to the floor. "Can I see her?"

Gladys held him from moving forward. "They have her in the operating room. We haven't heard anything, but I'm sure they're doing everything they can for her. They don't need you in there causing a ruckus."

"I went to Middletown and bought her a dress." He bent over and picked up the box. "She is going to look so beautiful in it." He held the box to his chest. "I stopped for gas and everyone was talking about a friend of the Iversons being taken to the hospital in the ambulance. I figured they had to be talking about Nora."

Mary was the first to see the doctor coming out of the operating room. His gown was soaked with blood. "Oh my," she said.

Duke set the box down. Everyone gathered to hear what the doctor had to say. The news wasn't good. Nora was far from being out of the woods. She had what is known as a molar pregnancy causing the uterus to begin hemorrhaging. "Sadly," he said, "by the time I got here, she had lost so much blood, the only way we could stop it and save Nora was to remove the uterus." Gladys and Mary let out a collective groan. Duke pleaded with the doctor to let him go see her. The doctor shook his head. "She's heavily sedated and in no condition to see anyone. Let's see how she does over the next ten to twelve hours."

Gladys dropped in her chair. Harry and Mary sat, too.

Duke watched the doctor walk away. "What did he mean? What's a molar pregnancy?

"Technically, there was no baby," Gladys said. "The body thinks it's pregnant, but there is no embryo."

"No baby? I don't understand."

"No one is quite sure what happens, but Doctor Gardener must have seen something in the test. Sometimes there's elevated levels protein in the urine. Medically, if they catch it early, they can do a D and C. Most of the time a woman will miscarry before they find out."

"So, there's no baby?" Duke said.

Gladys stood and put a hand on Duke's shoulder. "I'm afraid not." She hesitated. "Did you hear what the doctor said about having to take out the uterus to save Nora's life?"

"What does that mean?"

"Nora will never be able to have children."

Duke fell into the chair. He didn't say a word. He reached for the box, with the dress in it, and laid it across his lap.

Gladys again put a hand on Duke's shoulder. "I'm so sorry."

Harry helped Mary up from the chair. "Not much more we can do here. The poor girl is going to need to rest." Gladys nodded and the three of them started for the door. They had only gone a few steps when Gladys turned to Duke. "Are you coming?"

Duke didn't acknowledge the question; he just stared straight ahead.

***

Nora's mouth was dry. Her tongue felt glued to the roof of her mouth. Trying to open one eye, the eyelid felt like it weighed ten pounds. She forced the other one open and blinked a few times to adjust to the light. Her arm wouldn't move. It felt like someone had tied it to the bed; even her fingers were slow to respond. There were voices, but she was unable to decipher what was being said until she heard a familiar voice. It was Gladys'.

"She's waking up; let's get a doctor in here."

Nora felt a warm hand press against her forehead. It was her friend looking at her with concern on her face.

"C'mon, Nora, wake up," Gladys said.

Nora tried to speak but couldn't make her brain work in unison with her mouth. All that came out was "Ooooh." Her arm felt glued to the bed. When it finally responded, she ran her hand across the bandage on her stomach. Something was dreadfully wrong. The memory came to her in bits and pieces. Suddenly her eyes widened. "The baby!" she yelled. She looked at her friend. "Oh my God, the baby..." Her voice trailed off.

"Take it easy." Gladys' voice was even and consoling. "You've been through a lot. The main thing, we need you to do, is to get your strength back."

Nora turned away. "But the baby?" Her plea barely audible.

"You can't dwell on that," Gladys said. "A miscarriage is nature's way of expelling imperfection. We're lucky it didn't cost you your life. Everything else will take care of itself."

Gladys stepped aside when the doctor came into the room.

He checked Nora's pulse. "How are you feeling?"

Her lip quivered and her nod was barely detectable.

"You're a lucky girl," he said. "I didn't know if we were ever going to get the bleeding stopped. It was touch and go for quite a while." The doctor backed away. Looking at Gladys, "Do you work here?"

"No," she said. "But I am a nurse and a good friend of hers."

"I'll leave instructions with them at the desk," he said, and quickly left the room.

Gladys adjusted the covers around Nora. "Typical chicken shit doctor," she blurted. "Leave the dirty work for the nurses."

"I lost the baby, didn't I?" Nora braved a smile.

"Actually, there was no baby. You had a molar pregnancy."

"But I'll be okay? Right?"

Gladys' hesitation sent up a red flag. "What else?" Nora asked.

"You had massive hemorrhaging. In order to get the bleeding stopped, and save your life, the doctors had a tough decision to make."

"Meaning?"

"They had to take your uterus."

The realization of what that statement meant hit Nora like a bolt of lightning. She tried to hold back but couldn't stop from sobbing. "No," she cried. "Oh God, no."

Gladys took Nora's hand. "I'm sorry. I know this is hard to swallow." Just give it…"

Nora cut her off. Please, I just need some time…alone."

"That's okay, I understand. If you need anything, I'll be right outside your door." Gladys turned out the light. She heard quiet sobbing as she left the room.

Would Duke Lose, Too?

Not being able to have children was a crushing blow. Nora's emotions ran the gamut from hurt to anger, and from sorrow to guilt. She couldn't stop thinking about it and every thought brought more tears. Tears she tried to conceal when Gladys came back into the room.

"Feeling better?" Gladys asked.

"A little," Nora said, lacking conviction.

"Someone out in the hall is anxious to see you."

Nora turned to her side.

"He sat up the whole night outside your door. I sent him home to shave and clean up when I got here this morning. Can I send him in?"

Nora pushed with her hand. "No, not yet."

Gladys came to the bed. "I know you're upset, but this doesn't have to change things between you and Duke."

"I'm not ready to see him."

"You can't blame this on him," Gladys said. "The man loves you. He knows about the baby; he's good with it." Gladys stepped back. "And I'm not going to be the one to tell him he can't come in."

No sooner had Gladys left the room when Duke rushed in. He stopped midway across the room and then slowly walked to the bed. "How are you doing?"

Nora forced a smile. "Better."

Duke pulled a chair to the side of the bed. "Listen, I just want you to get well. They say you'll need time to recuperate; I want to help."

Haven't you done enough? Nora hated herself for thinking that way. Gladys was right, this was not his fault. If anyone was to blame, it would have to be her. She let things get out of hand in the first place. But the cruel fact remained, she would never bear a child of her own. Her grief surfacing again, she turned her head and cried. She cried hard.

Duke remained calm. He stroked her hand, repeating, "It will be all right."

***

Gladys had to go back to Chicago, but Duke showed up at the hospital every day at lunchtime and after work. Everyone was pleased with Nora's physical progress. She'd spend an hour or two in her chair and then be up walking in the hallways. Getting back and forth between her bed and the bathroom was a personal achievement. Her incision was healing and showed no signs of infection. The doctor was less enthusiastic about her mental state. She didn't smile, would break down and cry for no reason.

Duke tried to be understanding but sensed an ever-widening gap in their relationship. He tried to get her to talk about it, but every time he'd open the conversation, she'd go silent.

Both he and Nora were happy to see Gladys when she returned on the weekend. No one had to explain the situation to Gladys; the veiled happy talk couldn't hide the tension she felt from each of them. Maybe a little separation might help. Encouraged by Nora's progress, Gladys nudged the doctor to release her, saying some time at the farm would do her a world of good. Nora welcomed the change. Mary's cooking would be a wonderful improvement over the hospital's fare. Gladys also used her best diplomatic skills to convince Duke to give Nora some time to "gather" herself.

"I've lost her, haven't I?" he said, as Gladys walked him out of the room.

"Don't say that," she said. "You've just got to give her time. She's depressed and that won't go away overnight."

"How did this happen?" he asked. "One minute I'm a dad, I'm getting married, and the next minute, I lose everything."

Gladys felt the despair in his voice. "Don't give up, just give it more time. Come for supper Sunday night. It'll give me time to see where she's at."

"I'm afraid I lost her," he said again, walking down the hall.

Could Their Love Survive?

Duke was devastated. He never felt so alone. It's one thing to have never known love, but to experience it and then lose it was almost more than he could bear. He could only hope Nora would come out of her depression. Why wouldn't she let him help her?

Duke walked into his kitchen and looked at the cabinetry scattered about the room. He ran his hand along one of the base cabinets. They'd had plenty of time to dry. He pushed the sink cabinet in place, leveled it, and anchored it to the wall. He didn't stop until he had all the base cabinets leveled and anchored in place. This was his salvation; working kept him from dwelling on the fact he may have truly lost Nora forever.

***

Duke called Gladys on Sunday morning to make sure they were still on for supper. By three o'clock in the afternoon, he had finished hanging the upper cabinets. The doors all opened and closed. The drawers rolled in and out, and all the knobs and handles were mounted. It was time to put the rest of the room in order. He threw out all the odd pieces of lumber and scraps of paper scattered about. He organized his tools and painting supplies and swept the floor. Stepping back, he smiled, but couldn't shake the hollow feeling in the pit of his stomach. This was supposed to be Nora's kitchen; he built it for her. He dreaded the thought that all his work could become a constant reminder of a love he might never have.

*＊＊

Duke checked his watch as he mounted the steps at the Iverson place. Nora opened the door and stepped aside. She smiled but avoided making eye contact. Duke didn't know how to react. He wanted to hug her, hold her, kiss her, but felt frozen in place.

"Come in." Gladys' cheery voice broke the ice. "Let's go into the kitchen. Mom's got everything on the table."

Duke followed Gladys. "Hello," he announced. "Smells good in here." Stepping aside, he waited for Mary to direct the seating order. Nora would be on his right. He held her chair.

Nora sat and whispered, "Thank you."

"We have a gentleman in our midst," Gladys said.

Duke forced a smile. His cheeks flushed.

Harry picked up the bowl of mashed potatoes and put a heaping scoop on his plate. He passed the bowl to Duke. "I hear you're fixing up the Lawson place?"

"Been at it a while." Duke looked at Nora. "I finished putting the cabinets in the kitchen."

Nora smiled.

Gladys added, "Every woman's dream, a new kitchen."

"Not mine," said Mary. "I like my kitchen just the way it is. I know where everything is."

"I don't think Gladys was talking about you," Harry said. "Would someone pass the gravy?"

Duke put small portions of everything on his plate. Nora did the same. Gladys, with Mary's help, made sure there were no lapses in the conversation. Duke and Nora added smiles whenever someone looked their way. They both refused seconds, but each accepted a warm slice of apple pie for dessert. Duke finished first. He looked at Nora. "Would you like to take a walk?"

Nora pushed herself from the table. "Sure." She looked at Gladys. "Is that okay?"

"Oh sure, you'll do anything to get out of doing dishes," Gladys laughed. "Just teasing."

"The food was terrific," Duke said. "Thanks."

Duke took Nora's hand and walked her to the front door. In the yard, Nora pulled him toward the fields in back of the barn. "Let's walk this way."

"How are you doing? Are you feeling better...about?"

"I'm doing a lot better. Gladys has been super. She has a way of making me focus on all the positives in my life. There are no guarantees. I survived the war. I have loving parents...Sarah Jean..."

"You've got me."

She smiled at him. "I won't hold you to your proposal. Things are different now."

"Not for me," he protested. "Nothing has changed as far as I'm concerned. I still want to get married."

"I can never give you a child."

"That doesn't matter, it's you I want."

"That's sweet. It's what you say now, but what about in the future? You were pretty excited when you thought we were having a baby."

"I know." He lowered his head. "The thought of having a baby with you was beyond anything I could've ever dreamed about." His voice cracked. "But my dream has always been of you...having you...loving you. I just know, if we can be together, nothing else will matter."

Nora squeezed his hand. "I wish I could be as certain of that as you are."

Duke picked up a stone and threw it as far as he could. "Why is it every time I come this close to having you, the whole world blows up in my face?"

"Duke, listen to me." She pulled him to face her. "Now is not the time to make any long-range decisions. I know I can't, and I don't think you should either. I'm going back to Ely. My folks are still in the dark about all of this. It will give both of us time to think this out."

"When are you going?"

"Tomorrow. I've got a ticket for the afternoon bus."

"Are you still coming back for Christmas?"

"Let's see how things work out. I've got to start looking for a job. I've gone through most of my army pay." Nora started up the stairs to the house. "Are you coming in?"

"Nah, I'm going to head back home. Tell Gladys and her folks I said good bye."

Nora stood on the porch and watched Duke get on his cycle and ride down through the glen.

A Christmas Surprise

It was Christmas Eve. The snow had been falling since early morning, and now with the setting sun, Pine Lake looked like a real-life Christmas card. Having shoveled the first four inches of powdery stuff at noon, Duke cleared the additional four inches of snow from the driveway and sidewalk. Setting the shovel by the back door, he threw back the tarp that covered the wood pile. Grabbing an armful of split logs, he covered the pile, stomped his feet, and opened the back door. He was immediately greeted by an active golden retriever. "Sandy, behave." The dog settled and followed Duke into the living room.

After dropping the wood in the box by the fireplace, he took off his gloves and stoked the fire. The flames crackled as sparks danced up the chimney. He hung his coat and cap on the clothes tree, then tossed another piece of wood on the fire. The heat felt good as he rubbed his chilled hands. The dog nudged Duke's leg, prompting him to reach down and scratch behind the dog's ears. "It's getting cold out there; we'll have to keep the fire going all night." The dog lay on the rug in front of the fire. "I see you've got your place all picked out."

Duke reached behind the Christmas tree and plugged in the lights. He stood for a moment, waiting for the bubble lights to do their thing. The lady at the hardware store had said those motion lights and strands of tinsel were the newest thing in tree decorating. Before the war, he remembered his mom using strings of popcorn to decorate the tree. This was the first tree Duke had put up since coming to Pine Lake. A Christmas tree was no big thing to him, but he told Nora he'd have one. He also promised to have a room ready for her if she came back for Christmas

At Thanksgiving Nora had written with a lot of news about Sarah doing well in school and being chosen homecoming queen. She hadn't mentioned a thing about coming to Pine Lake. She also wrote she was working part time for a doctor in Ely, but still wanted to find a nursing job at a hospital.

Duke stepped to the mantel and took down the letter. He read it again. "Nope, she didn't say a thing about Christmas." He looked for a reaction from Sandy but saw none. He bent and gave the dog a pat on the head. "It's too bad; you would have loved her." This time Sandy barked and swished her tail.

Duke showed the letter. "Look how she signed it. *Love Nora.*" He brought the letter to his nose and was sure he was breathing in her scent. Walking to the window he pulled back the curtain. "Well, girl, I guess it's going to be just you and me for Christmas."

He put the letter back on the mantel and picked up a picture of Nora. It was the one he had taken of her sitting on the rocks above Sandstone bluff. He sat in the chair and laid the picture on his chest. Sandy got up and put her chin on Duke's leg. "I gotta tell you," he said, stoking Sandy's head, "I don't know how I'm ever going to get over her."

Sandy's head came up. She looked toward the kitchen and gave out a rough growl.

255

"What is it, girl? You hear something?" Then Duke heard it, too. "Hey, someone's knocking at the back door." He got up, checked the clock on the mantel. "It's too early for Santa."

Duke opened the door. The lump in his throat made it hard to swallow. He tried to speak but couldn't think of what to say. Tears gathered in the corners of his eyes. "You...you came...I didn't think...you didn't say you were coming." He wanted to hug her, kiss her, but didn't know if he should. She was a vision in a red wool coat with a large hood; snow covered her shoulders and the folds of the hood. He couldn't take his eyes off her.

"Aren't you going to invite me in?" Nora finally said. "It's cold out here."

Duke jumped aside. "Oh my God, Yes. Yes. Come in." He grabbed her brown suitcase and followed her into the kitchen. "How did you get here? The roads...it's been snowing all day."

Nora stopped in the middle of the kitchen and slowly looked at everything in the room. "It's really beautiful." She pushed the hood off her head and stomped her feet. "I wasn't prepared to walk in eight inches of snow. My toes are frozen."

Duke set down her bag. "Come by the fire. Let's get those shoes off." He pulled a chair close to the hearth. "Sit here."

Nora slipped out of her coat and laid it over the back of the chair.

Duke began unfastening the laces as soon as she was seated. "Your shoes are soaked." He pulled off her shoes and socks. He grabbed the afghan off the couch and wrapped her feet. "What happened to Sarah? I thought she was coming with you?"

"Maybe in summer. She was in a Christmas play at school and wanted to work as much as she could."

"She has a job?"

"Economy Drug Store, at the soda counter. She's saving her money to buy a grave stone for her mom."

Duke continued to rub her feet. "I can't believe you made it."

"I didn't think I was going to," she said. "The bus driver was going to stop at the junction. But by some miracle, we got behind a snow plow and were able to follow it all the way into Pine Lake. I had to walk from town to here. I'm surprised I remembered the way."

"You should have let me know. I would have met the bus and picked you up."

"On your motorcycle?"

Duke laughed, "I've got a pickup, too."

Sandy put a paw on Nora's knee. "I see that's not all you've got. Who's the new member of the family?"

"This is Sandy, pure bred retriever, runt of the litter. I needed her around so I would stop talking to inanimate objects."

"You've gotten a lot done in the house." She took her time to look at each decoration. "I love your Christmas tree."

"I promised you one," he said.

"I remember."

"Nothing's done on the second floor, nothing but a bunch of 2 x 4s."

"There are no..."

"Bedrooms?" He paused. "Not up there, but I did promise to have a room ready for you, didn't I."

Nora looked around. "Did you?"

"Want to see it?"

"I'd love to." She stood, holding the afghan on her feet.

"Wait, the floor is really cold." He dashed off and returned with a pair of his slippers. He unwrapped the afghan, knelt, and slid a slipper on each foot. "Not very stylish; I just hope you can keep them on your feet." Duke led the way. Nora shuffled across the floor trying to keep up.

He opened a double door off the kitchen. "One day this will be a formal dining room, but for now, it's your room." He lifted the switch and the room exploded with light.

"Complete with crystal chandelier," she said.

"It came with the house. It'll look good over a large table."

"I'm only teasing." Nora walked around the double-sized bed. She sat and gave an approving pat. She opened and closed one of the dresser drawers.

"The set is over a hundred years old. It's solid maple. I refinished all the pieces. The mattress is new, a J.C. Penney special. Do you like it?"

"It's beautiful."

"Are you staying?" he stammered. "That's silly, where would you go…on Christmas Eve…in a foot of snow?"

"And wet shoes." Nora shuffled back by the fire.

"Seriously, why didn't you let me know you were coming?" Duke sat on the edge of the couch.

"I wanted to surprise you."

"You did that for sure." This should have been the time to pinch himself to make sure it wasn't all a dream. "What are your plans? How long can you stay?"

"It all depends."

"On what?"

"My new job."

"Job?"

"I told you I was looking for a hospital job. Gladys wrote me Pine Lake had an opening for an emergency room nurse. I sent them a resume. I start the day after Christmas."

Duke was ready to leap to his feet but settled back on the couch. "Does this mean…"

"I'm planning on making Pine Lake my new home."

"You know what I mean; what about us? Will you marry me? I still have the dress I bought for you."

"Let's save that decision for another time. Right now, I have a job, and a very nice room…with a chandelier."

Duke scratched his neck. "This is Pine Lake; people are going to talk."

"Are you going to ask me to leave?"

Duke choked. "No, of course not. I was concerned…"

"I'm sure people have been talking about me since I left. And once it gets out that I spent the night…alone in this house…with you…well, one night or a hundred, it's not going to make much difference." Nora wasn't sure where all these thoughts were coming from. "Of course, they will trash you, too, for cavorting with a loose woman."

"I guess I never thought you'd…" He scratched the side of his head. "How long have you been thinking about this?"

"To tell you the truth, until a few minutes ago, I wasn't sure how I was going to handle…us. A few months ago, we were going to get married because we thought I was pregnant. It would have been a sham. And I'm not convinced that at some point in your life, you won't want a family. It would kill me to be the one to stand in your way. If we do get married, let's do it when we both feel it is absolutely the right thing to do."

His body language made it apparent that Duke was struggling with this. "What about your family? What about Sarah; what will she think?"

"I don't know. I guess everyone will just have to accept our decision." Nora saw the worried look on Duke's face. "I'm sorry, I've been shooting my mouth off about this; it's your decision, too."

"Personally, I don't give a damn what people say. I just don't want you to be hurt. Words on a piece of paper have no bearing on how I feel about you. I love you; nothing will ever change that."

"That's good enough for me, but for right now, I'm starving. I've been on a bus for two and a half days and I haven't eaten a thing today."

Duke jumped off the couch. "I made a great Irish stew earlier. It's a Christmas tradition in my family. I just have to warm it up. Do you like soda bread?"

"Never had any, but right now, everything sounds good."

Nora wrapped herself in the afghan and sat at the kitchen table. She watched Duke scurry from the sink to the stove, slicing, stirring, and tasting the varied parts of his meal. When he had everything ready, he lit the large red candle in the pine bough centerpiece and turned off the overhead light. Picking up his napkin, he smiled. "This has to be the best Christmas ever."

Nora nodded in agreement. She picked up her fork and speared a chunk of meat from her bowl. Duke ate, too, though he seldom took his eyes off Nora. Seeing her in the flickering candlelight, sitting at his table, all his Christmas wishes had come true.

Nora cleaned her bowl and ate the last morsel of bread. "That was so good, I can't believe I ate so much."

Duke picked up her plate. "Why don't you go curl up by the fire? I'll clean up a bit, make some coffee, and we can have dessert by the fire."

"Dessert?"

"Christmas cookies."

"You bake, too?"

"Nah, they're store bought, but I did make the soda bread."

Nora got up and settled in the chair next to the fireplace, wrapping herself in the afghan.

Duke came out of the kitchen carrying a tray with two cups of coffee and a plate of frosted cookies.

"You cook, you bake," she said. "I guess there are a lot of things I don't know about you."

"I hope I can surprise you every day from now on."

The coffee and cookies hit the spot, but soon Nora was feeling the effects of the long bus ride and the excitement of the evening. "I'm afraid I'm not going to last much longer. I'm going to need some sleep."

Duke set down his cup. "Let's get your room ready." He went ahead, turned on the lamp next to the bed, and pulled back the covers. "I don't have a furnace yet, but this feather tick should keep you warm. If you leave your door open, you'll get some heat from the fireplace."

Nora looked around. "You didn't show me your room."

"Not finished yet. Sandy and I sleep on the couch." Duke backed out of the room. "I'll leave the light on in the bathroom and crack the door, in case you have to get up in the night. Is there anything else you need?"

Nora lifted her suitcase onto the bed. "No, this is fine. I'm sure I'll be all right."

Duke went to the kitchen and began putting stuff away. He pushed in the chairs, blew out the candle, and wiped off the table. Movement caught his eye. Nora had stepped behind the door to get undressed, but from this angle, he could see her naked form reflected in the mirror. As soon as their eyes met, Nora closed the door.

Duke finished putting the last of the dinnerware back into the cupboard. He reached to turn off the kitchen light.

Nora stood in the open doorway. "I'm glad I brought along these flannel pajamas." Looking down, "Do you need your slippers back?"

"You keep them," he said. "I've got heavy socks. I'll see you in the morning, okay?"

"Thank you for a delicious supper." She started to turn but came back. "Oh, one more thing...Merry Christmas."

"It's been the best ever."

A Night of Surprises

Nora snuggled under the covers. Duke had been right; the feather tick did a marvelous job of keeping her warm. The crackle of the fire, the smell of burning pine, and the orange flickers of light dancing across her ceiling were very soothing.

Duke came out of the bathroom and walked past her door. She pulled the covers aside and watched him punch up a pillow and spread a blanket over the couch. As soon as he was settled, Sandy hopped on the couch beside him. Nora closed her eyes with one final thought: *Is this really going to work?*

"Nora, are you awake?"

Nora came out of a deep sleep. She pushed back the covers and saw Duke's silhouette standing in the doorway.

"What is it? What do you want?"

He came and knelt beside the bed. Reaching under the covers he found her hand and squeezed it.

"What are you doing?"

"Listen, I don't care if we ever get married. I want you to know that I will always love you, no matter what. I will cherish you and stand by you in sickness and in health, in good times and bad, now, and all the rest of my days." Before Nora could say a word, he got off his knees and started for the door.

"Duke?"

"I'm sorry to wake you. I just had to get that off my chest."

She watched him go back to the couch. He grabbed a log from the wood box and threw it on the fire. Sandy reluctantly moved as he straightened the blanket and crawled back onto the couch. The clock on the mantel chimed the hour. Sandy raised her head as the clock sounded for the twelfth time.

"Duke."

He rolled over to see Nora standing by the couch. "What is it? What..."

"It's cold in my room."

Duke sat up. "What do you want to do?"

She looked down at the couch. "Do you have room..."

Duke used his foot to push Sandy off the couch and held back the covers. Nora slipped in and backed up to him. He put his arm around her and drew her tight.

Sandy put her paw on the edge of the couch.

Nora poked Duke in the ribs. "Someone will have to explain to the dog who has the preferred spot in this bed."

Duke snickered. "No problem, I'll take care of that."

"And don't be in a hurry to take the dress back; we may need it sometime." She closed her eyes and felt safe in his arms.

About the Author

Joe Van Rhyn grew up in the sixties in the small resort town of Green Lake, Wisconsin. In school, Joe divided his time between sports and carrying the lead in a number of plays. He uses this theatrical background in his writing to build memorable characters, strong dialogue, and compelling story lines.

Joe has written many short stories and was a contributing writer for Thomas Gnewuch's 1997 book, *Green Lake Memories*.

Joe and his wife, Elaine, ran a successful promotional products company for many years. Retirement presented a new challenge: how to channel the creative energy that still churned inside him. Joe took to writing.

Where it All Began...

Battle Born is the follow-up book to Joe's first book in the series: *Born Yesterday*.

It's the spring of 1964; people in the resort town of Pine Lake, Wisconsin are skittish when a stranger is found unconscious in the park. His head wounds suggest he was severely beaten and he subsequently slips into a coma.

With nothing in his pockets, and no one coming forward, his identity remains a mystery.

Nurse Julia Parsons is enamored with the comatose patient and takes a special interest in his care. She sits by his bed each evening and talks to him hoping he will wake from his deep sleep. But waking only complicates matters when he claims to have no recollection of who he is or what landed him in the park. Overlooked clues send the couple on a journey across Wisconsin in search of his past.

Could her new friend be the love she yearns for, or will his previous life take him away from her forever?

Born Yesterday is available on Amazon. Signed copies are available by going to Joe's website: www.joevanrhyn.com.

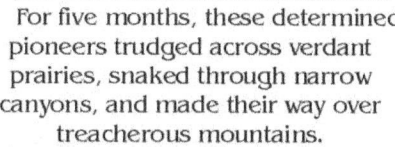

www.ingramcontent.com/pod-product-compliance
Lightning Source LLC
Chambersburg PA
CBHW070859180626
46817CB00003B/838

* 9 7 8 0 9 9 8 6 7 9 8 3 9 *